Carreta
de la Muerte
(Cart of Death)

also by Mari Ulmer

Midnight at the Camposanto

Carreta de la Muerte
(Cart of Death)

A Taos Festival Mystery

Mari Ulmer

Poisoned Pen Press
Scottsdale, Arizona

Poisoned Pen Press
6962 E. First Ave. Ste 103
Scottsdale, AZ 85251
www.poisonedpenpress.com
sales@poisonedpenpress.com

Printed in the United States of America

To my friends and neighbors of the valley,
toda la gente, for your smiles, help, and hugs;
and To Michele and Dan; Brooks and Dalton;
Sean and Jason;
and To Pat, Linda, and all the dreamers;
and To the spirit of Jim—forever.

ACKNOWLEDGMENTS

A big thank you to my brilliant editor, Barbara Peters; to Louis Silverstein who gave the first go-ahead and cheered me on; to Robert Rosenwald, the publisher who believed; to Jason Privette whose hard young hand slipped into mine at all the rough times; to the then Medical Examiner, Mr. Martinez and the people of the Albuquerque Poison Control who courteously helped me. May you have many years.

PROLOGUE

The attack on the Church needed an early start. In the pre-dawn hour the trees were a darker mass than the night sky, silhouetted almost black against it, but somehow suggesting they might be green. Headlights on, the driver saw only the gray highway as the car sped through the sleeping, still nearly all-Spanish towns of Chamisal, Vadito, Las Trampas, and Truchas.

While the communities flashed past, the sun gradually lit up the orange *barrancas*, the badlands, that reach crumbling, forbidding fingers of high rock into the hills and valleys around Chimayo. Here, at the edge of the Sangre de Cristo mountain range southwest of Taos, wind and rain and melting snow had shaped volcanic remains into rust, sienna, even pink rock spires, castles and pinnacles lying exposed beneath the vast cerulean sky. The highway rode a ridge between them, then dropped down into the green valley of Chimayo, a jade oasis visible from far distances. At the southeast corner, the land swept upward to form rose-colored Tsi Mayoh, the highest point. Below, neglected orchards showed ancient arthritic apple trees, still clinging to life. Past them, a road turned away around a corner by old adobe homes, now offering tourist enticements. It ended at a small squat adobe church known as the *Santuario*, the Sanctuary, because of its healing earth. A sand-colored hill rose behind it, frugally decorated with dark green piñon and juniper, but lavish with aspen not yet trembling gold.

A low adobe wall, rising up to mimic the shape of the hill at the gate, surrounded the church. Huge cottonwoods stretched out to protect it and square bell towers stood guard on each side. The church enveloped believer and non-believer alike in the dark mysteries of millennia.

Built two centuries ago by the Spanish at a place sacred to Indians for centuries, its atmosphere took one deep into that place where human and holy touch, and a glimpse can be had through the separating membrane.

The Indians first worshiped here, and still hold sacred a cave in Tsi Mayoh. They too know the healing properties of the dirt of this place.

The Spanish settlers built the church from the earth after strange events occurred, beginning when a *penitente* brother, Señor Abeyta, saw a bright blue light hovering above the ground near the river. He dug at the spot with his hands. Aiii! What was this? He pulled out the crucifix of *Nuestro Señor de Esquipulas*! This was same "black Christ" known for healing in Guatemala. First one, then another person came until a crowd gathered. They decided to carry the crucifix to the church in nearby Santa Cruz. The next day, they found it gone. The black Christ had returned to his original spot. Again the people processed with the crucifix to Santa Cruz. Again it traveled back. Recognizing the command of the Lord in this, the villagers built a church to house this crucifix of our Lord of Esquipulas. And he was happy there and blessed the church with miraculous healings.

Today, inside the Santuario, the sun provided only enough soft gray light to maneuver through the darkness. The contrast made the votive candles shine that much brighter through their red glass. The ever-burning candle in the hanging lamp above the altar also shone red, its light meaning God was present. But not for the intruder who walked quickly down the aisle.

The Church seemed twisted with age, crowded with the spirits of those who had come to petition God, to offer up their pain, to give thanks for healing. Prayers permeated the very walls, petitions soaking into the adobe through the decades and centuries. The floor was uneven, the pews and kneelers bent with age. Wood-carved *santos* and modern plastic saints crowded the altar along with both clothed and painted figures of Jesus and his Blessed Mother. Behind these and the rows of fragrant candles and bunches of flowers, the brightly colored *reredo* rose to the high beamed ceiling. The arms of Christ and Saint Francis crossed in the highest painting on this altar screen, symbolizing when St. Francis received the stigmata, wounded and bleeding in the same places as Christ. Bloody and emaciated, a powerful primitive figure of Christ on the cross dominated the center of the painted panels.

Spirits filled the Santuario, unfelt by the person slipping through the dimness. That one saw only cash value in the altar ahead, while hurrying past the Stations of the Cross. Time pressed because as soon as the priest unlocked the Church and rang the first bells, parishioners would quickly arrive for the dawn Mass.

The stranger turned left in front of the altar to the entrance to the mysteries. The doorway was low, the adobe walls thick. To the right in the room of the healing earth, dozens of candles burned. Despite the candles and crowding santos, the misshapen hole dug in the earthen floor focused all attention. The soft dirt filling it rivaled Lourdes with its healing powers. It was ever-renewing, soft as talc. The stranger turned away.

On the walls of the other room, believers had left "thank you" notes to God, prayers, pictures to remind God of who needed his healing, and large and small rosaries. Hanging crutches and walking sticks bore witness to miracles. Believers who had come bent and limping, held up by these devices, had left walking upright, without pain.

The santos jammed together on every surface put the intruder in a kind of frenzy at seeing the old and rare prizes. Nobody around here would realize the value of these objects. Better yet, nothing was recorded except the large Santo Nino. The baby Jesus sat behind glass, a smile hovering about his lips, beautifully dressed in pristine blue satin and white lace. The dress looked new and stiff in contrast to his infant face that was somehow old and wise, worn even. Worshipers had draped rosaries of all types, even rosebuds, around his neck. A plastic yellow Mickey Mouse head hung from him. Extra baby shoes lay near his feet, offered by the parishioners because, like the neighborhood *Santo Niño de la Atoche*, he wore them out as he went about doing miracles at night.

The thief looked around at the treasure-crowded shelves. The last bell was ringing. The choice had to be made quickly. A hand stretched up but the priceless santo was out of reach.

CHAPTER I

The call came just as Christy reworked a sentence in her novel. With a sigh, she set it aside and pulled out the will she had prepared. The Barelas had wanted to wait. Now they needed her.

Christina Garcia y Grant drove away from the high adobe walls of what had been her grandmother's *hacienda*, presently her own *Casa Vieja*, a busy bed and breakfast. Those walls provided a refuge from the world, and from the practice of law she had mostly left, while giving her a living so that she could write. But now she had a duty to the dying.

The car wrapped her in heat collected from the sun beating down on this breathless summer day. Dark with rain, thunder heads built higher and higher, towering in the west, threatening a monsoon downpour. The waiting stillness felt oppressive, heavy.

A cloud of dust hung in the air behind Christy's car on the narrow dirt road. Here in Talpa, just south of Taos, New Mexico, hidden little by-ways led to houses and mobile homes outsiders never saw. Many of the older people spoke no English and dated their forebears back to the Spanish colonists who followed the conquistadors. Christy wondered how her green eyes came from that gene pool. Maybe a blond northern Spaniard?

Christy only had a short way to go to the Barela home on a meandering lane crowded with *latilla* fences and fat cottonwood trees. Ripe apricots fell onto the road. Almost there, filled with foreboding, Christy took a drive that appeared to lead to a large hacienda. She parked past its entrance near an adobe wall and walked to the Barela's little place tucked in behind it.

The small house, made of sun-dried adobe bricks, sat in a yard of hard-packed, swept earth. Several men stood in the shade of an old gray-green olive tree keeping a death watch. Cigarette smoke hung in the lifeless air.

Recognizing them as *Hermanos* from Church, Christy wanted to ask about Señor Barela but first had to go through the ritual. "*¿Como 'sta?*" she called out as she approached the group. Some of the men were rough looking, biceps bulging out of muscle shirts, some business types. She noticed slicked back black hair, pony tails, one blow-dry style. These few men showed the variety that made up the Catholic lay society of *La Hermandad de Nuestro Padre Jesus*, the penitentes.

"*Bien, bien, gracias,*" they called back to her as cigarettes were dropped in courtesy and crushed underfoot. "*¿Y usted?*"

"*Bien, gracias.*" Anxious, Christy cut out the rest of the ritual to ask quietly, "How is Señor Barela?"

Heads shook. "Not well. No. He has trouble dying, that one. But he has had a good life."

"I'm sorry," Christy said as Señora Barela appeared at the screen door, wearing a cotton house dress.

"Come in, come in." She beckoned, her lips pursed together tightly to hold back the tears.

Lifting the papers in her hand toward the men, Christy said, "Be sure a couple of you stay. I have Señor Barela's will. It requires two witnesses if he's able to sign it."

The Hermano she knew as Leo Mares stepped forward from the shade into the hot sun. "He cannot read English, that one. Can you read it to him in Spanish?"

Trying to hide how defensive she felt, Christy answered, "No. You know how those of us at my age were punished for speaking Spanish at school. So then at home...Well..."

Los Hermanos exchanged looks there in the shadow, but Leo simply said, "I will come and read the will to Señor Barela if that's all right with him, and with you."

"Thank you. And one more of you as witness, yes?"

"Si. Si."

Ushering her in the door, Señora Barela wrapped frail arms around Christy in a hug. She was too thin. "Thank you for coming. *Mi esposo* needs to sign the papers pretty soon now. He is very weak."

"Yes," Christy answered softly. "I wrote the wills for both of you as you asked yesterday. I need to speak to Señor Barela to be sure he is still able to understand, and then Leo will read it to him."

Señora Barela gestured toward her purse. "¿Cuánto? How much do we owe you?"

"*Nada*, Señora. Hermanos such as your husband have done much for all of us."

They stood in a small immaculate front room. The combination wood and gas cooking stove at the kitchen end by the sink added heat to the already hot area. Shining clean linoleum covered the floor, its pattern and color long washed away. A row of painted white cupboards stood against one wall, a picture of the Sacred Heart of Jesus hanging next to them. Four cracked vinyl-seated kitchen chairs surrounded a scrubbed wood kitchen table. An old sofa sat off to the side. Beautiful wood-carved santos joined assembly-line plaster saints on every available surface.

Señora Barela led the way into an even smaller room where a bed was shoved up against one wall. Wearing several rosaries, a red-robed Cristo stood on a hand-carved bureau. The folds of the garment did not hide the emaciation of the figure. Painted blood ran down Jesus' compassionate face from the wounds made by his real crown of thorns. Candles burned in front of it and the other santos that stood near. Tall glasses painted with religious figures held many of the candles. Ribbons of fragrant candle smoke lay on the air.

Gesturing toward the gaunt bleeding Jesus, Señora Barela said proudly, "*Porque mi esposo* is Hermano, they bring the Cristo for him."

The shrunken figure on the bed barely made a mound under the bedclothes. He seemed concentrated into a small blue light of barely sustained life. In a nearly inaudible mutter, he was telling the gray beads of his rosary.

Hating to intrude, Christy said gently, quietly, "Señor Barela, I have brought the will you asked me to prepare. Can you hear me?"

"*Si, m'hija,*" he said on an exhalation. He clutched his rosary. "Yes. My daughter says I must have the papers for the lands *de mis abuelos*, from my grandfathers. She and her brothers want to sell them."

"Yes. That's why I made you the will. It will pass the lands legally."

Christy turned to Leo and asked him to read the short document to be sure Señor Barela understood. Then she called in Hermano Benjy to be the second witness. They crowded the little room. Husband and wife signed, the tiny Señora holding her husband's head up so he could see to trace his signature carefully.

Señor Barela gripped Christy's hand in his own, thin as a bird's claw. "*Gracias, gracias, m'hija.* This thing was important to me. I am done now." He breathed in and out a few times, and clutched at her shirt. Christy was confused.

Leo said, "He wants you to bend closer." Christy did and Señor Barela traced a trembling cross on her forehead.

"Thank you, Señor, thank you for your blessings."

"*Ahora, el tiempo.* It is time. *La Doña Sebastiana* waits. But I have trouble dying."

The others looked at one another.

On one more exhalation, Señor Barela breathed, "*¿La tierra?*"

Leo asked, "Do you want the adobe?"

Señora Barela nodded, ignoring the tears that ran through her wrinkles. Her husband whispered, "Si" so softly it was like a sigh.

Christy helped with the bed clothes as the grieving wife and Los Hermanos, with infinitely gentle hands, arranged an adobe brick at the feet of the dying man. It was to help him push off from earth.

"He has had a good life," Benjy repeated the Spanish mantra for the dying to Señora Barela. "His time is come."

"Bueno," Christy said. "I must go."

"Thank you. Thank you, Señora," Señora Barela whispered, reaching up to also mark a cross on Christy's forehead.

Christy touched Señor Barela. "I will pray for you."

"Pray that I go quickly, *m'hija*."

"Yes, yes I will," Christy answered, but she could not stay. The act of dying was the most intimate of all. She would not watch.

As she walked around her car to get in the driver's side, Christy glanced into the courtyard of the big house, recently purchased by strangers. She saw a miniature Cart of Death perched on the rim of a newly-installed fountain. A travesty. This was no Carreta like the Hermanos pulled for penance, carrying *La Doña Sebastiana* with her bow drawn. No, someone had carved and painted a silly, leering mockery, grinning in a flower-decked cart. Christy tried to be understanding, to consider that these people did not know the customs, but she was angry. It was not right: death as a garden decoration.

CHAPTER II

Desperately hoping no guests were around, Christy slowly pushed open the little gray-wood gate in her own hacienda walls.

Mac was sitting across the flagstone courtyard under the portal. He waved a bottle of beer at her. "May I get you one?"

Christy didn't feel like seeing anyone, not even her friend and tenant, Dr. Mac McCloud. "No, thanks. I'm going to shower and try to cool off."

Stepping around the random beds of summer flowers, Christy entered the hacienda through the kitchen. The dark red brick floor was so old the bricks were rounded and looked satiny.

The guests must all be out. The house had that empty feel.

Christy put her hand on the low adobe dividing wall as she stepped up the one small step into the dining room where the big wood table gleamed beneath the wrought-iron candle chandelier. Passing through to the Middle Room, she saw that Desire wasn't at the desk. Her receptionist must have taken off, leaving the phone and bookings to Mac.

Turning left, down two steps into La Sala, Christy just stood there on its polished brick floor and finally felt the cool stillness wrap around her. She looked up at the heavy *vigas* in the high ceiling. It was so lofty there had been a gallery in the old days, space for visitors whose children and servants slept on mats up there next to barrels of corn.

Santo Niño, the Baby Jesus, sat in his *nicho* on one side of the kiva fireplace, his friend St. Francis on the other side. "Please pray for the Barelas, both of them," she asked her saints.

Cool notes by Bach sounded from the CD alone in the dim room, its player hidden in an old Spanish chest The hacienda liked it.

Moving on to the back hall with the guest rooms on either side, Christy wearily climbed the spiral stairs to her room. She gratefully felt a breeze blow in through the cottonwoods outside her window.

Bells began to toll from the little *capilla* nearby on the Talpa highway. That meant Señor Barela had died. Receiving the news, one of the Mayordomos for the chapel, the *Capilla de Señora de Los Largos de San Juan,* had gone in to pull the rope that swung the bell. It knelled once for each year that Señor Barela had lived. Its deep tone sounded news of a death over the valley. As they had through the centuries, neighbors would ask who had died.

Christy walked to the window to listen. The sound of the tolling and the glory of the sunset insisted she duck under the low doorway and onto the little deck outside. As the bells rang the years in stately procession, great long steamers of golden coral shaded to a more intense apricot, changing second by second, filled with more and more luminescent pink across a sky of the purest azure. Christy's eye and heart were taken to the edge of divine beauty and then swiftly shown gray and the last embers of Angel Fire. Now, the penitentes, some of whom had been at the death watch, would begin the rituals that had taken place for centuries. With honor and respect they would prepare Señor Barela's body. Burying the dead was only one of the duties the Hermanos had taken on in this isolated mountain valley when there was little or no government. The poor and elderly needed wood chopped. There were chores to be done. Widows whose children needed discipline.

The *morada*, built of adobe clay, hunkered down in the earth, protected by white standing crosses and a life-sized Cristo dragging his cross. Prayers and rituals struggle to heaven here. Not for the Hermandad today's easy pablum and quick entry into the celestial. Many prayers and *alabados* and the smoke of the candles must rise to heaven to bring the soul from Purgatory.

A *velorio*, a wake, would find them holding vigil with Señor Barela's body all night. In the old days, at the home of the dead, Los Hermanos, friends and family feasted at eleven and then at three in the morning. The rosary would be tomorrow night. Next the funeral Mass.

At both of these, as they have for generations, the Brothers file into the ancient adobe church, singing their plaintive alabados, the hymns that bring in the sacred of the ages. These men are laborers, cardiologists, CPAs, farmers. The older ones are sinewy, extra fat burned away in their youth by harsh Wyoming winters where they went to herd sheep to support their families, or the fat sucked out in the dark of the mine where they labored underground. There are strong young men, too, some with the in-look of oddly shaved heads, some with pony tales. Their hands are hard. Together they are mostly Spanish, just a few Anglo, but all with the look of men who have glimpsed what lies behind the veil. The guitars sing, *"Adios, Madre mia, adios,"* the final goodbye.

La Muerte was in the air. Death's bow was drawn to shoot another arrow. *La Fiestacita* was tomorrow. The wrong time for a party.

Mamacita would have made the sign against the evil eye.

As Christy stepped into the shower, the phone rang. She remembered that her receptionist was already gone, and rushed to answer, "Casa Vieja—"

"It's Ignacio, Christy. *¿Que pasa?*"

"What's happening? I was hoping to shower and then rest before catching up on my writing. What do you want, Iggy?"

"Ignacio," he corrected automatically. "No one can trust a lawyer named 'Iggy.' I called to double check if it's alright for me to take Cindy to the Fiestacita tomorrow night. I'm new at this thing, being put on the Fiesta Council."

Christy smiled as she pictured the anxious frown on her friend's cherubic face, a soft face in contrast to his sharp mind. Iggy completed the circle of the older helping teach the younger. She was the mentor for Iggy, just as the feisty lady lawyer, Doris Jordan, honored with the title *La Doña Abogada,* had taught her.

Christy caught herself musing on how her beloved old friend pushed her into college and then on for a law degree. She dragged herself back. "It's too late to be asking that, Iggy! You've already invited her, haven't you?"

"I meant okay to have her to sit at the head table? First time for this foreigner from the east side of the State. Pretty heavy stuff."

"The Fiesta Council put you on because you've been so great about volunteering," Christy answered. "And as to Cindy at the head table, I don't see why not."

Iggy sighed. "Well, lucky for me. I already asked her. Then I had the thought...Well, I told her to meet me there by six, okay?"

"Sounds fine. We'll see you there tomorrow." Christy started to hang up, then, "Oh, Iggy?"

"Yeah?"

"I'm glad you're bringing Cindy. I really like her."

"Good. So do I," he answered wryly. "I'll go confirm with her right now."

Despite his considerable bulk, Iggy moved briskly as he cut across the Plaza from his office above the shops where the theater used to be. Cindy worked at El Museo, one of the stores below Oglevie's restaurant. A week from now this would be a bustling scene as people put up booths for the Fiestas. Right now, a number of tourists rested on the wrought iron benches or just wandered the new brick paving at tourist-pace. Few native Taoseños, or even relative newcomers like him, came here any more. They left the newly-renovated Plaza to the visitors, a Plaza that was all tarted up with new concrete planters, massive wood-slab lamp standards, and a copper-trimmed tourist kiosk. Worst was the new bandstand. Iggy wished he could have been here in the old days when this had been a run-down little community Plaza with nothing but some cottonwood trees, worn grass, the little bandstand, and a rail for hitching horses. People used the Plaza for socializing then, drinking, too, at the rowdy bar long since removed for fear of offending tourists.

Iggy stepped down to enter the wooden doors to the lobby for a number of shops. He couldn't see into El Museo since the glass was frosted, but the OPEN sign was still on the door.

Self-consciously, Iggy patted his black curls, gave his trailing little 'rat tail' a tug, and opened the door, looking for Cindy. She was almost obscured, so overwhelming was the impact of silver, gold, and painted wood, large Indian baskets and pots on the walls and high shelves, and gleaming counters filled with turquoise and silver.

Cindy stood behind the far counter, working on some papers. Her shining brown hair hung forward around her face. She looked up at the sound of the bell tinkling above the door.

"Ignacio!" Cindy's face radiated delight. "What a nice surprise. I'm just finishing up."

Iggy beamed. "I just wanted to be sure we're straight on tomorrow night. You'll meet me at the Fiestacita at about six o'clock, right?"

"Right. That's at the Kachina Lodge?" Cindy checked.

"Un-hunh. I'm told they take the tickets out by the pool, so just come on out and I'll watch for you."

"It should work out fine," Cindy said happily. "That's why I'm trying to get as much done today as I can. Dr. Bottoms said we could close the shop at four tomorrow so I'll be able to go home and change. Bobby gets off, too, but I don't think he's going to the Fiestacita."

"Where is Bobby?" Iggy asked, looking around.

"Working in back. We have the storeroom back there, you know. He's listing some new arrivals on the inventory."

Iggy looked more closely at the beautiful Indian and Spanish artifacts that had blurred together earlier in his first impression. "This really is a great place."

Cindy glowed with pleasure. "Don't you just love it? And it stays exciting because we get in really rare pieces that will go to the museum when it's built, ones that aren't for sale."

Iggy thought that Cindy outshone the treasures, but kept to the conversation. "Didn't you tell me that you sell stuff here?"

"Yes we do, and Dr. Bottoms puts a lot of trust in me. I'm responsible for being sure we only sell what he's approved, that I don't mix up any of the pieces that aren't for sale...Like right there by you. That *Carreta de la Muerte* is priceless. It's an authentic old one from a morada, a miniature of the one the penitentes pulled. That Cart of Death is the sort of thing Dr. Bottoms is bringing back to Taos where it belongs."

"Priceless?"

"Absolutely," Cindy answered. "Mr. Kelly, you know, the director at the Stoner Museum here, said to name our price he wants it so bad, but Dr. Bottoms won't sell."

"And you call this a miniature Cart of Death? Pretty big for that," Iggy commented, looking directly into Death's empty but somehow chilling eye sockets. "I'm nose-to-nose with old Doña Sebastiana here on the counter."

Cindy patted his arm affectionately. "I meant 'miniature' compared to the real thing."

He grinned back at those smiling brown eyes. "Well, this 'real thing' is ready to party ahead of time. How about a drink?"

Cindy shook her head. "I wish I could, Ignacio, but Bobby and I still have work to do."

Iggy's belly got in the way as he leaned across the counter, but he still managed to clasp Cindy in a big bear hug. "See you later."

CHAPTER III

Death was prominent at the party. Clad in the skeletal form of La Doña Sebastiana, she sat in her death cart and grimly surveyed La Fiestacita. Incongruously, a lovely black lace mantilla was draped over death's skull, falling to her bony shoulders. Her hands held a drawn bow.

Some might say that a late afternoon in New Mexico's high country was too beautiful a day to die. The Indians, though, might say it was a beautiful day *for* dying. One guest at the party grinned back at Doña Sebastiana's toothless grimace, sure that life is only worth living if Death is close at hand. It's the edge, the risk, that gives color. The closer the bone, the sweeter the meat.

Most of the vividly dressed partygoers ignored death. The Fiestacita was happening. The guests moved about the Kachina's patio or sat at the numerous round tables next to the pool. The sun shone with a particular clarity at this altitude, making the colors brighter, the shadows darker and more sharply defined. The sky was a hard summer blue. Doña Sebastiana's arrow remained cocked and ready to fire.

"*Vivan Las Fiestas!*" shouted La Doña Abogada.

"Vivan!" the crowd roared in response.

"*Viva La Reina!*" this Lady Lawyer, Doris Jordan, called out.

"Viva!" the group bellowed back.

"Viva!"

"Viva!"

Her speech opening La Fiestacita thus concluded, La Doña looked benevolently on the jubilant crowd, then resumed her seat at the head table. The celebration announcing the Queen was over. Fiesta week had begun!

At one of the many side tables, Christina Garcia y Grant laughed at Mac. "Isn't this great?"

"Sure is. And La Doña's doin' herself proud," Dr. McCloud added in his Florida drawl. This retired surgeon had come to Taos after his wife died, returning to the B&B they had loved together. Right now, he was able to sit back and enjoy the Fiestacita, his long frame relaxed.

"What is she," he asked, "some kind of Mistress of Ceremonies?"

"Well, in a way," Christy answered. "La Doña Doris is President of the Fiesta Council, so that puts her in charge of all the Fiesta functions including this Fiestacita, the 'little fiesta'. It's always the week before *Las Fiestas de Santiago y Santa Ana.*"

"Quite a mouthful, ma'am. I just thought it was 'Las Fiestas'."

Christy ran a hand through her thick, white-salted black hair, cut short and springy. "That's what we're losing sight of these last years," she regretted. "We forget that we're celebrating our Saints' days."

Mac sounded a little miffed as he responded, "All us newcomers—retired doctors and such—messing up the old ways, eh?"

Christy smiled at him ruefully, "Not you, my friend. Anyway, who am I to complain? Bringing *las turistas* to my bed and breakfast? Guess I'm like most native *Taoseñas, Taoseños...* We need the tourist dollar, but don't want them to change our ways."

"Or move here!" Mac supplied.

Christy grinned, her tone lighter. "That's right. Visas at the border. Only the good McCloud types allowed to move in!"

Dr. McCloud looked around at the boisterous crowd. "In all the times Betty Anne and I visited Taos, even took in the Fiestas a time or two, I never knew y'all had this blow-out the week before."

"Invitation only, doctor! Well, an occasional sale. Those other times were before you took up residence in my former sheep shed," Christy teased. Then, seeing the shadow pass across her friend's face, quickly amended, "I'm sorry, Mac. I didn't mean to make light of the loss of your wife."

Mac placed his large surgeon's hand lightly on Christy's arm. "I don't want you worrying over what you say, Christy dear. It's been more than a year since Betty Anne died, and a bunch of months since I came here to Taos. And I was often too busy, too self-important, to be much of a husband…Anyway, that was one good idea on my part, retiring early and doin' my own healing away from all our memories in Florida."

Mac brightened, the planes in his face shifting. "But I guess y'all find humor in tragedy. Else why that skeleton on the cart over there by the head table?"

Christy glanced over at the Carreta de la Muerte, then back at Mac with concern. "I hope you *can* see Doña Sebastiana as we Spanish do, Mac. There in the Cart of Death she is meant to be grim to remind you—all of us, I mean—of our sins, of how we may be cut off at any time, our struggle against death. She's also Death as a release, letting us leave our bodies and be with God." Christy paused, thinking of Señor Barela and the bells that had rung for him such a little while ago. "Sorry," she said. "I didn't mean to preach."

"Don't stop. I'm full of questions. Like, why the ox cart? And why Death at a party like this?" Mac asked.

"In the old days, Los Hermanos, the Brothers, dragged carts about that size as part of their penitential rites. They filled the carts with stones to make the penance more severe."

Mac interrupted, "Those are the penitentes we were involved with before?"

"Yes," Christy answered slowly. "A devout lay society, sensationalized and misunderstood." She shook her head as if clearing it. "No. I'm not starting on that subject! I'll just say that the Cart of Death, Carreta de la Muerte, is here because it's the theme of the parade this year."

"Death?" Mac questioned in amazement.

"Not as such." Christy bit her lip, trying to clarify. "Doña Sebastiana is serious in the Death Cart, but not always. The parade theme is the idea of enjoying life while you can. On the other hand, remember the saints."

Mac shook his head. "So old Lady Death there is reminding you to be good?"

"Yes, but we manage to make her humorous, too. There are lots of stories, Mac, where Death is a wily character people try to fool. In one, an old man and old woman are each complaining about how bad they feel. 'Oh, my back, my poor aching back,' the *viejo* says. 'Bah!' answers his wife. 'What do you know of pain, old man? I am the one who suffers with each step I take.' 'Aii,' argues the husband, 'but what of my bad heart, eh?'

"Just then Death walks in the door. 'I've come to take the poor sick old one,' she says. 'Take him.' 'Take her. I'm not sick. She is.' 'He is.' They argue."

Mac laughed. "No more death talk. Will you lookee here what's comin' at us!"

Seven strolling Mariachi players headed for Mac and Christy's table. Fiddles, violin and trumpets sang out. The blazing sound and their traditional costumes promoted the festive air of the Fiestacita. The group's five men wore tight dark blue pants with rows of shining silver buttons up the sides of their legs, and white wedding shirts with floppy black bow ties beneath their jackets. Its two women players substituted long blue skirts for the pants.

Christy looked from face to face, smiling. She knew them all, but her friends, Marty and Audrey, stopped playing long enough to give her a big hug.

Mac jumped up to shake everyone's hand. "Fine music!" he complimented the players.

"Sounding really good tonight," Christy added, smiling up at them.

Audrey grinned. "Are you ready for *La Marcha*?" she asked Mac.

He did his Groucho bit, waggling black eyebrows beneath his shock of prematurely white hair, shooting a questioning look at Christy.

"You'll find out what La Marcha is soon enough," Marty jumped in, "but we'll let you eat first, Mister, uh..."

"I'm sorry," Christy said, "This is Dr. Mac McCloud."

Her Mariachi friends wore curious looks, so she added, "He's living here now. Remember my bed and breakfast is at *mi abuela's,* my grandmother's, hacienda with the sheep shed in the courtyard? Well, Mac went to work on it, digging it out with a backhoe, renovating, adding on, and has made it into a little guest house."

The Mariachis grinned, nodded, lifted their bows and trumpet, and returned to playing. The music so close by was too loud for talking, so Christy and Mac watched the people congregated on La Kachina's patio. Groups formed, shifted, split, as the July sun sank toward the blue-gray mountains in a cobalt sky.

Clouds catching the sun, quickly turning to vermillion above, were challenged by swirls of color below in this largely Spanish crowd. The Fiestacita made one of the few occasions for the women to wear their full, broomstick fiesta skirts—blue, red, pink, plain and flowered—cinched in with silver concha belts most often set off by white ruffled blouses. And the jewelry! No one was shy about displaying heavy turquoise and silver bracelets, earrings, and squash blossom necklaces.

Not to be outdone, the men sported their best bolos, often with chunks of turquoise or wonderful Zuni inlays of Rainbow Man or Thunderbird, and big decorative belt buckles. Even the few men who wore sports jackets, instead of ruffled wedding shirts with full sleeves, still showed off bolos and belt buckles.

The Mariachis moved on. Mac turned back to Christy, smiling as he admired her smooth olive-skinned shoulders above the white ruffles. Her turquoise necklace brought out the green in her eyes. A silver concha belt accentuated her still-narrow waist. "I haven't seen you all decked out before. You could be the Queen of this Fiesta!"

Christy accepted the compliment with a grin, but corrected, "No, Mac. La Reina, the Queen, is over there with all her court."

"And a pretty bunch they are," he concluded, looking over at the bouquet of brightly robed young women wearing silver crowns on their long black hair.

"The buffet line isn't quite so long now," Christy said. "Let's get something to eat."

They worked their way through the tables, making slow progress because Christy had to stop so often to speak and hug. Mac stood tall and patient behind her.

Suddenly a tiny figure darted through the crowd, light blue fiesta skirt twirling.

"Mamacita!" Christy exclaimed, stooping a little to embrace her mother.

Ever the courtly Southerner, Mac took her hand. "Señora Garcia," he said gravely. "I saw you gracing the head table."

Her proud voice was surprisingly deep for such a small woman. "I sit at the head table because I am a member of the Fiesta Council. I am the one to give Christina the tickets, my invitation. Before when they call—Pablo's mother Conceptiona, he was in school with my son Patricio, she had asked me—and next Señora Sandoval, she—"

"Mama!"

"You are always so impatient, Christina. I am explaining to the doctor how many times I have been asked, but forever too busy—"

"Have any of you seen Cindy?" This time it was Iggy who interrupted Señora Garcia.

"We were talking, Ignacio," Mamacita said sternly.

"Sorry, Señora, but I'm really worried." Iggy chewed on his bottom lip and fidgeted, unable to stand still.

The buffet line moved forward, leaving their group behind. Mac silently steered Christy ahead, Mamacita and Ignacio following with them.

Turning back to her young attorney friend, Christy asked, "What's the big deal, Iggy?"

"This is serious, Christy!" Iggy said in a tone that made Christy contrite. They all had a tendency to downplay Ignacio's emotions. An opera buff, he also seemed to enjoy living his own life as high drama. Iggy thrived on crisis.

Iggy explained, "Cindy told me yesterday that she'd close the gallery early to get ready to come here. She was going to meet me by six for the dinner part. Now it's after seven and Cindy's still not here!" He ended in a near wail.

Standing next to him, Mac loomed over the younger man. He spoke gently, "Look here, Iggy, we're still in line for the food. Cindy probably knows how late these things run, especially with people enjoying a champagne fountain, and just didn't hurry."

Mamacita's curly white-haired little head turned from one man to the other, looking up at them with lively curiosity. "Who is this Cindy?" she asked. "Do I know her? Who is her family?"

Happy crowd noises rose and fell around them, but Iggy didn't feel like answering Mamacita politely. He'd sat at the head table being patient for over an hour. He was impatient with worry. "Cindy moved here by herself, a transplant from Eastern New Mexico just like me. There's no family to know about," he snapped at Mamacita, then turned on Mac. "And I know Cindy well enough to know she wouldn't keep me waiting like one of your Southern belles!"

Christy and Mac exchanged looks: Iggy would never speak to Mamacita that way unless he were genuinely upset. Christy answered for him, "Cindy works at one of the galleries, Mama. She's Ignacio's special friend, but I've gotten to know her, too. She's a sweet, gentle person."

The group reached the long tables of food lined up against the outside wall of the Kachina's dining room. Helping herself to salad, Christy noticed that Mamacita had somehow managed to insinuate herself far ahead along the buffet as usual. She smiled to herself, then gave Iggy her full attention. "I understand, friend. Cindy's not the type to be late. But things come up for all of us. She'll come rushing in any minute. You'll laugh at how worried you were."

"Well, I am worried! I get these feelings and I'm usually right. I'm not even hungry!"

That did bring a laugh from Mac and Christy. Iggy's appetite was a running joke with the Crew, a name the quartet, La Doña included, had given themselves.

"Not hungry, Ignacio?" came a booming female voice behind them. "I hope you don't have some infectious bug!"

"La Doña!" Christy exclaimed, happy to see her old friend. A fighter from way back, Christy's fierce friend had battled and won the war to be a lawyer at the end of the Depression.

"I had some gumption, too," Miss Jordan had said in one of her famous understatements. This gumption had earned her respect and the title of "La Doña Abogada," the Lady Lawyer. The people of Taos named her that all those long years ago when the town had few lawyers, and she the only woman attorney.

La Doña used both hands to adjust her embroidered, fringed silk shawl, bright with peacock colors. Probably doesn't know what to do without a battered, bulging briefcase dangling from one hand, Christy thought. But it was a beautiful shawl, as was her long, dark red velvet skirt, ancient though it might be.

"The head table has already been served and we've eaten, but thought I should leave the nobility and mingle with you peons," La Doña said gruffly. "What's the matter with our Ignacio?"

"I'm looking for Cindy," Iggy answered for himself. Anxiety clouded his face. "Have you seen her, La Doña?"

Still fiddling with her shawl, La Doña answered Iggy, "No, Ignacio. As far as I know, I haven't set eyes on your Cindy. But since I haven't had the pleasure of meeting the young lady, I can't give you a definitive answer."

In no mood for teasing, Iggy walked away stiffly to continue his search. Christy watched him, then concerned turned to Mac and La Doña. "Do you think we should do something? I know Iggy loves drama, but he's right. Cindy is a special person. She's not the type for a no show."

"Nothing to be done at the moment," La Doña replied brusquely. "I need to sit. Where's your table?"

Leading La Doña, Christy and Mac headed back toward their table and saw that it was already occupied by Mamacita and a middle-aged Anglo couple.

Mac grinned at the heaping plate of desserts in front of Señora Garcia, but Mamacita forestalled any comment. "I bring these for you." Then sadly, "They don't feed us the good desserts at the head table."

She turned to La Doña Doris. "You were at the head table, Presidente Doris. Perhaps if my Christina still practiced the law, she would be also?"

"Mama!" Christy was exasperated and embarrassed in front of the strangers. "First you object to my going to law school, then to my being a lawyer. Now you don't like it that I've burned out. Quit."

Mac didn't enter this familiar argument. In fact, he thought Mamacita did it for fun. Instead, Mac turned to introduce himself to the new couple. "Name's Mac," he said smiling.

"I'm Ted Nesbit, the famous artist," answered the bearded man."And this is my companion, Virginia Warren, from the Archdiocese by way of the Philadelphia School of Art."

Mac was speechless in the face of these credentials and presented by a famous artist no less! Luckily, Christy came to his aid with introductions. She then asked, "Don't you also own a gallery on the Plaza?"

"Yes, La Bonita."

"The Pretty? Um, well..." Christy was at a loss for words.

"A most reverential space," Virginia Warren chimed in, opening her eyes wide. "There is a sense of the universe brought down to the particular. Lute-like grace notes that in no way contravene the textile power of the paintings. Divine!" She giggled. "'Divine'! That is within my field since, of course, I have been coming to Northern New Mexico to catalogue church art for the Archdiocese."

"Of course," Christy murmured.

Mac refrained from looking at her.

"Church art?" Mamacita echoed, her voice eager. "Do you make a list of the paintings on our reredo at San Francisco?"

"The large screen behind the altar? Well, yes, as archivist." The words fell as if little plums from Virginia's cupid lips. "I research the provenance of all your art, paintings, *retablos*, santos—"

Mama frowned, pursed her mouth. "You know, then, that someone has stolen our San Francisco? The little santo who stands in el nicho by the altar? Gone, my friend who speaks for me to *El Señor*. This San Francisco has been with us all the days. He hears our prayers."

"Disgraceful!" La Doña interrupted. "I can't understand what lowlife would steal from a church! And it's not only Saint Francis Church. I have a client up in Chama who just yesterday told me about a theft from the church up there. Quite upset she was. Another Spanish import nearly as priceless as *La Conquistadora* stolen from the Cathedral in Santa Fe."

An awkward silence followed. Christy wondered why. Mamacita felt it. Something evil in the air, *muy malo*. She could see that Mamacita unobtrusively held her hands under edge of the table and secretly made the sign against the evil eye.

Ted Nesbit broke the silence. "The Conquistadora incident was quite some time ago, I believe."

Mama said, "'Priceless'? *N'importante*. La Conquistadora or our San Francisco cannot be measured in money. They are part of *nuestra familia*. They help us do what we cannot."

"Oh, come now, Señora. "Surely the theft of some forgotten, dusty old statue in a church—"

"*Castigo de Dios*," Mamacita interrupted. "Those who do this shall suffer Castigo de Dios and all their children and—"

"Punishment of God," Christy translated, anger in her voice.

CHAPTER IV

Music abruptly put a stop to all conversation. It grew louder and the crowd whooped. "La Marcha! Come join La Marcha!"

Christy jumped up, smiling and stretching out her hand to Mac. Mamacita appeared bereft, looking around like a confused little bird. "So many I don't know," she said. "In the old days I would know all the persons...*tios, tias, primos*...Now, *se esta muriendo todo.*"

"That one I know." Christy referred to the Spanish saying. "It's what we were talking about, Mac. Mama says that it's all dying out, the old ways."

Mac was touched. "Come join us in this march-thing, whatever it is."

Caught up in her sadness, Mamacita shook her head. "No, no. It is two-by-two, the couples...*Y ahora todo lo que tengo son anas.*"

"English, Mama. English."

"I *said*," Mamacita answered stiffly, "that all I have now is the years I've lived."

"Then we'll pair you with La Doña."

That lady immediately interrupted."Not this old war horse, Dr. McCloud. There's not much I can't do, but bending over under a long arch of arms is one of them!"

Christy turned, "C'mon, Mac, Mama! Look, they've already started."

Mac looked across now mostly empty tables to the center of the patio and saw the crowd moving into a ragged line of couples starting to circle.

The beat of the Mariachis called.

"All right! Let's go!" He grabbed the hands of both Christy and Señora Garcia. It was apparent Mac intended Mamacita would dance with *someone*. The older woman suddenly looked very pretty, blushing and shy.

Reaching the temporary dance floor, the trio joined a cluster of people waiting to merge with the still slow-stepping, circling dancers. Christy shouted at Mac over the din of voices and music, "Just do what everyone else is doing! Follow the leaders!"

An aristocratic-looking, blonde man about Mac's age stood alone in the hubbub. Christy smiled at him and he addressed her over the noise. "Er, I just arrived from Santa Fe. All this is new to me. I say, what does one do now?" His English accent was pronounced.

With a mischievous grin, Christy said, "Mama will show you."

For once, Mamacita was speechless, but the stranger had not heard Christy clearly. "What's that?" he called.

Again Christy almost shouted. "Mama, my mama, Señora Garcia. She'll show you."

"Right-o." A little bow. "Señora?"

The tiny woman and the tall Englishman fell in behind Christy and Mac as space opened up. Mac quickly picked up the rhythm and shuffling step, his arm around Christy's waist, and they were into La Marcha!

Two-by-two the boisterous crowd circled to the music, punctuated by occasional yips, fiesta skirts twirling colors. Around and around they went until Mac saw the lead couple turn sideways, still moving to the beat, and make an arch of their out-stretched arms. The couple next to the leaders up ahead ducked under those arms and, in turn, made a second arch.

By the time Mac and Christy reached the upraised arms, there were about twenty to pass under. Chuckling, stumbling, Mac was hard-put to bend low enough to get under the arms of so many shorter couples. Head down, Mac saw an endless-seeming forest of legs, and Christy's backside. Laughing and breathless, they emerged from the tunnel of arms and, in turn, held hands, arms upraised to make an arch themselves.

Next came a giggling Mamacita and the tall Englishman, he so tall and she so short they had difficulty making their arch. The man had to lean over so far for Mama that he looked like a question mark.

Music, laughter, noise! La Marcha!

Now the last couple passed under innumerable arms. Reaching the end, they split apart, circling in opposite directions, couple by couple following until the arch was gone. The men rhythmically moved one way, the women the other. The leaders then took the women into a smaller circle while the men formed an outside rim.

By now, the sky had darkened to a deep indigo tinged with a whisper of green, reluctant to give way to night. All encompassing serenity overhead; the noise of the Fiestacita in full swing below.

The circles were coming together again in couples but somehow to Mac's consternation, he was moved up, one person out of place. He faced a laughing and charming but unknown face, and Christy was with the Englishman.

Mac saw the blonde head bend down close to Christy's dark one. She smiled up at him. Mac thought the stranger suddenly seemed rather adept at La Marcha as the leaders now took the crowd of dancers into ever-decreasing circles.

Finally, faster and faster, louder and louder, the music reached a crescendo, all bunched tightly together, and with upraised arms and a great shout, La Marcha ended. Breathlessly laughing, some holding heaving chests, everyone headed back to their tables. The stranger had attached himself to Christy.

Mac was not pleased.

Naturally, Mamacita was already at the table. What did she do? scoot under legs? There La Doña remained chatting with the new people. Mac trailed Christy and the Englishman. They sat. He remained standing.

Christy smiled up at Mac and said, "This is Dr. Evelyn Bottoms, Dr. Mac McCloud."

"How do you do?" Dr. Bottoms shook hands with Mac. "Are you also in the Arts, sir?"

"No, I'm a surgeon. You say that you're an artist?"

"Fine arts, Ph.D." He coughed. "Harvard. I'm here on a mission to create a museum that recovers local artifacts."

The conversation stalled.

Nurturing an unexpected attraction to the Englishman, Christy asked, "Won't you stay and join our table?"

"No, no. I mustn't intrude longer on your party. And I really must return to Santa Fe." He stood as he spoke.

La Doña waved him down. "Don't be ridiculous, doctor. This is La Fiestacita! No strangers here!"

"Then let me treat all of you to a drink, if I may?"

"Champagne fountain's free," La Doña instructed. "Why don't you and Mac bring us each a glass?"

"Right-o." And turning to Mac, "Shall we?"

Christy watched the two tall men make their way through the tables toward the bar. Mac was lanky but solid, his shoulders wide in an elderly tweed jacket. Evelyn Bottoms was an equal height, but slimmer and put together more precisely in a beautifully tailored tan cashmere sports coat. Mac's white hair fell, as always, every which way, while the Englishman's blonde hair was a smoothly cut cap on a narrow head.

"A very pretty man," La Doña commented, following Christy's gaze.

Christy thought a moment. "Not 'pretty', La Doña. I don't like pretty men. But quite attractive, I'd say."

Shaking her head, Señora Garcia warned Christy, "Better that you stay with the one you have. *Un buen gallo, en cualquier gallinero canta.*"

"Mama! I don't have Mac. And what's with all these Spanish sayings tonight? How often must I have to apologize for being cool and not learning Spanish at home when they wouldn't let us speak it at school?...Remember Jaime? The teacher made him wear a wad of chewing gum on his nose all day. Punishment for speaking Spanish on the playground!"

Ignoring the outburst and looking both complacent and mischievous at the same time, Mamacita responded, "Then you should hear the English for what I said. 'A good rooster can crow in any hen house'!"

The two roosters stood waiting to fill seven plastic wine glasses at the champagne fountain. Mac, the Southern gentleman, tried to by-pass their previous chill with a friendly, "Fine arts, eh? Taos is supposed to be a good place to pick up art of all kinds."

"Oh, I'm not here to 'pick up art', as you say. I'm opening a museum and have a satellite retail gallery already in business on the Plaza."

Mac, not very good at small talk at any time, and uncomfortable with this character, could only come up with a feeble, "Great."

The awkward conversation was saved by a new voice. "Don't you find the idea of another museum redundant, Dr. Bottoms?"

The newcomer was a stocky man about Mac's age, wearing an unstructured gray silk Armani with a matching collarless shirt. He was shorter than the other two and had sandy hair in a brush-cut.

"Sorry to interrupt," the stranger said, looking at Bottoms intensely with sharp blue eyes, then turned to introduce himself to Mac. "I'm Jerome Kelly, the director of the Stoner Museum."

"Glad to meet you, Doctor. I'm Mac McCloud."

"I don't use the title," Jerome Kelly replied with a smile. "Don't want to put on airs with possible donors."

Mr. Kelly turned to Evelyn Bottoms. "Just wanted to suggest to you that what with the Millicent and Harwood, not to mention Fechin and Lineberry, we find the museum scene covered."

Dr. Bottoms bristled. "They do not fill the niche of the rare objects I shall retrieve," he retorted.

"Then why not donate them to the Stoner. We could use that Carreta de la Muerte, for instance."

"Our objectives are not the same."

Jerome Kelly smiled. "Sorry, Didn't mean to offend. We're all alike—museum directors, college presidents, foundations—have to keep pushing for those donations."

With a nod, he turned away.

"Luckily others here don't share Mr. Kelly's views," Dr. Bottoms commented.

"You've moved here then, doctor?" Mac did his part to turn the conversation to happier channels, while wondering why an English accent seemed to make the most ordinary statement sound intelligent—and himself like a clod.

"Oh, no, no," Dr. Bottoms, making his recovery from Mr. Kelly, laughed charmingly. "I'm rather a vagabond—off to New York one day, Europe the next, and then perhaps Santa Fe where I have my other gallery." He paused. "And please call me Evelyn, doctor."

"Fine. And I'm just plain Mac. But I bet if you spend any time in Taos, the place will get to you. You'll want to put down roots here."

"I take it you're a resident then. And your...uh, delightful Miss Grant is, of course, a native."

Mac didn't like the sound of native issuing from beneath that pencil blonde mustache. He also debated clarifying his presumed possession of Christy, since she was not his—yet. Mac settled for a noncommittal "Mmm."

Finding a tray, Mac carried the champagne back to the table. After the little flurries of thank yous as he passed the glasses around, Evelyn came up behind him. Mac noted that now he veritably sparkled with wit, embracing the famous artist and his long-haired companion. Christy seemed particularly entranced, especially when he launched into a description of his plans: "I'm not creating just one more museum. Just as the Smithsonian and others are returning Native American bones and religious artifacts, I'm searching the world for the precious Spanish Renaissance items carried off by collectors, though, of course, Northern New Mexico rather missed the Renaissance. Part of the charm, you see. None of the perspective, the depth, being developed in Europe of the time as witness the retablos, for instance, of the period, although there was indeed the Post-Renaissance—"

To Mac's relief, Iggy's abrupt arrival ended the burgeoning art lecture. Fellow was just beginning to hit his stride, too.

Iggy's face was flushed, damp with perspiration. His curls stuck to his forehead, despite the typical chill already overcoming this Taos summer night.

"Hello, Nesbit," Iggy said perfunctorily to the artist. Turning to the Englishman, he blurted out with no polite preamble, "Are you the Bottoms fellow they say is Cindy's boss?"

"Ah, yes, I own El Museo where Cynthia Williams is employed." Evelyn Bottoms appeared taken aback.

"You know where she is?"

"Sorry, Mister uh...?"

"Baca. Ignacio Baca. I'm an attorney here in town and Cindy planned to meet me here at six. Now it's almost nine o'clock! No Cindy! And that's not like her."

Dr. Bottoms was sympathetic. "I permitted the staff to close El Museo early so that Cynthia could attend this Fiestacita." Pausing, stroking his mustache, he smiled. "But surely, young ladies being what they are, there's no cause for alarm."

Iggy tried for control. "Apparently you don't know Cindy."

"Oh, but I do! A most responsible young lady."

"She sure is. And that's why I *am* alarmed. Will you come with me and check the gallery? Make certain Cindy left okay?"

Evelyn Bottoms glanced at his thin gold Rolex, "Sorry, Mister, ah, Baca, but I'm going to be late for an important engagement in Santa Fe as it is. May I assume that you have already queried Cynthia's friends? Perhaps rung up her apartment?"

"There wasn't any answer. If we could just go...?"

Dr. Bottoms stood up. "Sorry, old chap. Pressing business as I explained. Her friends?"

Iggy looked embarrassed, shook his head. "Well..."

"And her apartment? You looked there?"

Another sheepish head shake.

"You see? Perhaps a call upon the concierge of the apartment...A few telephone calls to her friends. Some other party may have rivaled this Fiestacita."

Dr. Bottoms turned to the group at the table. He sketched a small bow toward Ted Nesbit and Virginia Warren, then turned to La Doña, "Miss Jordan, it has been a pleasure."

He bent over Mamacita's hand, "Señora Garcia. "*Una gusta. Y muchos gracias.*"

"*La gusta es mia*," Mamacita answered happily.

Finally, he turned to Christy, "I so hope we will meet again. I would be buoyed immeasurably by your interest in my project."

Christy felt sexual tension between them, an undercurrent to her innocent response, "I hope so, too. You really didn't have a chance to explain it all to me."

A firm handshake with Mac. "Doctor." Then to Iggy, "Mr. Baca. I'm sure all will be well." Dr. Bottoms walked away. The departure was so sudden Iggy was left speechless. It was up to La Doña to add dryly, "A real charmer."

"I liked him," Christy defended.

Giving herself a little shake, Mama said, "We will see, hmm?"

Christy turned to Iggy. "I didn't like the brush-off you got. I think it's time you did some serious looking for Cindy."

Mac draped his arm across the back of Christy's chair. "I hear the dance is going to be country music. Want to show this Southerner the two step?"

Christy shook off the possessiveness, "Sorry, Mac. I'd like to, but I need to put the bread on to rise for breakfast. And you know how early I'll have to be up for my houseful of guests. We'd better go home."

"I guess I go home, too," Mamacita sighed regretfully, "but I do love to dance."

CHAPTER V

Tiny Señora Garcia didn't take up much room, but the three of them crowded the single seat of Mac's pickup until they dropped Mama off at her small adobe home in Ranchos de Taos.

Mac gallantly saw Mamacita to her door and waited until she had the lights on before returning to the Chevy.

"No need to scoot over," he said to Christy with a grin. "I like having you snugged up close."

Over her pique, Christy grinned back and remained where she was without comment.

"Your mama sure was quiet tonight," Mac said.

"She was excited," Christy explained, a tender note in her voice. "She told me that she'd been too keyed up to rest this afternoon when she got back from having her hair done. It was a big deal for her to go to a party like La Fiestacita without my father. Then to sit at the head table."

"I understand," Mac answered gently as, in order to let a car pass, he pulled to the side of the road that was too narrow to be two lanes. With no need to return to the highway from Mamacita's, Mac was taking the dirt road to Talpa, the one known as "The Road Under the Hill". Moonlight picked out white-blooming cactus on the banks of that hill.

They soon reached the intersection with the Talpa highway, crossed it, and drove on another dirt road.

Located in the tiny Talpa community, Christy's inherited hacienda waited to welcome them home. She had used her nest egg for renovation, remodeling, and more bathrooms to adapt the centuries-old adobe into a bed and breakfast.

I wish I was just going home to bed without worrying about breakfast in the morning, Christy mused. Sometimes it's hard to have continuous open house, never able to shut the doors and just slob around.

"Mighty quiet yourself," Mac commented. He negotiated the sharp bend in the even more narrow road near the hacienda.

"Sorry, Mac. I'm just worn out enough to feel a touch of self-pity. And I should be grateful that the bed and breakfast is staying full, giving me the luxury of trying to make it as a writer."

Mac's answer was simply the kind of silence that seemed filled with unspoken words. After a bit he said, "You have every right to want to boot everyone out occasionally. Even yours truly."

Involuntarily flashing on Evelyn Bottoms, Christy quickly answered, "No, not you, Mac. Never."

"Cherish that thought, ma'am," Mac said lightly. "And here we are."

The wrought iron lantern over the garage cast patterns of light on the small parking lot Christy had fixed across the dirt road from Casa Vieja. There were no street lights in Talpa.

The mood grew electric. Gently Mac lightly placed his fingers under Christy's chin and tipped her face up as he bent his head down to kiss her.

As he did so, Christy glanced at the guests' cars in the parking lot. "Mac, look!"

He moved protectively closer to her, but the mood was broken. "What?"

"There, that big car. Cadillac? Someone's sitting in it!"

"Well, maybe one of your guests had a fight with his wife."

"What if it's a car thief?"

"I doubt if a thief would wave! See there?"

An arm was stretched out the driver's side window. Christy laughed with relief. Mac got out, opened her door, took her arm and they crossed the little road to the hacienda. The silence now was filled with the tension of wondering what might have been.

The high adobe walls surrounding the house were gray in the dark, the ancient little wooden gate a different shade of gray. The adobe walls of the courtyard merged smoothly, indistinguishably, into those of the hacienda itself.

To the right of the gate, the light from the high kitchen windows fell on the road, but didn't reach this far. Farther right was the official B&B entrance, sporting the carved wood CASA VIEJA B&B sign. There, another wrought iron lantern lit the way for the guests.

The swamp willow brushed Christy's cheek softly as she opened the gate. Probably scarcely more than a twig when the walls were being built, the tree had remained in the wall and now, gnarled with age, it had broken the adobes to either side of it, completely insinuating itself into them.

Christy took a deep breath of the nighttime scent of the courtyard. The blooms were gone from the olive tree and with them their memorable fragrance. Gone, too, was the heavy Spring sweetness of hyacinth. Now, the scent of warm roses lingered from the summer day, mingling with the stronger notes of the night-blooming nicotiana.

"Beginning to smell like home to me," Mac said softly as he stepped around random flower beds, following Christy across the flagstone courtyard toward the kitchen door.

To the left, Mac's own quarters in the remodeled sheep shed were dark.

Giving one of the old wooden posts its usual pat, Christy crossed the portal and unlocked the kitchen door, noticing that the Don's Room was dark across the far side of the U-shape. Apparently those guests had already gone to bed. But as to the others, a light in La Escondida wouldn't show from here. Maybe Mr. DeWitt, who shared that room with his wife, was the guest out in the car.

Coming in from the night chill, Christy enjoyed the kitchen warmth. It brought memories of fires. She smiled, remembering guests who walked in demanding a fire in midsummer while she ran around turning on fans.

"Happy thought, m'dear?" Mac asked.

How comfortable he was, Christy thought. But they had almost moved to a new level tonight. She'd best forget her attraction to the Englishman. Hearing an echo of Mac's question, she answered, "Just guests and fires."

"Why don't you take off those party duds while I fix us some hot chocolate?" he suggested.

"Good idea, Mac. Thank you. I'm so wound up. Oh, damn! I forgot again. I still have the bread to make."

"Well, sit and relax first. Betty Anne always said that the best fun of a party was getting to talk about it afterward."

"I agree with Betty Anne. Be right back."

Remembering to duck under the low viga, which she often forgot after all these years, Christy stepped up one old brick step from the kitchen to the dining room separated by only the low adobe half-wall. The dining room depended for light on candles in the big old black chandelier, along with the kerosene lamps on the *tierra blanca* walls.

Next, turning on the night light in the Middle Room, Christy looked toward the door of the *Curandera's* Room. La Curandera, the healer, had been famous for her cures, and her room still had the two long adobe bancos, now furnished with comfortable mattresses, which the curandera had used for her patients. Christy kept quiet about the fact that the rear of the room (holding a new double bed) had been used to lay out the dead. The young couple, the Jacobys, had requested this room, he saying that its atmosphere was conducive to meditation.

Christy turned, stepping down into the great hall, La Sala. The days it held a gallery for visitors were the same days when the owners accommodated visiting sheep, or even oxen, in the courtyard. On that side, La Sala's many-paned windows reflected only darkness from the portal and courtyard beyond. But inside, the night light that Christy flipped on was enough to show the waxed shine of old brick floors, their gleam interrupted by soft Oriental rugs here and there.

Darker shadows indicated nichos holding Christy's beloved santos on the opposite wall on either side of the kiva fireplace, now cold.

Christy murmured goodnight to Santo Niño and San Francisco and stepped up again to the back hall. That blasted hunter, Mr. Keen and his wife, were staying in the Don's Room to her left, on the other side of her narrow iron spiral stairs to the second floor.

The tiny door to La Escondida was to her right. The bird-watchers were in there. Mrs. DeWitt had said she had to have that little nest.

Wearily, Christy climbed the spiral steps. Too bad that she'd told Mac she'd come back for hot chocolate. Better to be just going to bed.

Christy turned on the light by the bed, illuminating her comfortable sanctuary. The soft lamplight showed her queen bed with a puffy blue down comforter, and her big, Taos-style chair for reading, its cushions woven in random stripes of blues and lavender. A desk, also fashioned by Marcus, her favorite Taos woodworker, was topped with computer and printer. Her grandmother's braided rugs softened the shining dark red "blood" floor. Outside her window, the tops of ancient cotton-woods rustled in the summer night breeze.

With relief, Christy kicked off her shoes, quickly slipped off her heavy silver and turquoise jewelry, then undressed. Stepping into her long, soft, flowered robe, Christy was ready to pad downstairs barefoot.

Mac was waiting for her in the dining room. He had lit the side kerosene lamps. They shone on the old polished oak table where two cups of hot chocolate steamed.

"Thank you, Mac," Christy said, giving him a hug. She pulled back quickly, not wanting to move any closer to the romantic relationship interrupted tonight.

"Think nothing of it, ma'am," Mac answered with a happy grin. "I would have put on the bread but that's beyond my talents."

"I'm thinking more and more that my guests would rather have waffles in the morning than the bread that's haunting me tonight. They don't always have to have homemade bread do they?"

"Absolutely not. I'm sure they're all pinin' for waffles. Wouldn't consider fresh-baked bread."

"It's unanimous, then…" Christy tried to ignore her fatigue. "So what did you think of your first Fiestacita?"

"Great! Such a happy crowd. Gave me a different point of view for these up-coming Fiestas, too, less like a tourist seeing only those junky stands. Thank you for asking me."

"As you'd say, I was proud to have such a fine escort. Mamacita, too. You were sweet to her tonight, Mac."

Mac didn't want to be the first to bring up the Englishman, so he said, "I hope there was a good reason for Cindy to stand up Iggy. That poor boy was surely in a state!"

"'Boy', Mac? 'State'? You've gone all Southern on me. I'll need a translator soon."

"At least it's American," Mac teased.

Christy stiffened. "As opposed to Spanish, you mean?"

"Lord no!" Mac exclaimed. "You know me better than to think I'd make a crack like that. I was referring to Lord Bottoms' proper English. Makes me feel like a clod." Why hadn't he kept his big mouth shut? Christy was still riled and he sounded like some jealous bastard. Making moves on her, too.

"Dr. Bottoms is planning to do some fine things for Taos and *la gente*," she said coolly.

"I'm sure he is," Mac answered, his voice appeasing. "My trouble is feeling like a dolt around someone like that."

"Like what?" Christy fired back.

"C'mon, Christy, m'dear. I don't want to fight with you. This conversation just got off track. Let's talk about the party."

Christy took a breath, smiled and said, "Okay, Mac. But there's not much to say about the 'famous artist' and his date without sounding catty, is there? I don't like long graying hair on aged debutantes. Oh, I must stop! And I was afraid to look at you for fear you'd make me laugh."

Mac chuckled, "It was all I could do not to, and then when you pondered over his La Pretty gallery...!"

"Now, Mac. We mustn't."

"Okay. No more Mister Famous Artist and Miz Philadelphia School of Art...Say, Iggy seemed to know him, didn't he?"

Christy pondered. "Nesbit's gallery shows more than just his own stuff, and I think he's the one the other artists are accusing of embezzlement. Keeping the money he gets from sales of their paintings. Seems like Iggy said he's defending the man."

"Criminal charges?"

"Both, I believe."

At Mac's questioning look, Christy explained, "I mean there are criminal charges, but some of the artists are also bringing civil suits to recover the money due and force Ted Nesbit to give their paintings back, too."

"Some mess! What a low life! Pretty brazen of him to come to the Fiestacita!"

"Well, you saw that ego, Mac. 'Famous artist'! He probably thinks he can get away with anything."

"Didn't look like he was hurting, but if what you say is true, his attorney fees must be humongous!"

Christy sipped her chocolate."Yep." She yawned. "Our Iggy charges full rates when he's not working on his public defender contract with the state."

"This Florida boy doesn't know the Taos ins and outs, but I wonder why the Fiesta Council would invite Nesbit with all that going on?"

"Probably didn't. The Council would invite Miz Philadelphia since she's connected with the Archdiocese, and he came along as her date."

"Yeah. They were so close together at the table, they didn't know anything else was going on. Pretty bad for the image." He paused. "Speaking of images..."

"What, Mac?"

"I got to take the prettiest girl there!"

"Flattery!" Christy snorted. "What about La Reina and her court? You missed their visit to our table."

Mac shook his head. "No, ma'am. Couldn't hold a candle to my girl." Ooops. Now she'd grab hold of that "my girl" goof.

But instead it was Christy's turn to shake her head, smiling. "Mac, Mac. You're too much. And I'm too tired." But her voice was gentle.

There was no moon.

The Rio Grande was invisible far below the gorge bridge. One would only know the river was there by its barely discernible sound, something like wind brushing through high trees.

The gorge itself seemed a bottomless black rift in the desert, that rose on either side of that half-mile split of darkness, undulating away in miles of sagebrush. The barren land finally stopped at the surrounding mountains, which stood out blacker than the brilliantly starred New Mexico sky.

The late-night desert was dead quiet in the hours before dawn. Quiet, too, was the car that came to a careful halt a few hundred yards away from the sign that warned against stopping on the gorge bridge.

The driver took yet another compulsive look in the rearview mirror, then committed himself by popping the trunk lid. He fearfully slipped from the car, anxiously hoping to do the job before any headlights picked him out.

He ran to the trunk, unable to make himself open it all the way until he shot another look each direction. That done, the man pushed up the lid, cursing the luxury option that automatically turned on the trunk light.

A large and bulky black plastic bag reflected the dim light on its shiny surface.

In a frenzy of apprehension, the man braced himself. He had to lean over at an awkward angle to work his arms under the bag. Grunting, he lifted the bag with effort, but there was so much adrenaline pumping through his body that he was able to go at a near-run across the few feet of sidewalk to the railing of the bridge.

Did he hear a car? Was something coming? This was the part when he was truly committed.

A short judo-like shout and he heaved the bag and its contents up and over the rail. Endless seconds passed. The man waited for a sound, a splash.

Nothing.

Far below, the Rio Grande absorbed his secret.

CHAPTER VI

Christy awoke to a bright July day in a room still cool from the night's chill. She felt her usual early morning panic that she was late in fixing breakfast. Then she remembered she had no bread to bake. She had plenty of time. Nevertheless, Christy moved quickly to put on her long, lavender cotton robe, wash, and lightly make up. All the while she was thinking about last night's Fiestacita. Mac's aborted kiss was part of those thoughts. She hoped it wouldn't change their easy friendship.

Christy was soon hurrying down the difficult spiral stairway, her soft slippers making no sound. No sound either from the Keens or DeWitts in their rooms. Her thoughts turned to Iggy and his concerns about Cindy. She felt anxious as she passed through La Sala. It was dim, not yet reached by the early morning sun.

In the kitchen, Christy knelt by a cupboard, feeling toward its back for the Belgian waffle iron...What the hell was that! A piercing bird song right behind her?

She stumbled up too quickly, stepped on her robe, then caught the counter top. Mrs. DeWitt popped through the kitchen door from the courtyard.

"Oh! Mrs. DeWitt! I thought you were a bird." Unfortunate choice of words since the lady did indeed resemble a robin in her polished cotton khaki suit, orange blouse over massive bosom, and little pipe-stem legs ending in lace-up British walkers.

Mrs. DeWitt was unoffended. "Just what I wanted our little feathered friend to think. I was almost certain that I heard a

Townsend's Solitaire and was calling the fellow. Of course, he breeds in mountain forests, but is known to be fond of juniper. I thought there was just an off chance, you know, believing I heard him and noticing the juniper. That *is* a juniper by the back wall, isn't it?"

Christy was too bewildered to answer. Too early for this! The lack of response didn't seem to bother Mrs. DeWitt. "Just think! If I catch sight of that Townsend's Solitaire, I'll put him down in my Life Book, noting the sighting was right here at your charming hacienda!" Taking a quick sip of air, she continued, "A beginning bird watcher is likely to think him a thrasher, perhaps, even a flycatcher, anything but a Solitaire! Can you imagine that?" She laughed heartily.

"Uh, no."

"But tell me, now. Have you heard the Solitaire?"

Christy felt nailed in place by the little black eyes. "I don't know."

"You have memorized the bird songs, haven't you?" Stern.

Christy could only come up with a weak, "Well, I do have a bird book."

"But do you have the CD for Western birds?" Severely. "Learned their songs from it?"

"Uh."

Mrs. DeWitt was offended. "Please don't tell me you haven't even—"

Mac saved Christy by banging through the door, looking not at all like his usual easy-going self. "Is there a bird convention going on around here? I never heard so damn many squawks at the crack of dawn!"

Christy tried to warn Mac with a discreet jab but, oblivious, Mac continued, "What's the matter, Christy? I was just complaining about those lousy birds waking me…Oh, good morning, ma'am. I'm Mac McCloud. I live in the little—"

Christy interrupted. "This is Mrs. DeWitt, Mac. She and her husband checked in late yesterday. Just before we left for the Fiestacita. She's been—"

"Bird calling," the lady announced proudly. "One must be early at it. Such a symphony this morning! Although our hostess—"

A thin, middle-aged man rushed in from the Middle Room, cutting short the pending lecture about Christy's shortcomings. And she was too involved in her failings as a bird watcher to warn Mr. DeWitt to duck for the low viga above the step down to the kitchen. The top of his head cracked into the beam, but the man wasn't slowed. Rubbing his head, he said, "You should have seen the Kachina parking lot. With what I picked up on the Plaza last night, I've got all but Mississippi." He turned to his wife. "I told you the Kachina looked like the best bet."

Mac's black eyebrows almost disappeared into a disheveled lock of white hair. Christy, trying to hold back a fit of giggles, turned her back on the DeWitts. Her voice became muffled. "Excuse me. I have to start the waffles."

Mr. DeWitt: "If I might have just a piece of fruit? I want to find Mississippi, so I have to get back to the other motels before the cars check out." Then accusingly, "Your place is quite a distance from any of the centers."

"And just a bite of bran cereal for me," Mrs. DeWitt added. "The day *is* getting on."

Christy glanced up at the kitchen clock. Only ten til seven, and this was late for the DeWitts. Good Lord!

As she beat the eggs, Christy heard Mac behind her speak to Mr. DeWitt in a peculiar strangled voice, "Excuse me, sir. Ah, Mississippi what?"

"We haven't met. I'm Roger DeWitt. I collect license sightings. My wife has her birds."

"I just found out." Mac answered mildly.

"I have radio stations, too," Mr. DeWitt announced with pride.

Mac still seemed to have trouble speaking. "Radio stations?" he repeated.

"Yep. Saw you two come in last night just as I was starting my watch," he chuckled. "Er, not 'watch', I should say, 'my listen'. Very late is the best tracking time, you know. That Caddy of ours never lets me down. Last night I got Canada! Of course, this near the border, Mexico's no problem. No problem at all."

"Good. That's, uh, very good, Mr. DeWitt."

"Call me Roger."

"Uh, good, Roger."

Christy decided Mac needed bailing out. "Mac, would you mind setting the table and serving Mr. and Mrs. DeWitt? The cereal's in that cupboard. And maybe Mr. DeWitt would like some of the fruit compote."

A skinny arm reached past Christy. "If I can just snag this banana instead."

"Oh, fine."

Mrs. DeWitt, "And one for me, Roger. For my bran flakes."

"The coffee is ready," Christy offered helplessly.

"No, no, dear. Roger and I never touch caffeine. Just a spot of herbal tea?"

"Oh, fine," Christy said again, thinking, You're not sounding too bright, old girl. But damn! All this before seven when she liked to have everything under control before the first guests came in. Definitely rattled. She tried to sound pleasant, saying "I'll put the kettle on."

Thank God for Mac. He maneuvered the DeWitts into the dining room, saying, "Now if y'all will just have a seat here. We'll have that tea and cereal in just a minute."

The phone rang and Christy told herself to take a deep breath. This would be funny later. She called out, "Will you get that, Mac? I'll serve the DeWitts."

The kettle whistled. Christy grabbed two herbal tea bags—let them take their chances!—poured the boiling water over them and took them into the dining room. "I hope you like Lemon Zinger. I'll be right back with the cereal."

From the Middle Room, Christy heard Mac speaking courteously Mamacita. "Yes, Señora Garcia, I enjoyed the Fiestacita, and I thank you for inviting me."

Mac appeared to be listening to a long speech as Christy returned with the bran flakes for Mrs. DeWitt. No telling what Mamacita was saying to the "good rooster." Well, maybe not. She was pretty shy around Mac.

Christy came back to her waffles. She finished the batter, started the iron heating, and got out the fruit but needed Mac in the dining room to play host for the DeWitts. Apparently Mama was not suffering from shyness this morning.

In the Middle Room, Mac was listening to the deep voice. He was very fond of Christy's mother, but wished he could get off the line and go help Christy. She liked to start her mornings quietly. Not this way, birds and all!

He tuned back in at the mention of that lady by Mama, "...Christina. And such a sparkle in her eyes, no? Was it from dancing with the handsome stranger? She..."

Damned well better not be, Mac thought. 'Handsome stranger', eh? Wasn't that what they called the Devil in one of Christy's stories? Seemed he wasn't the only one who thought Bottoms was trouble.

Oh-oh, he'd cut out on Señora Garcia again. "...and you will have the pleasure to meet them all, *toda la familia*," la Señora was saying. "All the family, my sons, Patricio all the way from California and Juan from Colorado, and the wives and my grand-children, they will come for Las Fiestas. Then there is Odelia in Espanola. You will enjoy my family, Doctor, although if you had come to my house for Easter Sunday, you would have met..."

Mac drifted off. This was where Christy usually explained she had to hang up, but he didn't know how Mamacita would take it coming from him.

Mac tuned back in, finding that Señora Garcia was speaking a rapid-fire mixture of Spanish and English to the effect that some of the family would be in the Curandera's Room, that the curandera had been her mother's aunt and had cured many people thanks be to God. Mac tried to concentrate "...in there we will put Odelia and her husband, he is a Martinez, but not from here, because they have five children. The two sons, Fidel and Marcus, are in the Navy so they will not come, but there is Little Odie who will come from college in Denver, Colorado, and her sister Mary in high school, and Gabe, Junior. Why they name him Junior I do not know because he is not the first son."

Mac waited for Mrs. Garcia to take a breath, then, hoping not to offend, said, "I'm sorry, ma'am, but—"

"Aii! the breakfast. I am making you late for the breakfast that always gives Christina anxiety." Then abruptly, "You will be in my prayers. Bueno bye," and the Señora was gone.

Mac grinned at that Taos "Spanglish," stood up from the desk and started back to the dining room. The phone rang again. Damn! With a long sigh, Mac returned to the desk. "Casa Vieja Bed and—"

"It's Ignacio, Mac. I'm at the gallery waiting for that bastard Bottoms. I located him in Santa Fe at El Rey. He promised to come on up and open the gallery, but the sumbitch—"

"Iggy—" Mac tried, but Iggy wasn't to be slowed.

"He'll probably take his own sweet time! I already ran over to MacDonald's, brought a cup of coffee back. I'm here at the pay phone in the lobby under Oglevie's so I can watch for the creep. 'Nothing to be concerned about,' he says. Ha! That's a crock. Cindy never did come home last night. Bobby neither. I just may break down the friggin' door!"

"Iggy, Iggy. Hold on a minute. Just settle down. You're a lawyer. You know better than to break in."

"I'm sick of people telling me I'm over-reacting! I'll give him five minutes—"

"Ignacio," Mac spoke over him loudly. "You won't be able to look for Cindy from jail. Maybe she and this Bobby went somewhere. Maybe—"

"You're sounding like that bastard Bottoms, McCloud."

Mac lowered his voice, trying to calm Iggy. "Have you had any sleep?"

"How could I sleep when...?"

"Then, listen, Iggy. This is a doctor talking. You're not functioning properly on no sleep and lots of caffeine. Try to compose yourself before Bottoms arrives. You'll do better by Cindy that way."

"Thanks a lot!"

The phone crashed down in Mac's ear.

Damn! Mac worried. That's not our Iggy. And in the midst of that mess, the Keens were coming through La Sala from their room at the back plus here was the fellow that had the Curandera's Room with his wife. Damnation! No chance to tell Christy about Iggy. Have to try for a cheery 'good morning' when it already felt about noon!

"Good morning, folks. Come have a seat in the dining room."

Christy was just finishing with the table, the blue mats holding the lighter blue-and-white Mexican crockery. The big crystal bowl of fruit compote was in the center. She had already cleared the DeWitts' places.

Dressed in a loose-fitting black cotton shirt and baggy pants, the stocky young Glen Jacoby explained, "I had to leave Ruth alone. She's just a beginner at meditating, can't get into it with me in the room. That's why we wanted the Curandera's Room, though. The good vibes."

Pulling out a chair for his wife, Karl Keen said, "Well, young man, we have something in common. I often meditate when I'm stalking a trophy..." His speech trailed off as a breath-taking sight marched into the room in very high-heeled black boots.

Today Christy's receptionist was dressed in leather. Black leather pants hugged her tiny waist and tidy hips. A black leather vest curved over a pointy bust that was further revealed by a partially unbuttoned wedding shirt. Naturally, her jewelry was heavy metal, clanking bronze and iron.

"Hi, everybody. I'm Desire."

Stepping up from the kitchen with a platter of waffles, Christy was stopped short by Desire's regalia.

"How do you like my skins, Miz Grant?" Desire did a slow pirouette. "I thought with the Fiestas coming and all, I'd do something different, you know?"

"It's, ah, quite striking, Desire. And thank you for coming in early. Now, if you would—"

"But I couldn't get my hair right." She patted her blonde curls. "I wanted to spike it, you know? Like a biker's old lady? But it's so long and curly? Well, hey there!" Desire had sighted the pale thin young woman coming out of La Curandera's Room. "I'm Desire."

Long, straight black hair framed a small face dominated by huge black eyes. Or maybe it was the sight of Desire that widened them. "I'm Ruth," she said shyly, quickly slipping into the dining room to sit down next to her husband.

The phone rang.

"You want me to answer that, Miz Grant?"

Christy sighed. "Yes, please. That would be a very good idea, Desire."

Mac took over serving coffee while Christy helped her guests to waffles and suggesting, too, that cereal was also available.

Desire popped back into the doorway, again halting all conversation. "That wasn't nothing," she said. "Only somebody wanting reservations."

Christy took a breath before answering. Don't ask, she thought. Breathe. "All right, Desire."

She looked around at her guests, ready to make conversation. The young Jacobys were to her left from the kitchen end of the table. On her right was Karl Keen, small and wiry. Next to him, with blonde Texas big hair, was his wife Melba, a soft looking woman wearing many rings on her plump fingers. What a crew! And this without the DeWitts.

Karl Keen was addressing her, "...saying to young Jacoby here that I'm a trophy hunter." He held up his hand, palm out to stop the traffic. "Now I know some people—hunters even!—say they object to trophy hunting. Claim they do it for the meat or some bull like that. Not me. No, siree bob. I go for the trophy, maybe stalk it for years. Last elk I went after, trailed that buck for three years..."

"Guess that makes it premeditated murder," Mac muttered.

"What's that you say, Doc?" Mr. Keen leaned around his wife's cushiony breasts.

Christy waited. She had heard Mac's comment quite well.

"Ah, must be murder," Mac mumbled.

"Right you are! Murder all right. Stamina. Tracking the beast. Having to become one with it, the mystique of the hunter and the hunted. Takes it out of a man!"

The Jacobys looked as distressed as Christy felt. "Ah, Mrs. Keen, I take it you don't go out, ah, stalking?"

Mrs. Keen giggled. "Well, not always. And call me Bootsie! But you should see what Karly brought me from his last African hunt! The cutest spirally horn-things from...What was it, hon?"

"The gazelle. But don't go to Africa any more. They—"

"Made the darlingest towel racks in the powder room downstairs."

I can't stand this, Christy thought. I cannot stand it.

With a cross look at his wife, Karl Keen over-rode her loudly: "I was saying, don't go to Africa since those coloreds took over and ruined it. We have a fine game ranch in Texas. Can hunt about anything you want right from the jeep."

"Excuse me," Christy said weakly. She fled the table, almost running through the kitchen and out the back door.

"Shit!" She shouted under her breath. "Shitshitshitshit!"

The kitchen door banged behind her. It was Mac, looking worried.

"Are you all right?"

"I just had to scream 'shit' a few times."

Mac put an arm around her. "Know how you feel. That sorry excuse for a human being! Africans taking over their own country!"

"I'm going to throw them out. I swear, I'll tell them to leave right now."

"Well, Iggy's threatening breaking and entering—"

"What? What's Iggy doing?"

"Don't worry. He just had to holler at someone for a while. He's at that gallery where Cindy works, waiting for Dr. Bottoms to show up. And here you are, inviting a lawsuit. You two are having a day. But I'll tell you the same thing I told Iggy, 'Take it easy. Don't do anything rash right now.'"

"Okay, Mac. We'd better get back and rescue the poor Jacobys."

Christy and Mac returned to the table, where Glen Jacoby was apparently trying to change the subject, "Aah, what field are you in, Mr. Keen?"

"I'm an attorney. No clients taking up my life. Make them sign a little contract that they won't call me at home. Close the office at three every afternoon."

"So you can go kill something?" asked a little voice. Surprisingly, it was the shy Mrs. Jacoby.

Christy and Mac seemed to choke at the same time. Luckily, the phone rang again. And rang.

"Where's Desire?" Mac asked.

"Probably in search of a mirror," Christy answered dryly.

The phone continued to ring. Christy started up.

"I'll get it. I'm closer," Mac said.

The beautiful diction sang in his ear. "Say there, McCloud."
How the hell did the Brit know who it was? "Evelyn Bottoms
here. May I have a word with Señora Garcia y Grant?"

Iggy in a snit. Animal-murdering lawyers. Bird and what-
the-hell-else watchers. Desire in biker's drag. Now, precious
Englishmen affecting Spanish. Too much! Mac bellowed, "It's
for you, *Señora Grant*," then retreated through the side door
into the courtyard.

"HI-YA! HI-YA!" a startling voice rang out.

"Oh, m'God!" Mac jumped back. Jacoby stood in front of
him.

"Sorry. Did I startle you? I slipped out to get away from
that jerk and practice my karate. Usually I'm more into tai-
chi, but I needed to shout."

"Quite all right, Jacoby. I'd like to do a little shouting
myself. I wonder...Is this the way Fiestas usually start?"

Inside the hacienda, a worried Christy listened to Evelyn Bottoms.
"...so if you could just nip over here? We have rather a, ah,
sticky situation and your friend Ignacio has become more than
slightly obstreperous."

"What is it, Evelyn?" Christy asked sharply. "What's going
on?"

"I would prefer to discuss it when you arrive. Suffice it to
say your policemen are here—and since it *is* my gallery. Well,
I'm unacquainted with the legal system in the States. I thought
perhaps...?"

Concerned as well as irritated that Evelyn refused to explain,
Christy answered, "I'm not taking clients, Evelyn, but I'll be
right over to see what I can do to help."

"Thanks ever so." Bottoms hung up.

"Miz Grant?" Desire appeared behind her.

Christy stared at big blue eyes surrounded by black eyeliner.
"I thought a little more liner? Added something to my total
look?"

"Fine. Fine, Desire. Please listen. I'm going to have to run
out and—"

"I couldn't help hearing. I hope nothing bad—"

"No, I don't know. I need your help, Desire. I have to dress and get downtown as soon as possible, and with Ellie not coming in to clean today."

The wide blue eyes were concerned. "Sure thing, Miz Grant. What do you want me to do?"

Christy spoke rapidly, thinking of how much had to be done. "The kitchen and dining room. Then please see if the guest rooms need cleaning up, towels, all the usual. I'll find out if Mac can help you with the phone. Thank you, Desire."

Christy hurried through the hacienda to the stairs, hoping Desire had taken it all in and would be able to cope. Her mind whirled with thoughts. What had happened? Had they found Cindy hurt? Helpless? Why the police? Why had Evelyn refused to tell her anything? It must be something to do with Cindy or placid Iggy wouldn't be…what had Evelyn said? Obstreperous?

Up the spiral stairs. No time to worry about clothes. Into a pair of faded jeans. Grab a short-sleeve knit shirt. This white one was fine. Sandals. Quick brush of her hair, and back down the stairs to locate Mac.

She found him and Desire glaring at each other in the Middle Room, Desire in her black leather, arms akimbo, booted feet placed wide apart. "I'm telling you, Doctor, Miz Grant *said* for you to sit right here and answer the phone for me!"

"She said no such thing!"

"I'm sorry, Mac. Desire, I told you that we'd *ask* Dr. McCloud… Oh, never mind." She turned to her glowering friend. "Mac, I have to run down to the Plaza. Iggy was right. There is trouble at Evelyn's gallery."

Evelyn was it? "I'll come with you."

"No, if you don't mind, the biggest help would be for you to just listen for the phone. Desire's going to do me a really big favor and clean up the hacienda. I'll call and let you know what's going on."

Mac frowned. "What *is* going on? Has Evelyn Bottoms arrived in Taos now?"

"Yes, only he didn't tell me anything. Thanks for helping out. I have to run."

Christy was out the door. Sighing, Mac was left to deal with the biker's old lady, the great white hunter, and martial arts.

CHAPTER VII

Christy drove faster than usual down the one-lane dirt road in Talpa, hoping she wouldn't meet anyone and have to pull over. Worse would be to meet a pair of pickups "mating". That entailed vehicles stopped head to head while their drivers visited out the windows.

The summer monsoons having finally arrived, the hedge rows were shining green and as yet unmarred by the dust which would collect on them before the afternoon rain. Although not yet in full bloom, sunflowers, black-eyed susans, and chamisa added various shades of bright yellow. Fat cottonwoods shaded the road. Here and there high coyote fences cut off the view—except for the sky, always the vast burnished-blue summer sky.

Few would know that all these little feeder roads led to small clusters of trailers and adobe homes. Talpa was an old neighborhood, once a community unto itself. Spanish families, some dating back to the sixteenth century, had first divided up land grants, then increasingly created smaller holdings for their children and their children's children. The "Comanches" still came to dance and sing for all the "Manuels" on the first of January.

Christy turned the Buick right, onto the Talpa highway.

Out of Talpa, her musing turned to worry about what was going on at the gallery. Why the police? Was her *primo*, the Chief, there? Maybe not, maybe this wasn't a matter important enough to call in her cousin. Perhaps something minor? No, not if Iggy was so upset. Still, he was that way last night without any evidence of trouble other than that Cindy had stood him up.

The Talpa highway came to a Y, joining Pueblo Sur. Driving north, Christy saw the dominating mass of Taos Mountain looming up against the impenetrable sky straight ahead. The Pueblo's Sacred Mountain still showed scraps of white as did the other mountains ringing the valley. Looked like this year there would be snow until August if the rains didn't melt it.

The tourists weren't out in numbers yet, so Christy was able to make good time heading toward downtown. The strip of motels, car dealerships, and fast food places passed in a blur as Christy said a prayer for Iggy.

Reaching the Plaza intersection, Christy aimed for the parking lot across the street from Oglevie's. She paid a strange-looking character she didn't know, feeling her customary stab of regret that Louis' service station no longer occupied the opposite corner. Like so many local businesses, it had been torn down and a tourist shop sat where that fine and friendly man had welcomed her for most of her life. She smiled remembering the time he had stepped out to stop traffic on Kit Carson Road so that she could safely back out.

As soon as Christy entered the lobby below Oglevie's, she saw a crowd of spectators in front of El Museo Gallery.

Christy pushed through the people craning for a look and came face to face with two policemen standing in front of a yellow crime scene tape. An unknown Anglo officer stepped forward to stop her but, thanks be, the other policeman was her young primo, cousin Jaime.

"Jaime! *¿Que pasa?*"

Not one to forget the courtesies, her cousin smiled politely and asked, "*¿Como 'sta*, Prima?"

Christy was impatient. "Fine, Jaime. Fine What's happening?"

Shaking his head, Jaime ignored the question and tried to be firm. "You can't go in, Prima Christy."

"I have to." Stretch the truth a little. "I represent the gallery owner and he's in there."

Jaime looked sad and flustered at having to turn her down. "Sorry, Prima, but the Chief said to keep everybody out."

In a tone cross with anxiety, Christy said firmly, "Jaime, stop all this nonsense! Either let me in or call Chief Garcia!"

Jaime unhappily debated the two evils: disturb his boss or break the Chief's orders by allowing his cousin to cross the line. A third: see Christy *really* get mad!

"Duck under the tape," Jaime said with a sigh.

Fearful of what she'd find, feeling shaky, Christy opened the curtained door of El Museo.

Inside, it seemed like every cop in Taos' was present—doing what, she didn't know. One had a sketch book, another took pictures. Although Christy recognized almost all of them, they seemed too involved to do more than nod. Worry kept Christy from taking in much of the gallery. Long counters dull with fingerprint powder, walls covered with elaborate crucifixes, high shelves of ancient pots and baskets.

Christy heard shouting from the back. She ran along a short corridor, glimpsed an office to the left, and found herself in a large storeroom that suddenly seemed very small.

The shouting stopped at her entrance.

Christy's peripheral vision took in cartons, shelves, rows of santos and retablos, paintings, shipping supplies, but her eyes focused on one thing. A covered mound lay on the floor. The sheet wasn't large enough to hide the blood. A thick puddle of dark red blood on the floor.

In a black haze, Christy felt a large arm around her waist. She heard a concerned voice. "Prima, Prima Christy. You shouldn't see this. Don't faint. Sit here on this bench." Still in a mist, Christy felt her cousin Barnabe's big gentle hands helping her sit down.

"Who?" She asked weakly. "Who is it?"

Iggy's loud voice rang out. "Don't faint on me, Christy! I need you!"

Christy looked up at her friend, his round face red, curls matted with sweat, his Fiestacita clothes from the night before all rumpled and stained. "Thank God, Iggy! You're all right! For a second, I was afraid—"

"I'm not all right, dammit! That's Bobby there on the floor, the guy Cindy worked with, and I can't get these bastards to *do* anything!"

His concern for Christy vanishing, Chief Garcia looked like an angry bear towering over Iggy. "I have explained, Mr. Baca, that we already have an APB out on Miz Williams and are doing—"

Iggy interrupted. "Christy, your primo thinks Cindy had something to do with this mess. He won't treat it as a kidnapping!"

Uh-oh...

Puffing out even more, the Chief roared, "One more word out of you, one more fucking—excuse me, Prima—word, and you'll be out of here so fast! Cuffed maybe!"

"Just you try, you—"

"Stop it! Both of you," Christy shouted. "Iggy, be quiet."

Both were surprised into silence.

"Now," Christy said in her usual soft voice. "Primo Barnabe, please tell me what's happened."

Before Chief Garcia answered, Christy saw Evelyn Bottoms hovering anxiously behind the Chief's bulk.

Unexpectedly standing at parade rest, Barnabe spoke. "I was told that Dr. Bottoms came in from Santa Fe to open the gallery at the insistence of Mr. Baca. These individuals claim they first entered together and, after discovering nothing in the public portion, came back here and found the deceased on the floor. He has been identified by Dr. Bottoms as his employee, Roberto Mascarenas. Mr. Baca was also able to make an identification. There are indications that the place has been burglarized. The medical examiner is on his way.

"Formal statements have not yet been taken, but the two gentlemen seem to agree that they remained together while first contacting 911 and then awaiting the arrival of the police and paramedics. Upon my arrival, Dr. Bottoms was allowed to call you."

At first, Christy was so surprised at hearing her cousin speak this officially that she didn't take in his words. Then they sank in and she looked around the storeroom, seeing past the terrible mound on the floor to a large crate, its boards hanging in broken pieces of wood.

"I tell you, Christy," Iggy was speaking loud and fast, his cherubic face twisted, "the bastards killed Bobby and have made off with Cindy! We have to do something *now!*"

"Stop it, Ignacio!" Christy said loudly to get through to him. "You're not helping Cindy."

She turned to her cousin. "Why did they kill Bobby, Primo? What do you think has happened to Cindy?"

"There appears to have been a struggle. The deceased had a ski mask in his hand and was stabbed in the throat with a small sharp instrument." Barnabe couldn't maintain the formal jargon. "I'd guess more than one perp was involved. I knew Bobby and he was no weakling. No defense wounds on his hands, so the stabbing was likely unexpected. We'll know more from our own M.E. before the body is sent to Albuquerque."

Words, official words. Hard to comprehend. A young man was dead, for God's sake!

"But as to Miz Williams...The robbers, having already killed the deceased had no reason not to kill her also, if she was an innocent bystander."

Iggy started to interrupt. Christy hushed him.

Chief Garcia continued. "We know nothing about the young lady. She's not from Taos. So, on the face of it, it would seem Miz Williams was either an accomplice or witnessed the whole thing and somehow got away."

Iggy's short heavy body shook, his words were jumbled.

Christy took Iggy's arm and led him toward the door. "Iggy, dear, I can see you're about to explode with worry, but you won't help Cindy acting this way."

"But, Christy, Cindy is so special. I won't say we were in love yet, but she cared about me. She saw past all this fat and liked the man she saw inside. I'm more to Cindy than a fat slob with a good brain."

"I hear you, Iggy. But I also know you're too stressed and exhausted...Afraid for Cindy, up all night, tons of caffeine. Please go home and let me work for Cindy. Trust me, my friend."

Iggy continued. "I need to be here—"

Christy interrupted. "I will handle it, Iggy."

He slumped, turned and left, looking back at Christy once.

The Chief was still rumbling, however. "And you, Dr. Bottoms, you report to the station. I want a statement from you as to what was in that crate and what else has been taken."

Christy said, "I represent Dr. Bottoms," at the same time Evelyn told the Chief, "Sorry. I'm afraid I can't help you there. My staff appear to have been shipping a purchase to a customer. I have no way of knowing…"

"You surely have an inventory?"

Dr. Bottoms shrugged, "I'm afraid I left that up to Cindy. Now that she—what do you chaps say?—has flown the coop…" He gestured, palms up.

Christy ignored this, saying only, "I'll go with Dr. Bottoms to the police station." She turned to Chief Garcia, "He *is* allowed to have his attorney present."

"All right, all right. I'm going to seal this place, leave a guard, and call in the State forensics team. We have to send everything we get to them to be analyzed anyway."

Christy remembered an earlier, more innocent time. Then the Taos Crime Lab was a little blue van with—always—four flat tires.

CHAPTER VIII

It took Christy longer to get out of the Plaza traffic mess than to drive the few blocks north to the Taos police station.

She pulled up on the side of the building, which used to be a bank's drive-up window, and smiled despite her upset state, thinking of the jokes that had been made about that. "A cop to go" had been one. Lately, that Taos sense of humor had been displayed in a rash of miniature plastic cowboys and Indians appearing everywhere, glued on gallery doors, mail boxes, sculpture. And, thinking of sculpture, what about when they erected the life-size red metal horse at the bank? The next day those bankers found criticism in the form of a "deposit" on the ground beneath its tail.

A dark blue Infiniti pulled up to park beside her. It was Evelyn. Christy was immediately brought back to the present with all its horror and shock.

"Thanks ever so," came his cultured voice. "I appreciate your assistance, lending a solicitor's helping hand, so to speak."

"Just for now," Christy warned. "I *am* pretty much retired and, anyway, couldn't do justice to a client's interests. No time."

"I understand," he answered, taking her arm. "If you will simply see me through this meeting with your rather intimidating...uh, cousin, is it?"

Christy smiled. "Yes, Chief Garcia's my primo, my cousin. Some people tease me over the number of primos I have in this town. But don't be alarmed. He's just a big bear of the 'teddy' variety."

They entered the police station into an open area with a counter running across the back. Louisa, a young Spanish woman stood behind it, her pretty face brightening at the sight of Christy.

"¿Como 'sta, Miz Grant?'

"Bueno, Louisa. ¿Y usted?"

"Bueno, gracias, y su familia?'

"Bueno, gracias."

Evelyn Bottoms stood to one side, seemingly bemused at the stylized exchange.

"A terrible thing, no?" the young woman asked.

"Yes, it is, Louisa. Chief Garcia asked us to come by."

"I'll see if he's ready to see you."

With the Chief's okay, Louisa led Christy and Evelyn Bottoms down the hall, past busy cubbyholes, to Chief Garcia's office, a sunlit corner room with windows open. The summer breeze felt good. The temperature must already be up to seventy.

Smiling, the Chief lifted his large, muscular bulk from his chair and came around the desk to embrace Christy. "I didn't get my hug this morning, Prima," he said. "A crime scene is no place for such things."

"You helped me, though, Barnabe. The sight of that shape on the floor, the blood!"

"Try not to think of it, Prima."

The Chief turned, hand outstretched. "Thank you for coming in, Dr. Bottoms. I'll only need a short statement from you."

Returning to his desk, Chief Garcia added, "I'll buzz for someone to take it down."

Christy and Evelyn were still standing.

"Sit! Sit!" he ordered.

They sat. Christy noticed that this put her cousin's back to the light, while making his visitors face the glare—an old interviewing technique.

A tall, awkward young man entered, carrying a pad and a cassette recorder. Chief Garcia introduced him as Officer Arnold. They began with the preliminaries of names and dates, and Dr. Bottoms' understanding that his statement was being recorded.

That done, Chief Garcia said, "Now," in a businesslike tone. "Dr. Bottoms, if you will please state, in your own words, the sequence of events leading up to the discovery of the body."

Evelyn Bottoms smiled at the big policeman, and shrugged, gesturing palms up. "I'm happy to oblige, but where do you want me to start?" Before Chief Garcia could answer, he added, "I assume the incident occurred yesterday? Friday? Not the day before?"

The Chief answered, "I try not to ever open a case holding preconceptions. We'll know more when the body is examined. Have to send it to Albuquerque to the O.M.I., the medical examiner's office, for that. But," he mused, "rigor having set in, the blood congealed...Neither one gives us an answer at this stage."

Choking back her distaste, Christy commented. "Never having had a murder case to defend, I'm out of my depth here. But haven't I read or heard something about rigor mortis leaving the body after a certain time?"

"Not certain, Prima. The onset is within two to six hours and is complete in about the same time length of time. Rigor lasts twenty-four to forty-eight hours and then starts to exit the body in a period comparable to its setting in."

Christy's legal training was to be precise and this certainly wasn't. "So you've got a big time span, Barnabe, from start to finish."

Dr. Bottoms looked from one cousin to the other, forgotten as they involved themselves.

"That we do. And those times are affected by a number of factors. The temperature and the physical condition of the deceased. Younger and stronger, like our Mr. Mascarenas, and the rigor comes on faster and lasts longer."

He hesitated, then added, "Of course, I've learned most of this at seminars. Luckily, I haven't had a lot of experience with murders here in Taos!"

"Thank God for that!" Christy acknowledged. "But surely, common sense would tell us the robbery had to have happened yesterday. Someone would have noticed if the gallery had been closed any longer. And then there's Iggy."

"Oh, si," Chief Garcia bristled, "Yes, there certainly is Mr. Baca!"

"Now, Barnabe. You know Iggy wasn't attacking you personally. He was exhausted and out of his mind with worry." She paused, ignored a "Harumph" from the Chief, and continued, "But still, I'll ask him when he last talked to Cindy."

Stiff with the memory of Iggy's insults, Chief Garcia said formally, "That is a matter for the police, counselor."

Christy didn't answer. Of course she'd talk to Iggy, but no need to argue and further rile her cousin now. Instead, telling herself to maintain her composure, she looked out the window behind Barnabe where she could see the top of Taos Mountain.

Chief Garcia turned back to the Englishman. "It would appear that the incident occurred sometime yesterday, but if you'd start when you first arrived in New Mexico, doctor?"

"Of course. Now, let's see. I had flown into Santa Fe, staying—"

"Excuse me, Dr. Bottoms. Flown in, when?"

"Yes, certainly. Flown in from New York Thursday evening."

"Commercial flight?"

Shaking his head, Evelyn smiled deprecatingly. "No. I have my own Lear. More efficient, you know, considering my extensive traveling."

"Evelyn's involved in a world-wide effort to bring back many of our treasures, Barnabe," Christy inserted proudly.

Not to be deterred the Chief only nodded and persisted, "The Santa Fe airport? What time?"

"Yes, Santa Fe," he answered patiently. "And the time? Oh, well before dinner. I checked into El Rey Inn as usual." A nod to Christy. "Charming, but not your bed and breakfast. Then drinks and dinner with friends at eight. And back to my room alone for the night." He smiled.

Chief Garcia kept boring in. "If you arrived Thursday, Doctor, why haven't you cleared up the puzzle of when the robbery occurred? Why didn't you discover the robbery earlier?"

Evelyn threw out his hands in a gesture of helplessness. "No opportunity, Chief Garcia. Friday morning, I must admit I slept rather late, then enjoyed a bite of breakfast at the Inn before attending to my affairs in Santa Fe. I have a small gallery there also, you know."

"You didn't call or come to your gallery here?" Christy's cousin sounded skeptical.

Dr. Bottoms shook his head sadly, "No, no. I believed it to be in good hands. Now...?" he shrugged, then looked over at Christy with a smile. "And your lovely cousin can tell you that I only arrived in Taos Friday night, well after your delightful Fiestacita had already commenced."

Chief Garcia looked a question at Christy.

"I don't know when Dr. Bottoms arrived in Taos, Barnabe. But I saw him come out on the Kachina patio just as La Marcha was starting. He danced with Mamacita and then joined our table."

Evelyn said politely, "If I might interject? Unless we find to the contrary from the medical evidence, it appears most reasonable to assume that the break-in and murder occurred sometime early Friday when El Museo was without customers." He paused, then added sorrowfully, "Unless, of course, it was no break-in and our Cindy let them in."

Christy felt a stab, hearing those last words. She didn't want Iggy's girlfriend responsible for any of this horror, but Evelyn's comment raised a point: "How in the world did those killers get away, Barnabe?"

The Chief pondered, "Well, unless Bobby and Cindy *both* were accomplices, they wouldn't have been there at night. Since the Mascarenas boy is dead, we'll have to assume daylight, and that's your question, Prima." He paused. "But think of those Plaza crowds now with Fiestas coming up. I'd say that if the bastards kept their cool, they could take off the ski masks and stroll right out of the gallery with no problem."

"Except for Cindy!" Christy answered. "What *are* you doing to find Cindy?

The Chief wasn't to be diverted any further. "Later." He turned back to Evelyn, "So you spent all day yesterday attending to your affairs in Santa Fe?"

Uh-oh. Christy saw her cousin was getting a little antagonistic. "Dr. Bottoms explained that he has another gallery down there, Barnabe. And, as I told you, has been very busy tracing old santos, retablos, paintings and such like to bring back here where they belong."

"Doctor?"

"Yes, Señora Garcia y Grant is quite right. I visited my Santa Fe gallery, made calls, saw curators...a tiring day."

"All right. Now, let's consider the robbery itself. When will you be able to tell me what was taken? And who would know what was worth stealing? I won't say 'killing for' because we all know these *malcriados* don't value life that much!"

Evelyn shook his head. "I just don't know, Chief Garcia. As I explained to you over there, I trusted, perhaps not wisely, but I trusted Cindy to keep the inventory. Religious and other Spanish artifacts are arriving all the time to be stored pending the opening of the museum itself.

"As to knowledge? How am I to know with whom she shared descriptions of value? Many items are, of course, priceless. The Cart of Death, for instance."

"But out in the open?"

"I have a security system here and at my other storage facility."

The Chief wasn't satisfied. "Surely you're not telling me you don't check the books either?"

Evelyn remained unoffended. "But, of course I check them. Not, however, on a day to day basis." He again lifted his shoulders, held out his hands.

"I think Dr. Bottoms has covered it all, Barnabe," Christy said.

"Not yet, he hasn't. What about the crate? You claim you don't know what was in that?"

Evelyn shook his head, put his index finger to his mustache. "Chief, Chief, you saw what I did. An empty crate. No label. I could conclude from that that an item was to be shipped to a purchaser, rather than being delivered. But I speculate only." He paused. "One hopes that Cindy had made the requisite notation as to item, buyer, and so forth, but..." Another helpless shake of his blonde head, seeming somehow vulnerable.

Chief Garcia sighed. "All right. For now. I'll expect you to do what you can about producing an inventory for me, up to date or not. You know what you have purchased or brought back here, what you've stocked for retail trade. And I'll want your best efforts on both what's missing and what might have been in that crate. An item that large...!"

Christy stood. There was tension in the room—and in her shoulders. No cousinly comradery right now. "If that's all, Barnabe? You'll let me know when forensics have finished and Dr. Bottoms can examine his gallery?"

Primo Garcia answered without his usual cordiality. "I'll do that, counselor," he said stiffly.

Chapter IX

As they waited for his statement to be typed, Evelyn asked Christy to have lunch. She hesitated. While she'd been protecting Evelyn's interests and sparring with Barnabe, the old trial-lawyer high took over. Now, the let down, and thoughts of Bobby's murder came rushing in. She was sickened by the thought of food.

Evelyn attracted her from the start but she didn't want the attraction. Why risk disrupting her growing relationship with Mac? Now new feelings to contend with...Still, it was only lunch. "Thanks. I'd like that."

He suggested a restaurant a few blocks south of the Plaza intersection. It wouldn't have been Christy's first choice but she went along, following him there in her car. She tried to hold the death image at bay and think of other things, but her mind filled with the horror of Bobby's body on the floor.

When Christy pulled up alongside the Infiniti in the restaurant's parking lot, she took a moment to try to settle her stomach with deep breaths.

Evelyn came around the car to take her arm in a rather proprietary fashion. Still upset, as well as feeling a little uptight and self-conscious, Christy distracted herself by admiring the brightly blooming wild flowers along the path.

The pleasant main dining room was large and open, the white-clothed tables farther apart then in most restaurants. However, Christy felt it lacked the old Taos feel as did the nouvelle cuisine on the menu.

Looking around the dining room, Christy saw that it also lacked any Spanish faces. Certain places in Taos did not make her people feel comfortable.

The waiter presented a wine list, but Evelyn said, "We'll see what the lady will have first."

"The salmon, please," Christy answered, sending Evelyn into a study over which wine would best suit.

Finally, the little flurry of ordering ended and there was a pause. Evelyn gazed directly into Christy's eyes and then looked around, "Rather nice."

"Yes." Now, that's a witty rejoinder, Christy old girl. And it's Evelyn who looks nice in that lovely, soft Harris tweed jacket, the muted shades of tan going nicely with his creamy Oxford shirt and brown tie. Few Taos men would be wearing any kind of jacket. There were not many places in Taos where she'd feel out-of-place in knit shirt and jeans. Maybe not the jeans so much as the sandals. Bare feet in sandals just didn't seem the thing here.

"You know," Christy said. "Two older friends of mine made adobes for one of the first hotels here. They were paid one dollar per one *thousand* bricks. They didn't complain. They were proud of bringing home that dollar."

Evelyn shook his head, then said, "I want to thank you for your assistance today."

Christy answered, "No problem," but was immediately recalled to the morning. How could they be sitting in a restaurant, making weighty decision about wine and lunch, when Cindy was somewhere terrified or dead and Bobby was a bleeding body?

Evelyn smiled at her again. "Ah, but I'm fairly certain that there would have been considerable problem with Chief Garcia had you not been present."

"You're not a suspect," Christy disagreed. "You have all day Friday covered."

Evelyn chuckled. "An alibi, I believe it's called. Nonetheless, your cousin fairly exuded disapproval of my careless ways."

The dining room was stiffly quiet. Christy felt slightly stiff herself. "I do hope you can provide him with an inventory, Evelyn. What was stolen might provide a clue as to the thief, answer whether this was a random break-in or if the robbery had a definite purpose behind it."

Evelyn responded solemnly, "I understand your implication that Cindy may have told them what to steal." He sighed. "I confess to leaving too much responsibility to Cindy. Perhaps I am too trusting."

Christy didn't believe she had implied any such thing. She spoke crisply, "I doubt Cindy had anything to do with the robbery. From what Iggy says, Cindy was a very special person. I knew her, too, and liked her." Hearing an echo of her words, she quickly added, "Listen to me speaking of Cindy in the past tense. I'm praying she's very much alive and well!"

Christy's words dropped into the room's quiet as the waiter arrived and poured the wine into Evelyn's glass. Evelyn then held his glass over the candle to check its clarity, sniffed its bouquet, rolled a taste on his tongue, pronounced it satisfactory, and nodded at the waiter to pour Christy's. At least he didn't sniff the cork, she thought, and gratefully took a sip.

"To return to our conversation," Evelyn said, "I must fault myself. Who knows if our Cindy was tempted by the treasures and found the temptation irresistible? Or perhaps a chance word to a less-than-savory acquaintance?"

Drinking some wine, Christy forced herself to consider the possibility Evelyn raised again, then answered, "I don't know. It just doesn't feel right. I think it's more likely Cindy somehow got away as Barnabe suggested and is frightened and hiding right now." She paused, and continued somberly, "I'm really afraid that's the best we can hope for. Iggy's convinced she's been kidnaped...or worse."

Evelyn gave his head a little shake, straightened in his seat, "Let's speak of happier things." He smiled at Christy. "I understand your obvious distress. I feel it, too. But one mustn't be morose when one has such a charming companion."

Christy had felt sexual tension underlying the serious conversation about the robbery. Now she wanted to deflect any personal topics he had on his mind. The time and her mood were all wrong. She tasted the fresh, nutty flavor of her white wine. "Please tell me more about your plans."

"Ah," Evelyn's face lit with joy. "My plans, yes. In our limited exchange last night, I began to tell you. I'm building a museum south of Taos, you see, near the new golf course. I intend to bring back as many of your treasures as I am able to locate and," he gave a little chuckle, "can afford to buy back. Some good people do donate when approached properly."

Evelyn smiled and continued, "Those items of a religious nature will first be offered to, say, the moradas, if that was their original provenance. The remainder will be on display in the museum here where they belong."

"Yes!" Christy answered, then added, "But I'm surprised you would even know about our moradas."

Evelyn reached over to touch Christy's hand lightly on the table. "How, dear lady, could one study religious art of the region and not become aware of the moradas, the buildings devoted to the prayers and rituals of the Penitentes?"

"Los Hermanos, La Hermandad, the Brothers, the Brotherhood," Christy said automatically, then added, "Excuse me, Evelyn. I corrected you too sharply. It's just that Los Hermanos have had so much unfair publicity. They have actually been *stalked* by outsiders. "

"I understand," he answered gently.

"No," Christy replied, but this time in a more subdued tone. "I don't believe anyone can understand who hasn't lived here and known Los Hermanos. Then you read about your friends and neighbors and it's wrong and unfair!" She paused and then felt compelled to add, "La Hermandad is a fraternity made up of all kinds of people—accountants, computer programmers, financial planners...Nor do they practice 'ritual torture'. That's one stupid dictionary definition I read. The definition didn't mention that it's in remembrance of Christ that the Hermanos help the old and needy, as well as conduct special rites."

Evelyn clasped the hand that Christy had carelessly left lying on the white tablecloth. "I know the Penitentes had problems with the Church in the nineteenth century—"

Christy interrupted, removing her hand. "No longer. The Brotherhood was officially recognized by the Church in 1947. And the Bible itself refers to devotion to Christ by imitation.

It's likely La Hermandad grew from the lay order that Saint Francis himself began."

"There now," Evelyn said soothingly. "I'm not arguing your point at all, although you must admit to flagellation and other practices that drew the name 'Brothers of Blood'."

Christy opened her mouth, but he continued smoothly, "I was going to say that the Penitentes' troubles commenced at about the same time that imported priests tried to rid the area of true folk art in the form of santos and brought in junk saints by railroad boxcars." Evelyn's eyes twinkled. "In fact, one might damn the railroad. The classical period of *santero* work and the most magnificent *bultos*, your statues of saints, were created in the period between the full use of the Santa Fe trail and the coming of the railroad." He paused, smiling into Christy's eyes. "Ah, but you listen well. Pardon the lecture. Let me pour you more wine."

"No thanks, Evelyn," she said. "Enough wine, but I'd be happy to hear more. I enjoy your enthusiasm. What you might not know is that soon after the first influx of Anglos, many of la gente, the people, gave up all sorts of beautiful handmade objects, not just the santos and retalbos but furniture, quilts, more. The unscrupulous convinced them to buy new—"

"And took them off for a song, I know!" Evelyn finished for her.

Christy shook her head sadly and listened to more stories from Evelyn.

The elegant waiter arrived with their nouvelle cuisine. Christy's stomach rebelled.

CHAPTER X

Feeling like it was his penance, Mac actually welcomed aching knees as he knelt to pluck the spent purple and yellow pansies that bordered taller summer flowers. He was trying to ease the irritation he felt with himself that came from being upset that Christy had not yet returned. He disliked the thought of her at that bloody crime scene and with that slick English fellow. Refreshing the pansies excused lying in wait for the lady.

Mac lifted his head as he heard a car approaching down the dirt road. It went by, and he angrily decided some questionably wilted blooms had to go.

Another car. Ha! The "chunk" of a heavy car door closing. Mac got very busy yanking at a clump of grass poking up through the flagstones.

Christy came in through the little blue-framed gray door set into the wall next to the ancient swamp willow—blue that kept out evil because it echoed the color of the Blessed Mother's robes.

Mac fought the urge to accuse "You're late!" He and Christy had an unspoken agreement not to invade one another's space. But why in hell was she looking so flushed and sparkling?

"Hi, there!" Christy sang out. "Weeding the garden again! What a treasure you are, Mac."

Mac stood up, brushing dirt off the knees of his faded jeans, the "treasure" making an effort not to show any resentment. "So, how did it go? Your mama called with news of a murder."

Christy smiled. "Lots to report, Mac. Just let me get a Pepsi and I'll join you. Too much wine and my mouth's dry."

Mac's own smile felt phony as he answered "Fine," and wondered what she meant by too much wine.

Coming back out the kitchen door, Christy aimed for the comfortable wrought-iron chairs under the portal by the Middle Room door. "Come sit in the shade," she called to Mac. "It's too hot out there in the sun."

"Too hot?" Mac teased. "I'm just starting to feel warm. What's the temperature? All of maybe eighty degrees?"

"That's hot, you cold-blooded Floridian. I brought you a Pepsi, so come sit."

"You're in good spirits," Mac commented, sitting down on the other side of the round table from Christy.

Christy's smile faded. "Oh, Mac, that's just an act. It's so sad. It's hard to get my mind around Bobby Mascarena's murder. That's who you heard about. He was killed in the robbery. Young and alive and then, in a heartbeat, a lump of bloody flesh on the floor. And Cindy, who should have been working with him, is missing."

Mac took both Christy's cold hands. "I understand. As a doctor, I've seen more death than most, but never become immune to the sort of feelings you're having. Best thing to do right now is focus on the living, see what we can do to find Cindy."

Choking up, Christy only nodded.

Thinking of a diversion, Mac said, "Before I forget, some people called for a reservation, only they want to know about rafting first."

Christy sighed, then nodded. "I'll call my friend Mary to ask about conditions as soon as we go in. She's an expert rafter with her own company and will know for sure."

"I saw some people out the other day when I was coming back from Santa Fe," Mac offered.

"Right. But some keep on trying even when the Rio Grande's too low. Mary will know if there's still good white water." She mused. "Probably is, what with all that late snow we had for run-off, the monsoons late, too."

"Now," Mac settled back. "Tell me all about it."

"Well, Barnabe seems to be leaning more toward Cindy being an accomplice or maybe a witness hiding out. But at lunch Evelyn said—"

"Lunch?" The question popped out before he could stop himself.

Christy gave him a cool look, perhaps a little defensive because of her unwanted attraction to Evelyn. Realizing the wine was having some effect on her, Christy stifled a sharp reply. Instead, she said mildly, "Yes, lunch at that restaurant south of the plaza.

"But you don't like—"

"The food was delicious," Christy interrupted firmly.

Just then the Jacobys emerged from the Middle Room, acting so uncomfortable that Christy immediately knew something was wrong. Glen Jacoby was out of his karate black outfit and into a snug pair of jeans and an easy blue sports shirt. His wife Ruth still wore her Taos-style long trailing skirt. Right now those beautiful black eyes were even bigger as she looked everywhere around the courtyard but at Christy.

"Uh, Miz Grant," Jacoby said hesitantly, "Ruth and I have been talking it over. And we, uh, think it would be better if we checked out. Early, I mean. Like this afternoon. We'd pay the full bill, and everything."

Dismayed, Christy also felt sorry for the young couple. "What is it, Glen?" She asked gently. "What...?"

"Oh, it's not you, Miz Grant or the hacienda or our room," he interrupted.

"Tell her Glen," Ruth put in her soft voice. "Tell her what we were saying about that creep."

"That hunter and his wife," Jacoby said in a rush. "We just can't stand being around people like that."

Oh, Lord! She had totally forgotten the scene at breakfast with all that happened since then. "Glen, Ruth," Christy answered. "That's not right, you two feeling forced out. I'll ask the Texans to leave."

Mac started to remonstrate but Glen overrode him. "No, Miz Grant. We can't let you do that, wouldn't be comfortable. We'll just—"

"Yoo hoo! We're back!" Melba Keen sang out as she and her spouse bustled in through the courtyard gate, each carrying an armload of sacks from the stores.

Although the wiry Keen was as tall as his wife, she seemed to loom over him in her plumply-filled brilliant turquoise pants suit. Her bright yellow curls shone in the sun.

Christy rose. The Jacobys faded back inside.

The Keens dumped their parcels on the glass-topped table and Keen commenced reaching around in them as he said, "Now you just sit yourself back down, Miz Grant. I bought us some Wild Turkey and we'll all have us some bourbon 'n branch. Mother, bring these nice folks some water from the kitchen."

Christy remained standing, attempting to control her anger.

"Miz Grant? Miz Grant, will you come in here?" Desire, in all her black leather biker finery, stood in the Middle Room door.

"What is it, Desire?"

"I really think you should come here, Miz Grant, you know?"

Temporarily giving up on this situation, Christy went inside.

The Jacobys waited at the desk, their bags on the floor beside them. Ruth smiled at her shyly as Glen said, "We just wanted to quietly pay our bill and leave, but—"

"I told him people don't ever leave here early," Desire interrupted crossly, her pretty face considerably more focused than usual. "Not our guests! Not at Casa Vieja Bed and Breakfast. They're happy here!" she wailed.

Taking in the Jacobys' determined faces and their luggage, which they must have already packed before they made their announcement outside, Christy decided there was no point in further discussion. "Make up their bill, Desire," she said firmly, then turning to the young couple said, "But only through tonight. I'm very sorry other guests have made you uncomfortable and I won't have you paying for tomorrow."

The Jacobys exchanged a pleased look, "Okay. Thanks," he said.

Desire forgot her indignation at Christy's words. "Oh, wow! Who was it? What did they do?"

Ignoring this, Christy shook hands with the Jacobys, saying, "Good-bye and please come back. We'll give you one night on the house. I promise our guests aren't usually like this."

Christy detoured through the kitchen for another Pepsi before confronting the Keens, and then came out the kitchen door.

Melba Keen was apparently reciting their days' event to Mac who wore a rather glazed expression. "...and there we were at the Taos Inn for lunch with that table of Mexicans right next to ours! They must have been artists because they were complaining about not getting their work into any of the galleries." Diamonds flashed in the sun as her hands fluttered. "And I wanted to just speak right up and say to them, 'Bone lazy, that's your trouble. Everybody knows you Mexicans are just bone lazy'!"

Speechless with anger, Christy contemplated throwing her Pepsi into that pudgy face.

Mac's hands gripped the chair arms. He took a deep breath. "Such a peculiar and meaningless expression, Mrs. Keen. 'Bone lazy'. Is that one of your quaint Texas idioms?"

Blink. Blank look, then a giggle and, "I told you to call me Bootsie," waving plump little hands aimlessly.

Christy didn't look at Mac as she felt words come rushing. "The artists about whom you're speaking were probably Spanish, or Hispanic as more politically correct *gringas* say, and, yes, they've found it necessary to form their own association and open their own galleries," breath, "although *my people* were here creating works of art before *your people* got out of the Dark Ages, if you ever did. Santa Fe was a busy city before Columbus ever thought of his little journey."

Bootsie giggled again.

Keen said, "Have a bourbon 'n branch, Miz Grant. No need to get your bowels in an uproar."

Christy was again speechless. Apparently this pair left wakes of destruction behind them wherever they went and were totally unconscious of it!

Bootsie turned her attention back to Mac. "What I was telling you, doctor. It was the funniest thing! After lunch, Karly had to use the Little Boys Room and I was sitting in the lobby waiting for him, just people-watching, you know? And all these girls were coming by, all tricked out like you wouldn't believe! I saw they were applying for a maid's job at the desk...Well, I ask you! Just who did they think they were with their hair done all fancy and all?"

That was it!

Clamping her mouth shut to hold back all she wanted to say, Christy strode quickly over to the Middle Room door, entered, and slammed it behind her. "Women! Not 'girls'! Hardworking. Taking minimum wage...!" Storming past Desire who gazed after her wide-eyed, Christy turned up the stereo loud, but kept on going. She imagined the Keens trailing after her through La Sala. No sanctuary there. She moved quickly up the spiral stairs in an adrenaline rush. In her room, she flopped down in the big chair.

Deep breaths. In one, two, three, four, five, six, seven. Hold one, two, three. Out, one, two...Clench each part of your body. Relax. Clench. Relax. Breathe again. Meditate.

Okay, Christy told herself, you were angry about the Jacobys being forced out by those turds before they ever came through the gate. You're a trained attorney. They're just stupid, don't know what they're saying. Bigoted little minds...And anyone who'd shoot game from a jeep! Ignorant, too, talking about native Africans.

It's wrong to let people like that upset you so when truly awful things are happening right here! Bobby Mascarenas dead. Murdered. Cindy missing. Poor Iggy...

But what to do about those damned Keens?

A large shape loomed up on the landing outside her room. Mac. She had been contemplating so deeply that she hadn't heard his steps on the stairs.

He bent over to rap on the frame of the little door, open to the summer breeze.

"Come in, Mac."

He stood there, still bent, peering in. "Are you still irate?"

"I've calmed down. Come on in. Don't stand there looking like a question mark."

Mac, smiling at her, eased through the little doorway, ducked under the particularly low viga there, and crossed the room to sit in her desk chair. "I didn't want to interrupt, but have a suggestion to make."

"What am I going to do with Keen and company?"

Mac waggled those black eyebrows. "Well, you're the lawyer. I surely don't know what you should do, but I suspect you might get into a mite of trouble throwing out guests who've done nothing but be their obnoxious selves."

"Right. But, Mac, I need to make a statement. It's like that movie, *Gentlemen's Agreement*—if I don't *do* something, I'm condoning them."

"The Great White Hunter," Mac intoned solemnly. "And could you ever really relate to a woman calling herself Bootsie?"

"And anyone who'd make towel racks of little gazelle horns..." starting to giggle.

Mac laughed, too. "They're so awful they're unbelievable! Blasting that woman like you did!"

"How is she?"

"Impervious. That's the trouble with those types. They don't hear what they're saying in relation to others and they sure as hell don't hear anyone else!" He paused. "But I didn't tell you about my suggestion."

Christy was still smiling. "What's that, doctor?"

"I still need to check on Iggy, then what say we go out to dinner? You need a break from all your guests, even Birdwoman and License Plates. Let's just have a happy time away from the hacienda. Okay? And nary a thought about anything violent."

Christy considered a minute, then: "Thank you, Mac. I'd like that. Just let me shower and change. I need to wash off those people and all the rest of today. One thing, though. After we see Iggy, I'd like to go to the six o'clock Mass before dinner."

Mac looked questioning. "Saturday night?"

"Yes. This evening, it's the Talpa capilla at six. Okay, Mac?"

He hesitated. "The roof might fall down if I walked in the door."

"Please join me. I want to pray for Bobby, and for Cindy's safe return, and ask for some guidance..." Christy trailed off.

Mac stood, smiling down at her. "I'd be purely honored, Ma'am, to escort you. So. Iggy, then Mass, then dinner."

Wanting to offer Christy something special, Mac added, "What about the Trading Post? I know you love it."

"And I'd get a hug from Kimberly. Now *there's* a someone who can make jeans elegant."

Mac looked puzzled.

"Never mind. I'm just comparing the atmosphere there to another place—noisy, happy Italian with great food, to too much quiet and nouveau cuisine. I guess it's the owners, like Kimberly who make a difference.

"Trading Post it is then!" Mac squeezed Christy's shoulder in passing. "See you anon, m'lady."

The bells were ringing when Christy and Mac, true to his reluctant promise, arrived at the little Talpa capilla. The bells momentarily took Christy back to when they tolled for Señor Barela, but then she smiled. These rang fifteen minutes before Mass to call the men in from the fields, the women from changing diapers, oiling vigas, *toda la gente* of the neighborhood. "Leave your chores. Come celebrate the Mass."

Long ago, the people built it as a mission church when the journey to the St. Francis Church was too long and dangerous on foot or horseback. And to this day, many homebound, who needed the Eucharist brought to them the rest of the month, on this evening made it to the capilla, twisted hands gripping canes or bent over, hunchbacked, so bad was their bone disease.

The capilla was small, room for four only on wooden benches on either side of the aisle. The tall windows made no pretensions with stained glass, but had long white, perfectly ironed, starched curtains hanging the length of them. And so close to the altar, the worshipers were part of it, part of the little white-painted trellis that arched over the tabernacle to one side, part of the santos who sat on each cross-piece of it, part of the candle that burned to promise God's presence by its light. The mayordomos were careful to see a new one placed there before the old candle could go out.

In the center in the place of honor stood *Nuestra Señora de San Juan de Los Largos.*

Christy remembered, as a child, her delight in the small side room, a vestry. It had a closet for the priests and another full of decorations for the seasons and boxes of bright-colored paper flowers for everyday use. But best of all were the contents of the little trunks. Beautifully sewn tiny dresses of satins, rayon, velvet and silks—pink, blue, white—decorated with lace and rick-rack, lay one on top of the other, filling each trunk with a wardrobe for Our Lady. A cloak of pink velvet had a fur-trimmed hood for when she went out on procession.

Nuestra Señora was of painted wood, stiff, primitive, but her parishioners made more soft, lovely clothes than the mayordomos could change every week for a year. They loved her. They watched, too, to see whose gown she was wearing. And sometimes requested she wear someone's rosary for a special prayer.

Lost in memories Christy hadn't noticed Mac's contained squirming. Now she noticed the heads turning and the whispers. Tourists seldom wandered in here. Who was this man with Christy?

"Be brave," she muttered as the bells rang again, announcing the start of Mass.

The guitar players, standing by the front pews, readjusted booted feet on the wood seat, knees cocked up to brace their instruments and hit it joyfully. *"Buenos dias, Señor/ Buenos dias, mi Dios..."* ushered in Father Joe.

Outside, the late afternoon sky was still heat-washed summer blue, the July sun bright. Dark, lowering storm clouds walked the ridges, their heavy rains missing Taos.

Part of the canyon walls of the Rio Grande gorge were turning blue-gray in the shadows. The river was cold. The rafters had called it a day. None of them had seen the heavy bundle in black plastic as it bumped along, scraping against rocks.

The plastic was tearing. An icy white hand was emerging.

CHAPTER XI

The phone's harsh sound shocked Christy awake in a room dim with early morning light. The clock radio's red numerals showed 5:33. Couldn't be Mama this time, Christy thought groggily, talked to her last night. Must be bad news. Christy grabbed at the receiver. It was Mama.

"I knew it would happen after what you tell me of that poor girl, the friend of Ignacio, although you did not bother until last night to call your mama and by then the whole town knew of the robbery and murder—"

"Mama! I did call you. Why...?"

"I hear it just now on the Early Hometown News, but Señor Martinez does not say who."

"Mama. What...has...happened?" Christy enunciated crossly.

Her tone aggrieved, Mamacita said, "I am trying to tell you, Christina. A body in the river. Search and Rescue—"

"Oh, God! Who is it? Cindy?"

Impervious to Christy's frantic interruption except for an automatic, "Watch your mouth, m'hija," Mamacita continued, "Search and Rescue radios they have been called to take a body from the river at Pilar—"

"Who, Mama? Who?"

"...which was found by rafters camping overnight. 'No further information is available at this time'."

Christy plumbed for hard facts. "Did the radio just say 'body'? Not a woman's body?"

"I tell you exactly what is on the Early Hometown News."

"Okay, thank you, Mamacita," Christy said. "This is very important. I have to go now and try to get to Ignacio before he hears it. He'll go crazy thinking it's Cindy!"

"What will you do?"

"I don't know. I have to think. I'll call you later, okay?"

For once Mama didn't try to prolong the conversation, saying simply in her gruff voice, "I will pray for Cindy and Ignacio."

"Bueno bye."

Wide awake with an adrenaline rush, Christy threw on her long robe. Running her hands through her hair, she thought, Tell Mac."

Christy didn't realize she was still barefoot until she felt the chilly landing of the outside stairs beneath her feet. Never mind. She hurried on down the steps. They were so old that the wood felt tender.

The softness of a summer early morning calmed Christy as she took deep breaths of the gentle air and felt the quiet of the predawn courtyard. Though morning was coming, the courtyard still cradled night in its walled shadows. The sky was a gray veil pinned by a yellow moon.

Christy ran across the cold flagstones to Mac's little house. "Mac! Mac!" She rapped again.

Mac opened the door looking both groggy and worried, his white hair disheveled. Lifting a robe from the floor, belting it over pajama bottoms, he grabbed her hands. "Come inside. You're barefoot. It's *cold* out there, girl! What's the matter?"

Gratefully Christy stepped onto the rug in Mac's warm little nest. Shock was setting in and she shivered. Mac put an arm around her as she told him, "They've found an unidentified body in the river at Pilar. I'm so afraid that it's Cindy. We have to break it to Iggy before he hears about it. And not the phone. That kind of call is awful."

"I know," Mac answered sympathetically. "Iggy is already distraught. Damn! I was going to take the Texas Keens off your hands this morning, but I'd better go to Iggy...Wait. I just had a thought. Can't you call your cousin, the Chief, first, find out who the body is?"

"No use. If Barnabe's been informed, he'll already be on his way down to Pilar." Christy thought for a moment. "I guess you're right, that you'd best go to Iggy. Don't worry about the Texans, they're pretty minor compared to this. It's a tragedy for someone. I just pray it's not Cindy."

Mac nodded. "Well, it could be an accidental drowning, but prepare yourself. It most likely *is* Cindy. We don't have that many bodies around here."

When Christy left, Mac quickly pulled on Levis and a sports shirt. He grabbed a light cardigan, too, the temperature being only in the low fifties, and then thought to take his medical bag. He hurried out the door, glancing over at the kitchen-dining room wing. No lights shone in the windows under the portal. He hoped Christy was back upstairs, getting warm.

Mac smiled as he realized the Birdwoman wasn't out chirping yet. Have to check the parking lot to see if the husband had already gone off to hunt down license plates. It would be better for Christy if they were at breakfast, diluting the impact of The Great White Hunter and wife. Too bad the nice young couple had left.

Opening the little gate set into the adobe wall, Mac ducked to pass through to the road. There he stopped a minute, struck by the sun popping over the eastern mountains into a delicate blue sky, not yet hardened by heat. Taking a deep breath of fragrant air, he thought, God! I love this place...But no time for dilly-dallying. Must get the hell over to Iggy's before he takes off on his own.

Starting the car, Mac soon negotiated the Talpa dirt road, and turned right onto the highway. The houses on the south side lined the rim above the Talpa-Llano valley as did their counterparts across the valley pastures. The Jicarita mountains rose beyond the Llano ridge.

Making another right at the Y, Mac saw Taos Mountain loom straight ahead. To his left, he could see the sagebrush flat lands stretching west to mountains with names strange to his Southern tongue. The sun had reached these western plains, but the near slopes of the eastern mountains were still dark.

Mac sped toward town down an almost empty road. Most of Taos still slept. The few cars he met were probably heading for early Mass at St. Francis. Time to figure out how to tell Ignacio, how to handle the situation. For sure Iggy would want to go to the scene at Pilar. Mac would have to go with him.

Mac walked across grass damp with dew to Iggy's apartment in the back. He saw to his surprise that Iggy had a door bell. Taos didn't have door bells. This one rang a few notes from *Carmen* but there was no response. Mac rang again and knocked.

Finally, a sleepy Ignacio opened the door, curls wild and rat tail trailing undone. "What the hell…! Mac! Why are you here at this hour? Is it Christy? God no! Cindy!"

Mac stepped inside, gripped Iggy's shoulder. "Take it easy. Christy's fine, but she heard a radio bulletin—"

"What?"

Mac could think of no way to soften the harsh news. "An unidentified body's been found in the river at Pilar."

"Oh, m'God! Cindy! They've killed Cindy!"

Mac shook Iggy's shoulder. "You're not listening, man. No one knows yet. It could be anyone—some man, some rafter, accidental drowning."

Iggy broke away, ran toward the bedroom, calling back, "I'm going down there!"

Mac followed him. "You're with me. We'll take the Chevy."

"Whatever you say, just get the fuck there!"

A few minutes later they were in Mac's truck and speeding back through a still-sleeping Taos. Iggy urged Mac to run the stop signs as he took the new back way. Mac compromised with some hesitation stops on the empty roads.

They soon passed the remaining little businesses and were headed down the hill toward the St. Francis Church.

"I'm not speeding through here, Ignacio, so just don't say anything," Mac commented, seeing the yellow blinking light ahead at the Church intersection. The parking lot behind the Church was full. The early Spanish Mass must still be in progress.

As they started up the next hill, Iggy said, "Okay! Let's move!"

Mac knew the State Police liked to wait along here on the long straight stretch but, sympathizing with Iggy's urgency, picked up speed. Although the road seemed level here, looking in the rearview mirror Mac could see that they had been steadily climbing. Taos was laid out behind them tiny against the mountain and in the great sweep of sagebrush plains slashed by the enormous gorge. The near-vertical sides showed gold in the early morning light.

Iggy's hands were balled into tight fists on his knees, his eyes straight ahead. His body leaned forward as if he could help move the truck along. His voice was tight with tension. "That goddamned Bottoms! If he had just opened the gallery Friday night when I asked him! Stupid, self-important prick!"

"It may not be—"

Iggy turned to shout at Mac, "Yeah! Yeah! God knows I'm praying it isn't Cindy." His voice dropped, "Sorry, Mac. But how many bodies are ever found in the river? And Cindy gone since Friday." He stopped talking abruptly and turned his face toward the window.

With a view of tree-covered mountains straight ahead, Mac took the pickup through the horseshoe curve just a little too fast. It was well-banked but the right-hand side was a drop-off that had claimed many lives. "Hang on, Ignacio. Not long now."

No comment. Tension filled the Chevy.

Pilar was on the descent past the next bend. Oh, no! A road block was set up by the Yacht Club hostel. State troopers. Patrol cars slewed around every which way, naturally. As Mac recalled, about half a mile farther down from this little community of Pilar a short side road went down to a small beach on the Rio Grande.

Mac stopped and a State trooper approached the truck. He leaned in the window, saying politely, "There's been an accident, sir. Proceed slowly until you're on the other side of it."

Thinking quickly, Mac answered, "I'm Dr. McCloud, Officer," indicating his bag. "I'm answering a call on the drowning," which was true, as far as it went.

"Do you have some identification, doctor?"

Mac fumbled for his driver's license, wondering how he was going to explain Iggy's presence. The trooper didn't ask, just touched his cap, and said, "That's fine, Dr. McCloud." He scribbled on a page of his citation book. "Just show this to Officer Benz at the turn-off to the beach. He'll let you through."

Mac started up again, exchanging a look with Iggy.

He showed Officer Benz his pass and maneuvered past more official cars down the narrow road to the beach that rounded out into a bend of the Rio Grande.

People. Officers. More yellow tape. Then the tragedy: a khaki Army blanket lay over a shape on the sand and rock beach.

Iggy already had his hand on the door handle, ready to jump before the truck was stopped Mac reached his long arm across, grabbing Iggy. "Hold it, Ignacio."

"Cindy!"

Mac spoke with authority. "You don't know. And if you want to find out, you'll use your head. Go leaping in there and you'll get us thrown out."

"But—"

"Just wait a minute! I have some idea how frightened you are, terrified it's Cindy, but I'm counting on the usual bureaucratic confusion to get us over there for a look. Don't screw up, for God's sake!"

Breathing heavily, Iggy reluctantly let go of the door handle. Another deep breath. "Okay, McCloud. What's your plan?"

"I carry my little black bag and walk over there like I know what I'm doing. You stay put!"

Iggy started an objection, but then forced himself to think. He nodded at Mac and reluctantly leaned back against the seat.

Carrying his medical bag as planned, Mac walked briskly toward the group of officers around the body on the other side of the tape.

As he got closer, groups began to sort themselves out. There were the rafters, a small group huddled together, looking shocked and frightened: some in wet suits, some still in life jackets forgotten in the tragedy. Close to them were the spectators who always seem to emerge from nowhere at any accident. Mac caught bits of conversation as they pointed and chattered in excitement: "Over there in the rocks…" "Found the body…" "Had to get…"

Mac's gaze was drawn from the pitiful bundle to the other side of the Rio Grande. There, a few skinny trees stuck out from large black, glistening boulders splashed by the river as it cut itself a deeper curve. Not very grande here, the river wasn't more than sixty feet across.

Nearby was a less frightened, more professional looking bunch, the Search and Rescue team. Seeming awed, stunned, grim, unlike the spectators they were quiet,

Mac spotted Sheriff Aaron Mason, a chilly character he'd met once before. The man looked like an ascetic: severe face, fine-featured, glasses, old-style military crewcut, tall. He had a couple of his deputies with him.

Good. There was Chief Garcia by himself.

Two State troopers walked toward Mac, determined looks on their faces. Mac called past them, "Hey, Chief Garcia, Sheriff Mason, I hope I didn't keep you waiting too long?"

The troopers relaxed. Mac stepped over the yellow tape. And, thanked God that apparently neither the Chief nor Sheriff were going to ask the other who called him. Just maybe he'd be able to carry off this bluff.

The two men came to meet him, Chief Garcia shaking Mac's hand and speaking first. "Good to see you, Dr. McCloud. You can take a look, maybe give us an approximate time of death. Search and Rescue found the body over there, caught in that rock. Had to go in and bring it here to the beach."

Feeling concern for Iggy, hating to ask, Mac questioned, "You've identified the body?"

The Chief followed his own thoughts, "I'm out of my jurisdiction, but got the call and came down to see if this had anything to do with our murder-robbery."

Sheriff Mason gave Mac a puzzled look. "We've called Mister Martinez, the M.E. What are you...?"

Thinking fast, trying to head off the question of who called him and breeze past why he was here when the medical examiner was coming. Mac quickly answered, "Good thing you did, Sheriff. Drownings are tricky. Were you also able to I.D. the body?"

"Small time hood, drug dealer. Name of Clive Castle."

Mac felt light with relief. He impulsively turned to wave at the truck to let Iggy know, but saw he had slipped up to the edge of the taped off area. Mac missed something the Sheriff said, and was now being looked at suspiciously. "Doctor?"

"Yes, Sheriff.?"

Chief Garcia broke in. "With this Castle's record, he *could* have been one of the killers, but not planned. Not his style. Only if cornered, I'd say. On the other hand, I know Bobby must have struggled with one of them, and this guy's face looks punched." Trailing off, the Chief shook his head. "What doesn't fit that kind of unpremeditated violence, there's wire around his neck."

Mac didn't want to get into some theoretical discussion for fear Iggy wouldn't be able to contain himself. For this reason, he abruptly left the Chief and Sheriff and approached the sinister blanket. The officers followed.

Pulling back the sheltering cover, Mac saw a slim white male before the awful stench overwhelmed him. Drownings had a terrible smell, worse than anything on earth. Turning away for a quick gulp of air, then turning back, Mac squatted down and lifted one of the body's hands. He examined it.

Still gagging from the foul odor, Mac rose and walked away a few steps, then said, "That body's been in the water some time."

"Since after the robbery Friday?" asked Garcia.

"I don't know, Chief," Mac answered politely. "Just two days is cutting it pretty close, considering its condition."

Chief Garcia didn't want his theory messed up. "How can you tell?"

"Two things. One, the epidermis, the outer skin with all its marks, scars, hair, so forth, is gone. Fingernails, too. The body is down to the dermis. That takes a considerable period of time in cold water with a current like this river."

"But—"

"Wait. Let me finish. That godawful smell results from at least the start of adipocere, the fatty tissues of the body reacting with water. The whole process takes at least a year, but I think it has begun. Of course, I'm no pathologist and haven't seen that many drownings..."

Sheriff Mason had been glad for the Taos Police to be taking the body off his hands. Now he said, "Looks pretty fresh to me. Seems like the perps could have fought anytime, way the man looks."

"No," Mac answered. "That fresh look, almost like a baby's skin, is the result of losing the epidermis over quite a spell."

The Sheriff: "We'll get it down to the O.M.I. right away. They'll know."

Mac agreed. "They sure will. Internal organ decomposition, or lack of it, will be a major indicator." Mac paused before asking casually, "By the way, you all recognized the man, mentioned his name. What was it again?"

"Clive Castle," the Chief answered and then turned with the others at the sounds behind them.

Iggy was struggling with two state troopers. "I have to see! I have to be sure!"

The Sheriff's cold blue eyes narrowed in a glare, but the Chief said, "Aw, let him in."

One quick look and Iggy turned away, retching.

CHAPTER XII

When Mac left Casa Vieja, Christy ran back upstairs to dress and put something on her cold feet. She then hurried down to prepare breakfast for her guests.

So much had happened, it felt later in the morning than it was. But no, still "Sunday morning silence" and no one around yet.

Soon, Christy slid muffin tins into the oven, then moved quickly to the dining room to set the table.

Although Christy worried deeply about Iggy and what he and Mac would find on their terrible errand, on another level she also wondered why the DeWitts hadn't made their early appearance. Nary a cheep.

Christy saw a note on the coffee maker on the small table in the corner. "Gone birding. Don't worry about breakfast. We helped ourselves to some fruit." A sketch of a robin was the signature. Nice people. Christy felt ashamed of making fun of them with Mac. They had a sense of humor, too, Mrs DeWitt apparently realizing she resembled the bird.

Lord, now she'd face the Keens undiluted, no good people to serve as buffers. As Christy took the place mats and Mexican crockery from the corner trastero, she pondered dealing with that bigoted pair. She was in no mood to be gracious and wondered if it was even moral to be polite.

Back in the kitchen to finish preparations, Christy prayed that the body was not Cindy. Please God bless her and hold her safe wherever she is.

Christy welcomed the comforting, spicy scent of the muffins coming from the oven. She had time to step outside.

The old brick floor of the portal had reddened from the dampness of the dew. Standing under the overhang, Christy could feel the night's cool still held by the portal. Most of the courtyard remembered the night, too. The fat lilac bush stood shadowed in the corner near the Don's Room; and the roses, colors muted by shade, held their breaths, waiting for sunshine before springing into their full scent and intensity. The sun, already warming the adobe wall above it, would soon reach down to Mac's little guest house.

"Yoo hoo! Where are you?" Mrs. Keen sang out from the kitchen.

Sighing, Christy turned back to the house.

Mac had a different Iggy with him on the drive home. Shaken, yes, and pale, but the rigid tension was gone.

"Some relief, hunh?" Mac glanced over at his passenger as they topped the rise, leaving Pilar behind them.

"Hell, yes! I'm still really concerned about Cindy, but thank God that wasn't her back there!"

"You know anything about the dead man?" Mac asked.

"Yeah, even though he looked real different. Used to have a lot of beard, moustache, but I recognized Clive Castle, pot-grower and dealer. I defended him on a drug bust." Iggy pondered. "I wouldn't have expected him to be the violent type, but who knows what happened?"

Mac took the horseshoe curve more slowly than he had on the way down. "No, if he was dealing, not a desperate user, seems like he wouldn't need to go in for what was probably a daylight robbery."

Behind the low protective wall, the stubby growth clung to rocky ground that fell sharply downward on the left. To their right, the mountain kept on climbing, ignoring the road cut into it. Thickly forested with piñon and juniper, the area was popular with rock hunters in search of staurolites, naturally-formed little crosses. Deer abounded there, too.

Both men were silent, thinking.

On the straight piece before Ranchos, Mac said, "Well, the advanced condition of the body is a puzzlement but this Castle probably *was* involved with the murder-robbery. Not likely to be unconnected. I can't see Taos having a crime wave of homicides, but still...You know any other possibles in town?"

"You mean because of my criminal defense work?" Iggy asked rhetorically. "I can't breach any client confidences, but that character you met at the Fiestacita, Ted Nesbit? He's been charged with embezzling from the artists, some other shady deals. And he's a gossip—would know if Bottoms had stuff in there worth the risk."

Mac remembered his impression of the "famous" artist and objected, "He didn't seem the type for anything so physical. And what about the motive? He need cash that bad?"

Iggy reached back to tug on his rat tail. "Ethically, I can't say, but I guess it wouldn't be any breach to tell you that everyone knows Nesbit's going to have to come up with a good bit of money if the court orders restitution. Plus, if he's been doing what he's charged with, he'd know where to fence whatever was taken."

Mac didn't reply as he started to pass the car ahead, then reconsidered and fell back. "So," he pondered, "Nesbit's got a damned good motive. Could've hired Castle to do the dirty work. But with that wire around Castle's neck, that takes us back to the problem of Nesbit and violence. Did he kill Castle? Throw him in the river? Oh, hell! Leave that for now. What else have you got?"

"Quite a few art scandals going," Iggy answered. "The former director of the Millicent Rogers Museum was convicted for some sort of thievery in California. Jerome Kelly's at the other museum and I've heard he wasn't checked too closely. Then we have the clients of our friend La Doña. She's representing a pair of gallery owners who are taking bankruptcy, Tad Spunk and Julian Horse."

"Sounds possible. What sort of folks are they?"

"Don't know. I've just met them casually." Iggy grinned. "And luckily for the rest of us, not many bankrupts turn violent. I only know about them because they're having a big reception and auction this week, trying to cash in on the Fiesta crowds to sell off as many assets as they can."

Mac saw that they were approaching the hill down into Ranchos and abruptly changed the subject. "What do you want to do, Ignacio? Head straight home? Go over to Christy's? Grab a cup of coffee at some cafe?"

"Coffee at a restaurant," Iggy answered. "I think I might be able to eat some breakfast now."

Thinking of how they all teased Iggy about his appetite, Mac smiled to himself, but didn't comment. Instead, he said, "Then let's stop at the Guadalajara Grill. I want to call Christy, let her know. She'll be worrying."

Iggy grinned. Where but in Taos would you find a popular restaurant attached to an automated carwash? On top of that, gossip had it defunct because it didn't arrange for water.

Christy had done something she had never done before, placed the breakfast on the table for the hunter and his wife, poured their coffee and then said, "A situation has come up, so please excuse me."

Now she sat at the desk in the Middle Room, anxiously waiting for news. No point in calling Mamacita until she knew something. She could call her friend Nancy, share all her worries with her. Funny. Christy wondered if other people were like her: waiting for a phone call, her mind would fill with all the people she could phone—and tie up the line!

Or she could take the cell phone and go grocery shopping...

Christy jumped when the phone rang, then answered, "Casa Vieja Bed and—"

"It's me, Christy," Mac interrupted.

"Thank God! I've been waiting..." She fearfully asked, "Is it Cindy?"

"No. Not Cindy."

Christy groaned with relief.

Mac continued, "It's the body of a man, some drug dealer. Name of, ah, Castle. Clive Castle. Know him?"

Christy hesitated, then remembered. "That's the one Iggy talked to for information on the Los Alamos case."

"Sure. I'd forgotten. Maybe never heard the name."

"Tell me what happened! Was it an accident?"

"Nope. Poor bastard had a wire around his neck."

"Oh, Lord! Then was he—?"

"The Chief thinks he was one of the ones involved in killing Bobby Mascarenas, then got it himself, but there are problems with that."

"Why? What's going on?"

"Look, Christy. I'm calling from the Guadalajara. Iggy wanted to eat, naturally."

"Naturally. But at least he must be feeling better."

"That he is. Anyway, we'll talk when I get home."

"Okay, later," Christy agreed, reluctant to let him go.

Christy had no time to think of Mac's news before the phone rang again. It had to be Mama. It was. "Christina! Why are you not at Mass?"

"I told you last night, Mamacita, that we were going to the six o'clock then."

"What of the body in the Rio Grande. Is it that poor friend of Ignacio's, the *muchacha* with no family?"

"No, Mama. It was not Cindy."

"¡Ah, *gracias a Dios*! God is good! *¿Pero, quien?* Who?"

Christy answered as best she knew, but Mamacita was still not satisfied. "*¿Pero*, what of Cindy?"

"No news. And I'm afraid that until she's found, Primo Barnabe will keep on thinking she's a suspect."

"Si, I hear the gossip that this *muchacha* helped in robbing the store of Dr. Bottoms, pero I say, '*Vale mas ser al que van a jusgar, que el que van a enterrar.*'"

"Mama!"

Sigh. "One would think you would know the sayings. I *said,* 'It's better to be the one being judged, than to be the one being buried'!"

Briskly she added, "*Ahora!* What of your brothers and sisters and Las Fiestas, eh? Will you have the rooms for them or do you have those who pay for the bed and breakfast?"

"You know I've saved the whole hacienda, Mama!" Deep breath. No quarreling. "Tell me when Patricio, Juan, and Odie, and their families are coming. Do they all want to stay here?"

As Mama began to answer, the Keens came clattering out of their room, burdened with luggage, dropping some.

"Sorry, Mamacita, some guests are checking out. I have to go help them."

Sigh. "If you cannot speak to your Mama...I will pray for La Cindy, and for you, m'hija. Do not involve yourself in danger! *La gente mala* walk the streets of Taos. *Muy malo!*'

That Spanish Christy knew. Wicked people. Much evil.

CHAPTER XIII

Christy believed passionately that Iggy's three close friends had to do something to help him. Iggy himself felt they were such a tight knit bunch, although so disparate, that he'd named them the Motley Crew. And the Crew couldn't abandon Iggy to this relentless limbo of fear and uncertainty. But what could they do that Barnabe and his police couldn't? Hoping to figure out a plan, Christy had called them to meet at the Apple Tree Restaurant after they all did some investigating.

Right now, she and Mac were in the lobby under Oglevie's. Steps to the restaurant led up from there with a planter of greenery underneath. Christy and Mac were gazing at the brick floor.

"Well, this isn't helping much," Christy said. "Let's just make up our minds and do it!"

Mac stared at his piece of floor. "Yeah, but do we come right out and ask the shopkeepers if they saw anything or act like tourists?"

"I say start here with Chantel's and just ask," Christy decided, pushing open the door as she spoke.

"May I show you something or would you rather just look?" the pleasant middle-aged man asked.

Christy took in an array of icons, retablos, cards, and especially deep blue fat glass hearts interspersed with the other merchandise.

"I'm afraid we're not customers," she apologized. "We wanted to ask you about the day of the robbery at El Museo, last Friday."

"Nothing, "the man answered. "As you can see, or can't see, the merchandise pretty well hides the window. I don't get a good look at anything in the lobby."

Mac asked, "Did you go in or out? Notice if the CLOSED sign was up?"

The man shook his head. "Sorry. Nothing at all."

Christy and Mac thanked him and left.

They visited From the Andes, wonderfully scented with wool and candles. There were elaborate multi-colored candles, Guatemalan saints, wool and alpaca ponchos.

A helpful dark-haired woman could give them no information and, next, Lombardi's Antiques was locked but had no window to the outside.

Tico's Studio had hundreds of various clay Storyteller figures and Indian art; La Chiripada a wall of wine and displays of the local wines, ristras and garlic. No help either place.

Open Space Gallery was an artists' co-op where the members took turns showing paintings, pottery, and beautiful woven garments. It was next door to El Museo.

This time Mac took a turn asking.

"Why, yes, I may have seen something," the young blond woman said. "Two men were going into the shop just as I unlocked. I noticed them because they seemed to be pulling something over their heads."

"What did they look like?" "Did you tell the police?" "Did you see them leave?" "See Cindy?" Christy and Mac both pounced with questions.

Looking taken aback at this barrage, the woman said, "I'm sorry. I didn't pay much attention, not knowing it was anything sinister. Fairly tall—one more so than the other—an impression only of Anglo. And, No, I'm sorry, I didn't see Cindy and Yes, I did tell the police."

Although she tried, the woman was unable to give them anything more.

Thanking her, Christy and Mac walked back through the lobby and outside. Their mood slightly lifted because of a crumb of information.

Christy looked around the Plaza, trying to think of somewhere else to try. She saw the place that used to house Rexal Drugs and one of her favorite memories tumbled into her mind.

"See catty-corner over there, Mac?" She pointed. Mac looked baffled. "Well, that's the spot of one of our family miracles."

"Miracle?"

"Yes. That's where Tia Porfy levitated."

"Levitated?"

"It was many years ago. Would have to be. I don't think it would happen the way things are now with the tourists and not all Spanish like before.

"Tia Porfy and Mamacita were shopping on the plaza. There used to be a general store, dry goods, all sort of places for the people. Well, they'd just come out of Rexal's when Tia Porfy gave a little whoop, and levitated!"

"You mean like off the ground?"

"Absolutely. She was clutching a little white patent purse in front of her and she flew into the air and down, then back up. Each time giving that little whoop."

Mac shook his head. "You're putting me on."

"No way. Whoop! Whoop! White patent purse and all. Mamacita didn't know what to make of it, but they both took it in stride. Tia Porfy levitated all down the block."

"Christy!"

"Trust me, Mac. Some of our saints did it, though Tia Porfy's certainly no saint. But one of my favorites was Saint Joseph of Capernum. He was a monk and his duty was to set the table for the monks' dinner. He started regularly levitating in the refectory which would have been okay but he was dropping the pottery as he flew around the ceiling. The brothers had to assign him different duties where his levitating wouldn't be so costly."

Sighing loudly, Mac took Christy's elbow. "Let's join the others at the Apple Tree."

Following this afternoon of investigating, Iggy and La Doña waved at Christy and Mac from where they sat at a comfortable wooden table on the patio of the Apple Tree Restaurant where they had previously agreed to gather for coffee and dessert. Christy and Mac found the mood wasn't good. La Doña and Iggy had taken the shops on the periphery near Oglevie's in case either the thieves r Cindy were seen on the street. Depression infected the team after the excitement of hoping to find out something.

They had opted for the shade of the bent old apple tree because Iggy thought the eighty degree day was too hot. Christy, however, continued to feel an occasional frisson unrelated to the temperature. The returning thought of the body in the river caused it. This was not Taos—not violent robberies; Bobby Mascarenas knifed; Cindy missing, maybe dead; and the horror of twisting a wire around a man's throat and dumping him into the icy waters of the Rio Grande.

Beneath the steely blue summer sky, Christy gazed around the patio and tried to absorb the beauty of the flowering vines on the high latilla fences, picking out a deep purple clematis here, a hummingbird drinking from the fluted orange trumpet flower there. She was trying not to fall into the morose mood emanating from Iggy beside her.

"Well, m'dears," La Doña addressed them in her brusque voice, "That does it, and a good afternoon's accomplishment it was, too. We've canvassed every merchant under Oglevie's, checked out those nearby, called some at home, talked to every waitperson at the restaurant...There was that one who said Cindy wasn't any better than she should be."

"What in Hell's that supposed to mean?" Iggy flared.

La Doña explained calmly, "An English expression that speaks for itself. Rather critical...And we saw that lovely child in the place catty-cornered."

"Woman, you mean," Christy corrected. "Not child."

"Hmmm. Yes. Well, that *person* states she saw Cindy go in the lobby doors early Friday morning about nine, and nothing else. From that point onward, not one of our witnesses can testify to anything other than that they saw the CLOSED sign in the window throughout the day. Interesting."

"'Interesting'!" Iggy mimicked bitterly, pushing aside his fudge cake. "Why didn't anyone see Cindy leave? Why haven't the police found her? Oh, God!"

Mac and Christy exchanged looks: Iggy's desperation seemed to be escalating. Hoping to distract him, Mac said, "So, we have our witness to two men and the CLOSED sign. That pretty much pinpoints the time the robbers went in—"

"Sure." Iggy's tone was sarcastic. "'Pinpoints' to the whole f-ing day, that is."

Mac refused to be insulted. "No. Shows it was so early no one reversed the sign to OPEN. But that's *in*. Will someone explain to me how the killers, as well as Cindy, could get *out* of the gallery without being seen?"

"Kidnapped," Iggy muttered into his hands.

"Well, think, friend." Mac sat forward. "I can see how one or two men could slip in with just that passing observation from Open Space. But, assuming you're right and Cindy was abducted, we're still left with my question of getting her out."

La Doña began to answer, but Mac wasn't finished. "And don't forget that the pair, if that's who the artist saw, were carrying something large enough to fit in that crate found open."

"The crowds," La Doña said firmly. "Nor am I forgetting anything, young man. Wrap up the booty and look like all the rest of the tourists with their parcels. Friday saw week-end visitors along with the influx who plan to make a stay of it through Las Fiestas. All the bandits had to do was walk out casually with a big package and, say, a gun in the child's side."

Iggy groaned.

Christy placed her hand on Iggy's. "We'll find her."

"How? We've talked to everyone. Maybe some tourist saw, but there's no way to trace them."

Mac was momentarily distracted from Iggy's speech as he thought how pretty Christy looked, flushed from the heat and their rapid walk. He returned to the problem. "Let's start from the other end."

He turned to Doris Jordan. "Who do you know in the Arts Community that might have both the motive and gall to pull something like this?"

Somehow managing to look cool in her shapeless tweed suit and tan blouse, La Doña looked at Mac sternly. "Why pick on the Arts Community, bless their internecine little hearts?"

Mac looked so taken aback that Christy had to smile despite their somber mood. "La Doña means fierce in-group battling.

They all go to each others openings, unless they've had a spat and show it by staying away—"

"I do not believe I need an interpreter, Christina. Answer my question, young man."

"Because it appears that despite what seems to have been a struggle with Mascarenas that may have interrupted the robbery, the men knew where to go. Opened only that one crate and made off with its contents."

"And Cindy," Iggy added sadly, then added more vehemently, "One of them brutal enough to strangle poor old Clive with a wire. God! I saw the body!"

"Maybe not," Mac soothed. "Maybe not. Remember, I thought Clive had been dead a much longer period, making his death unconnected."

La Doña allowed herself a sympathetic look at Iggy and then returned to Mac. "I represent several artists, some galleries, but I cannot see any of my clients becoming murderous thieves, Dr. McCloud! Anyone at all might have heard of particularly valuable merchandise."

"That's true, La Doña, but it's also true that this didn't begin as a murder. Perhaps you have a client that was simply desperate for money, knew what worth stealing, and the plan went wrong."He paused "Iggy mentioned a bankruptcy?"

La Doña sat even more erect, "If you are referring to the Spunk-Horse partnership, I can assure you that neither is prone to criminal behavior."

Mac pressed her, but in a soothing manner: "Yes, ma'am, but Christy and Iggy here say they're not well acquainted with those folks. I'm not asking you to violate any confidences if you could just tell us something about this Spunk and Horse? And anyone else you can think of," he added quickly.

La Doña considered. "Rather ordinary young men, in their forties, I'd say. Came here from California, flashing about their cash, grandiose plans."

She paused, picking her words in order not to say anything that wasn't already public knowledge. "Messrs Spunk and Horse bought a large home on Placitas. That purchase took money, naturally. Then they splurged on renovating and creating a rather elegant gallery."

"And ran out of capital?" Mac urged her on.

"That and being misinformed about the naiveté of the locals, having had in mind they could buy up cheap all sorts of goodies with which to stock their gallery. They were knowledgeable about the old Taos art scene as well as Spanish religious articles, but rather dim as far as thinking the people here wouldn't know the worth of what they had."

"So, sharpies who weren't?"

"I believe you could sum them up that way, Dr. McCloud. Forced into bankruptcy—having an auction Tuesday, as a matter of fact, but nevertheless innocent of any wrongdoing."

Then with a wicked gleam in Iggy's direction, she added, "However, one hears that is not the case with those represented by Ignacio. Mr. Nesbit is an example, I believe."

Iggy pushed back his chair and half rose as if he were about to bolt. "Talk. All this talk is wasting time. We have to find Cindy."

"Sit down, Ignacio," La Doña commanded. "This is no time for hysterics. Now is when we should organize a list of suspects and proceed to find out where each was on Friday."

The lady lawyer nodded to Mac. "And determine what was stolen and where it is. No small task! Work, Ignacio. Stop emoting and get to work!"

The High Road ran from Taos to Chamisal, Penasco, Las Trampas, Truchas, and Chimayo, ancient beads on a string of Spanish settlements. From Chimayo one could go into Espanola or continue on to Santa Fe.

The High Road seemed to follow the spine of the earth, running along sky-scraping mountain ridges, sometimes through thick rusty-red barked ponderosa pine and blue spruce forests, their floors patterned with sunlight and needles, sometimes on the bare backbone itself where the land dropped away on either side to reveal spectacular vistas of far-off dun, yellow, sienna carved sandstone and lime.

The driver of the car was immune to the beauty and the views of snow-covered peaks, the glimpses of tidy little farms down below. Instead the person thought of the priceless artifacts held in the small adobe churches of these towns. The Santuario at Chimayo was the best, of course, so many people having brought old, beloved santos, retablos, and rosaries in thanks for miracle cures from the healing earth. They donated in prayer for this holy place. The altar and side rooms were absolutely crowded with treasures!

The thief was smart to have made this particular return trip on a Sunday afternoon. After the morning Masses, that was the one day of the week when one could count on no one being around a Catholic Church! Well, except for the Santuario, of course. Apparently, as far as could be determined from reconnoitering, it had a steady stream of both the faithful and simply curious. The specialist's particular type of entry there would take more thought, and there wasn't that much time left.

Today's target was Las Trampas, Spanish for "trap".

The car leapt forward as the driver accelerated, taking the curve too fast. So damned many curves on this road!

Cool, I must keep my cool, the person chided, easing off the gas pedal. Remember, if you remain composed, you have an unshakable cover. That and the fact that you're unnoticed by the average person. The thief smiled, thinking about what cretins the majority of people were. It was delightful to be far more clever than the most intelligent of them.

Las Trampas, and then maybe, just maybe, Chimayo and the Santuario! There was that very special santo. The problem was to figure out how to reach it.

CHAPTER XIV

Christy was up early in order to catch the DeWitts. She wanted to do something special for them. Guilty conscience, she acknowledged, just feeling ashamed for laughing with Mac behind their backs. But no shame about the Keens. Thank God the Great White Hunter and Miz Bigot had departed to pollute other surroundings!

Rounding the last curve of her spiral staircase, Christy heard loud thumps and saw canvas bags sailing through the air from La Escondida. Then, preceded by her impressive bust, Mrs. DeWitt emerged, little black eyes bright.

"Just clearing out our teensy nest, dearie. Off to new fields! That's how the female troglodytidae does it you know."

"Troglo...?" Christy murmured overwhelmed.

"Common house wren," Mrs. DeWitt interpreted impatiently. "Every Spring the male wren arrives first and carefully builds a nest for his mate. Then she comes along and scolds him, quite amusing to hear, pitches out all his efforts and builds herself another nest."

Mr. DeWitt ducked carefully through the little door, smiled at Christy, and began loading himself with luggage.

"May I help?" Christy asked him, but Mrs. DeWitt jumped in to say, "No, no. We're accustomed to carrying our own little sticks and fluff, aren't we dear?"

Mr. DeWitt grunted, bent over, gathering up more bags. Once upright, though burdened down, he announced, "Last night was a real winner!"

"Not now, sweetheart, wait until breakfast. I have my own small success to share with our hostess, too, you know."

Bemused by how many cases Mr. DeWitt could manage, Christy said abstractedly, "Than you are staying for breakfast?"

"Oh yes, this is a travel day for us. No birding until migration ends. One makes sacrifices. But I must be at the Bosque by mid-afternoon when our friends return. Whooping cranes are said to be making their home there!"

"Uh, right. I'll have your breakfast ready shortly. And since you two are my only guests, how about Eggs Benedict?"

Heavily weighted, Mr. DeWitt strode purposefully toward the front. That thin wiry frame must be pretty strong.

Mrs. DeWitt replied, "No, no, dearie. A bit of fruit, a bite of cereal, and my herb tea."

Christy fled.

She had just entered the kitchen when Mac wandered in the back door, looked around, and waggled his black eyebrows in his favorite Groucho imitation. "Where's the smell of baked goods? The bustle of mine hostess preparing breakfast?"

Christy grinned at him. Comfortable old friend, right now looking freshly showered, his white hair curling up a little at the edges.

"I get to play hooky," she answered. "No one here but the DeWitts and they only want cereal and herb tea!"

"Hmmm," Mac pondered. Then, "Be right back," and he was gone.

What was that all about? she wondered. No matter, here came the guests.

Feeling as if she were cheating, Christy showed them the variety of cereals, placed the fruit bowl on the table, prepared the tea.

When the three of them were seated, Christy with her coffee at the head of the table, the DeWitts on either side of her, Mr. DeWitt said, "Now my news! Last night, just on the off chance, I decided to slip into the parking lot of that bed and breakfast, the hacienda on the other side of town. Really don't know what made me do it. And there, right there, was a Porche with—get this!—a German license plate! How do you like them apples?"

"Uh, fine. I mean marvelous! That's really, uh, terrific!"

Mr. DeWitt stripped his banana with gusto.

Mrs. DeWitt tapped Christy's hand, rather like a peck, she thought. "Remember, Mrs. Grant, that I said I had a wee surprise for you?"

Christy nodded.

"And that we went birding in the mountains yesterday?"

Another nod.

"I saw, well, I'll tell you the common name for this most uncommon bird. I saw a white-eared hummingbird!"

"White-eared?" Christy choked.

"You are right to be astounded, my dear. The *hylocharis leucotis* is normally found only in the mountains of *Old* Mexico and as a rare, very rare, visitor to Arizona! But New Mexico? Ha! Well, Bert and I were slipping about among the trees when I thought I heard the sound of a tiny bell. 'Could it be?' I thought to myself. Creeping closer, glasses at the ready, I made my find! Yes, indeedy, I spotted the little lady, red-billed, bold white stripe behind the eye!

Mrs. DeWitt allowed a moment of quiet awe, then: "Now you will ask, 'How can you be sure it was not the more likely broad-billed?' And I will quickly answer, 'Because the little darling had *spots* on her throat and was *not* uniformly grey!'" She sat back in triumph.

At a loss, Christy finally managed, "Congratulations!"

Mrs. DeWitt looked at her husband, "Now, Bert, if you will...?"

"Hunh? Oh, right."

They sat in silence while Mr. DeWitt loped out of the room and returned with a package which he handed his wife. She presented it to Christy with a flourish, saying, "I was rather giddy with joy over this entry in my life book and wanted to share it with you." Little finger peck on the hand, "And you have been lax, you must admit. Bird calls. I've bought you the bird call CD!"

Christy was truly touched.

Christy was still at the desk in the Middle Room. The DeWitts had just checked out. And Desire sashayed, the only word for it, in on high-heeled cowboy boots, a long stretch of legs, short-short ragged cut-offs, and an artfully tattered off-the-shoulder top. "Did you manage all right without me over Sunday?"

"Yes, Desire. What's the costume this time?"

"Don't you just love it, Miz Grant? I'm still doing a contrast to Las Fiestas, you know?" She ran a hand through disheveled blond curls. "I dressed like that old tv show I just loved when I was little? *The Dukes of Hazard?* Where they had those cute girls and a sheriff and funny cars?"

Christy nodded. This seemed to be a morning for wordless nods. She thanked God for no guests today, a double thank you since Ellie wasn't coming in for the housekeeping either.

"My Gawd!" Mac stood in the doorway.

Desire put an extra wiggle in her pirouette for Mac. "I guess you like my outfit, Dr. McCloud?"

"I'm speechless, Desire."

Christy grinned. "I'll leave you the desk, Desire, and take the good doctor to the kitchen." She led Mac off by the arm, as he gawked back over his shoulder.

"If I can pull my wits together, I brought you a surprise."

"I've just had several," Christy said dryly. "What's yours?"

"I thought after all those wonderful homemade breakfasts you turn out, and bein' as how you're off duty today...Well, I ran down the road to buy it, thinking that you might enjoy some awful junk!"

Mac reached into the sack and hauled out a donut oozing chocolate cream. "Ta-dum!"

The phone rang. It was for Christy. Evelyn Bottoms. And in a state of agitation.

Chapter XV

Mac drove down the road on another errand that Christy knew nothing about.

Admit it, he thought, Evelyn's call has a lot to do with this sudden desire to talk to Chief Garcia. Some nerve, Bottoms saying that the Chief was keeping him in town and it would be much more pleasant if he could stay at Casa Vieja! Luckily, Christy had put Bottoms off, saying she wasn't sure when all her relatives were arriving for Las Fiestas. Be honest, McCloud. Lucky for whom?

This jaunt had been spur of the moment. Now he had to prepare an excuse for seeing the Chief, while attempting to give Bottoms a push out of Taos. It wasn't jealousy on his part, he told himself, just that he didn't trust that character, didn't want Christy hurt.

Mac turned at the new intersection, taking the back way which still had something of a country look, a good many empty fields and vistas to the far mountains. The developers wouldn't neglect it much longer, Mac mused. It was a good thing that Taos Land Trust had been trying to preserve what they could for views. Of course they also wanted to keep as much land in its natural or agricultural state as possible.

Ha! Mac thought, as he saw a prairie dog. Now that's serendipitous. Think of the land and a prairie dog sentry appears. Having noticed one, he spotted several others on watch for the community. If the guard sensed danged he give little high yelps to warn the prairie dog town.

Mac liked the little creatures that resembled squirrels, always sitting on their hind quarters when being sentries, usually at the head of a burrow whose winding passages would even include a separate place for bodily functions. He knew they were often exterminated and blamed for carrying fleas spreading the plague, but he didn't want them wiped out. And he'd bet a fortune not one horse or cow ever broke a leg in a prairie dog hole.

Distracted by little critters, it seemed no time before Mac reached Placitas, the road along the backside of the Plaza.

When Mac entered the Police Station, Louisa glanced behind him, apparently looking for Christy.

"Good morning, Louisa. Any chance of me seeing Chief Garcia?"

She smiled and said she'd see, leaving Mac time enough to hope he didn't make a fool of himself.

Louisa returned. "Come on back, Dr. McCloud. The Chief has an appointment coming in, but he can see you for a little while."

Barnabe Garcia rose to shake hands with Mac, his expression curious. "Please sit down. What can I do for you this morning?"

"Thanks for taking time for me, Chief. I wanted to apologize for Mr. Baca's behavior at the river yesterday. He was close to Cindy and distraught, thinking the body might be hers."

"No problem," Chief Garcia answered, his expression remaining quizzical, obviously not accepting this as the reason for Mac's visit.

"I also wanted to find out if there was any word on the body yet, check if my med school training was correct. Condition of the corpse? Time in the water?"

The Chief leaned back in his chair. "Not much from the O.M.I yet. Just confirmed what we surmised, that Castle had been badly beaten and strangled with that wire. That, not drowning, was the apparent cause of death. The medical examiner's office is over-worked, so I'm afraid they won't have any details for us any time soon."

Casually picking up on this, Mac said, "Well, I was wondering about that, Chief. Time, I mean. Seems Dr. Bottoms is chafing at the bit to leave town, get on about his business."

The Chief gave Mac a sharp look, but answered mildly, "I have quite a few questions for Dr. Bottoms. I'd like to know what was in that crate and who he's acquainted with that would have also known."

The Chief paused, his scrutiny of Mac seeming to sharpen. "Funny thing. We're sending the whole crate to the State forensics, but first we did our own pretty close examination. Found a long strand of black hair."

"Black hair?" Mac repeated in surprise. "Did Cindy have black hair?"

"No, she didn't, but you're not thinking. The crate wasn't big enough to hold Cindy's body. Anyway, it didn't seem to be a hair from a woman's head. This hair was exceptionally coarse. I don't know, more like a horse hair, maybe?"

"Could it have been human hair?" Mac was intrigued.

"Yeah. Odd. We'll get our answer when they take a look down in Albuquerque. They do amazing things with age, sex, and so on, but makes me wonder."

"Well, I sure do, too," Mac answered. "Too bad your investigation has to wait on Albuquerque for so much."

The Chief nodded. Mac had more questions, but the Chief glanced at his watch, a signal to Mac that the interview was over. He stood, ready to leave—and Christy walked in. Damn! Bottoms was behind her. "Mac!" Christy exclaimed.

"Why, hello there, Christy, Dr. Bottoms." Mac turned back, shook hands with Chief Garcia, and hurriedly escaped. Caught in the act!

"What was Mac doing here?" Christy asked her smiling cousin.

The Chief held his massive hands far apart, shrugged, but there was a glint in his eyes. Then, becoming less genial, he turned to the Englishman, saying, "I have a number of questions, Dr. Bottoms, but wonder first why you thought it necessary to bring your attorney with you again."

Christy spoke for him, "Evelyn called me after you contacted him, Barnabe. He's just not used to our ways and wants me here to be sure that there's no misunderstanding."

Chief Garcia continued to look at Dr. Bottoms, not Christy, "You mean you think you need an interpreter? Quaint locals?"

Christy began to speak, but her client got the words out first, "No, Chief Garcia," he answered unruffled. "Not at all. I simply have so many business dealings, I'm accustomed to being accompanied by my barrister."

The Chief winked at Christy, "'Barrister', eh, Prima?" When she had no response, he turned to his phone intercom: "Louisa, send in Officer Arnold, *por favor.* I want him to take a statement."

As they waited, Christy asked, "What news, Barnabe? Any word on Cindy?"

"I was just speaking to your friend about that," he replied in a non-answer.

A rap on the door and Officer Arnold entered, once again quickly arranging himself in an unobtrusive corner.

Chief Garcia returned to business: "Now, Dr. Bottoms," he sprang his surprise, "Will you please describe your relationship to a Mr. Clive Castle."

"Just a minute, Barnabe, you haven't established that Dr. Bottoms had any acquaintance with Castle."

"You are not in court, Counselor," he answered mildly.

"That's all right, Christy," Evelyn soothed with a smile, then looked at the big policeman. "I had no knowledge of the man, Chief Garcia. I only heard of the discovery of his body when I spoke to Miz Garcia y Grant this morning."

"Has he had occasion to visit your gallery?"

One finger stroked the pencil mustache. "As I have explained, sir, I did not know the man and thus have no way of ascertaining if he was one of many who visited El Museo. Indeed, from what I have been told of the man's reputation, it seems unlikely he would have had an appreciation for my treasures."

Irritated, Chief Garcia snapped, "I'm not talking about art appreciation. I'm talking casing the place."

Evelyn Bottoms spread his hands, palms up, "Obviously, not to my knowledge, Chief Garcia. However, one must wonder if the person was a friend or, say, cohort of our Cindy, mustn't one?"

"Okay, doctor," the Chief said gruffly without answering the rhetorical question "Let's get back to your inventory and the contents of the crate."

"He's explained that, Barnabe," Christy interceded.

"Please, Prima. Your answer, Dr. Bottoms?"

A shrug, wistful look. "What can I say? I travel most of the time, buying back many of your splendid artifacts, sometimes, say, ten to twelve purchases at a time. You would be astounded at how popular the artifacts have become with collectors—Japan, Germany, my own little isle."

Chief Garcia watched him impassively, no sign of his impatience other than fingers drumming on his chair arm.

Evelyn Bottoms shifted position, crossed his legs. "Yes indeed, I wander the world. As to the inventory, that was among Cindy's duties, as I believe I previously explained. Mistaken trust, perhaps, but nevertheless, Cindy was responsible for keeping the record of my many purchases when they arrived here in your charming town."

The Chief sighed, shaking his head. "You must have some idea of what was in the crate, Dr. Bottoms."

Hands gesturing, a sheepish look. "Again, my ignorance is embarrassing, sir. But how could I know? There was no shipping label, but perhaps Cindy removed it to catalogue an in-coming shipment. The alternative, of course, was that she and Mr. Mascarenas were preparing items to send to a purchaser. Already some little fame had spread. El Museo ships worldwide."

He turned to Christy, "Only those things which I felt could properly be sold, my dear. Lesser Indian pots and baskets, for example. The true treasures, the articles unique to the culture or brought in by the Conquistadors, were held for my future museum."

Chief Garcia spoke sharply, "Who or what do you know about black hair, doctor?"

The man blinked, then smiled. "Black hair? Is this a local joke, Chief Garcia?"

"No joke," the Chief answered grimly.

Mac left the police station feeling routed. He decided to see if Iggy was in his office so drove back the way he'd come to the Plaza parking lot. Cruising the lanes slowly, he thought that his intention to park here had been pretty silly, it being near noon in the high tourist season. Maybe a chance in Our Lady of Guadalupe's lot…Yep, there was Christy's friend Louis waving him in, pointing out a shady place, too.

Mac decided to try his Southern tongue on the Spanish formula with, "¿Como 'sta, Louis?"

Louis' face was made for smiling, and now he beamed, answering, "Fine, fine, Dr. McCloud. How are you?"

"Fine, thanks."

"And Christina?"

So much for trying Spanish.

Mac crossed the street, passing a gallery located where his barber shop had previously been. He strolled onto the open square of shops around the center Plaza.

Funny to think he'd never been to Iggy's office, but he knew it was over there above the old movie theater. More changes: now the theater was closed and the new Storyteller multiplex was just off the main drag.

Mac walked along the west side, and began looking for the entrance to Iggy's second floor office. There it was, just before La Fonda hotel that housed the D.H. Lawrence paintings. Mac climbed the wooden stairs, thinking how appalled the big-city firms would be at this remnant of typical small-town law practice. The days of yesteryear, he thought.

An open door with hand-painted gold lettering, IGNACIO BACA, ATTORNEY AT LAW. No one in sight in the small reception room.

"Hey, Ignacio, it's Mac McCloud. You in there?"

"Come on in, Mac," Iggy called from his office.

Iggy was at his computer, sitting in a good-looking brown leather executive chair. Otherwise, the overhead pipes and cracked leather couch did not provide a prosperous image.

"I think of Cindy every minute, but decided I'd better try to get some law work done," Iggy explained. "I can't sit around crying like a baby."

"Good for you," Mac answered, shaking Iggy's hand. "But you're no baby. Only naturally upset, I'd say. Anyway, I'm the one feeling like a kid right now."

Iggy's serious expression lightened slightly, "Yeah? What've you done?"

"Went to see Chief Garcia on my own. Wanted to see if I could nudge him a little, get our friend Bottoms out of town."

"What's the matter with that?"

"I hadn't said anything to Christy, naturally. And she and Bottoms walked in on me."

That brought a grin. "Uh-oh."

"Uh-oh's right. No words were exchanged, but she's going to want to know later what I was up to."

"So you feel the way I do about that bastard?"

"Probably not as intensely, but he grates on me. Too precious. And the way he keeps latching onto Christy! Claims he needs her help, but she's not even practicing law any more."

"Yeah, I know." Iggy looked glum again. "I don't suppose the Chief had any news about Cindy?"

"No. Nothing much on the body in the river either."

Iggy put his head down into his hands. "That body, Mac." His voice was muffled. "No word since Friday. I'd better get used to the idea that Cindy is gone."

"I don't have any words of wisdom—just what I used to tell the families of some of my patients—keep praying and yet try to adjust yourself, be prepared for bad news." Mac paused. "But I'm not helping you any with this kind of talk. Why don't we do something?"

"What?" Iggy's tone was listless.

"Well, La Doña had that plan yesterday, checking out her bankrupt pair and your Nesbit. Before we do that, we could start with you telling me what you know about the dead man Castle."

Iggy stood, began pacing in front of the long, old-fashioned windows. "I represented him on a drug bust. He was strictly small-time. Not a bad fellow. I just can't see him involved in armed robbery or something as sophisticated and probably difficult to fence as whatever they were after at Bottoms'."

Mac stood, too, and stretched. "Did he have buddies we could investigate?"

"Not that I know of. Pretty much a loner, mostly hung out at his cabin in the mountains, grew some pot up there."

"You real busy right now?"

"Not if I can help Cindy. What do you have in mind?"

"Thought we might get a bite to eat, then go about this methodically. Pay some calls on some galleries."

"Let's do it!" Iggy answered with new vigor. "And then tomorrow we'll check out that auction. But don't forget Bottoms while we're at it."

"Oh, I won't forget Dr. Bottoms," Mac answered grimly.

CHAPTER XVI

Naturally, Iggy wanted lunch before they started their investigations. He chose Bravo for the size of its sandwiches and its array of delicious desserts. Mac just plain liked the food.

When Iggy was replete with tiramisu and they had said their goodbyes to Jo Ann, the friendly manager, they faced how in the world they were going to be investigators and where to start.

Iggy said, "Since we're already driving, let's do that part first. Then we can hit up the galleries on Kit Carson and just have to fight for a parking space once."

"Sounds fine to me," Mac answered. "Want to take the Chevy?"

"When we can ride in the Diva and listen to opera? No way." So they headed to Iggy's elderly Chrysler Imperial.

Iggy already had the CD of *The Magic Flute* in his sound system that was many generations younger than the Diva. "Needed to try to be upbeat," he explained.

"Where to first?"

"First you turn that thing down," Mac complained. "Then let's take them as they come. Your Famous Artist Nesbit, then Spunk and Horse since they're on Placitas, too, away from the other galleries, then maybe that other museum. See what, uh, Director Kelly thinks of friend Bottoms."

"By then we'll be ready for Cafe Tazza and then do the Kit Carson galleries," Iggy added.

As it turned out, they didn't even need to stop at Nesbit's since they could see the CLOSED sign hanging from the board that carried its name, La Bonita, carved in curlicues.

Mac smiled remembering Christy's translation of it to "The Pretty?", then turned serious. "Doesn't look like Famous Artist is trying to make up the money he's accused of taking from the artists."

"You'd think he'd be open with the crowds coming in for Fiestas," Iggy answered. He sped up, casually turning the volume higher for a favorite aria.

Mac gave him a look, but only said, "I think Spunk and Horse are right along here, too."

"Yep. That big converted adobe up there."

At the elegantly simple sign, they pulled into a drive containing the typical Taos variety of vehicles, often a clue as to which group its owner fell into.

The front door stood open, so Mac and Iggy stepped inside. The nearly bare walls gave the gallery a naked, vulnerable feel, nor were the number of people present that the vehicles outside would suggest.

A big, muscular man was wrestling with a painting to be hung. A slighter man and a young woman took it from him.

"Hello there, gentlemen," the big one said. "I'm Tad Spunk. Afraid we're not doing any business today but a mega auction tomorrow. How about stopping by then?"

"Well, we wanted—" Iggy began at the same time Mac said, "Sure thing."

The other man finished hanging the painting and turned with his hand outstretched, "Horse, Julian Horse is the name. Hope we can expect to see you tomorrow."

Both men smiled at Iggy and Mac and moved away together.

"I think we've just been kicked out," Mac said.

"We've got to get some answers," Iggy answered. "This isn't finding Cindy! That's why I didn't want you to let that Spunk get out of questioning."

"We'll find out more if we keep it casual. Hang in there. Let's see what we can uncover about Bottoms from the museum director."

Since the relatively new museum was housed in a compound just off Placitas, the drive was a short one. Leaving the car in the graveled parking lot, Mac and Iggy followed a path to a blue wooden gate in an adobe wall. Ahead, heavy carved wooden doors stood open.

Mac took the lead in introducing themselves to the short, wide receptionist, liking the fact that the museum didn't have to put on airs, as his mother used to say.

"Mr. Kelly can see you right now," she said on her quick return, and led the way to an office that overlooked a courtyard where a full-size copy of the Cart of Death sat on the red bricks.

Jerome Kelly came around from behind his desk, hand extended, spiky sandy hair escaping his apparent attempts to make it lay flat.

"Hello, there, gentlemen," he said. "Nice to have you here at the museum, but my guess is that you don't come as tourists."

Iggy and Mac shook Mr. Kelly's hand and then sat in the comfortable leather chairs he indicated.

"Afraid you're right," Mac answered, crossing his legs. "It's something of a fishing expedition."

Jerome Kelly returned to sit behind his desk. He raised sandy eyebrows, but smiled. "I can't imagine what fish you hope to catch here."

Iggy's feelings were barely contained, "We're checking out Evelyn Bottoms. What do you know about him?"

Mac regretted that Iggy couldn't maintain his more subtle courtroom style. "Sorry to be so abrupt," he said. "We thought since you were in the same field you might give us some background on Dr. Bottoms. We're doing a little independent research into the tragedy at his place. Attorney Baca here is particularly concerned about the missing young woman."

Jerome Kelly looked somber at the mention of Cindy, but then grinned. "Well, I can't say I accuse you two of being over subtle," he said. "I don't want to say anything libelous."

Mac and Iggy both pricked up at that, Mac saying, "Mr. Baca's an attorney and I'm a doctor. We're accustomed to keeping confidences."

"Well, in that case…" Jerome Kelly shrugged, his friendly open face turning serious. "Let me just say that Dr. Bottoms does not appear to be known in museum circles."

Mac saw Iggy ready to pounce and stepped in first, "And…?"

The museum director reached forward, then drew his hand back. "Sorry. I'm accustomed to getting my pipe at stressful moments. Stopped smoking, though."

Mac thought Iggy would burst. "You were going to comment…?"

"Well, yes. I don't want to be quoted, but I worry about a couple of things. There's really no niche for a new museum for one thing. Ours here fills in with Hispanic art from the early santeros up to the present with Our Lady of Guadalupe riding a motorcycle as a gangbanger."

Even Iggy laughed at that one. Then they waited.

"So there's that," Kelly continued. "The other is more difficult." He again reached for the nonexistent pipe.

"Well, let me just say that his so-called mission to bring back ancient Spanish artifacts would be an ideal scam. Who's to say what he's bringing in from generous donors or, in the alternative, what's going out?"

Iggy and Mac exchanged a look.

"There now," the director commented ruefully. "I've said too much. Please remember you promised not to quote me."

Thanking him, Mac and Iggy left. They were scarcely out the door when Iggy punched Mac's arm. "See there! We'll nail that Bottoms yet!"

CHAPTER XVII

Back in the Chrysler Imperial, Iggy smacked the steering wheel. "See? See what that Kelly says?" He deflated abruptly. "Well, it's a start anyway. One professional who's never heard of him before."

"I agree. Jerome Kelly's given us some interesting information, but we've still a long way to go. Like who were the thieves that the witnesses apparently saw pulling on masks."

Iggy's mood darkened more. "You're right, Mac. We're no closer to finding Cindy.

"Nothing more than that Bottoms may be a phony and that's just bolstering up what we already believed."

Mac tried for an up beat. "Then let's get going on the galleries. See what we can pick up. Maybe suspects that are more viable."

Iggy drove to a lot behind the rows of galleries on Kit Carson. They made their way around walls and up steps, walked by Roberto's on its little lane, and came out by Total Arts Gallery. Mac admired the paintings in the window. The more realistic ones by Barbara Zaring imprinted the mind with sunset mountains while looking at her abstracts, explosions of joy. Unfortunately, that gallery was closed, but anticipating the next, Mac asked, "How do we go about this?".

"We'll stop in where I know the owners and see what we can pick up," Iggy said, his tone still grim. He didn't even mention a snack at Cafe Tazza.

"Then take it easy," Mac said. "Don't scare anyone off."

Iggy didn't answer.

He led the way into the Parks Gallery first. A slim blond woman came toward them quickly, her smile welcoming.

Mac's gaze was drawn to a number of arresting vermillion paintings that led his eyes to their darker centers. The artist, Marsha Skinner. He was also taken with several multimedia works of ancient wisdom by Melissa Zink. Mac surprised himself with the pleasure they gave him.

Iggy was speaking with the woman he introduced as Joni. "Just showing my friend, Mac here, around the galleries. You being one of the best. Well…"

Mac liked the space, open and contemporary, although created in an old building with creaky wood floors, but Joni had no gossip to offer as Iggy tried to draw her out.

Mac made his attempt, "What Iggy didn't tell you is that we're investigating the robbery-murder at El Museo. We're just wondering what might be being said about it in the Arts Community."

Joni said, "I wish I could help but I'm going to have to lock up for a little while. I need to pick up my son. There's always talk. Maybe you all can pick up more information at the Spunk-Horse auction tomorrow."

That ended that and after goodbyes, they went next door to what was actually part of the same building; it had once belonged to one of the founders of the Taos colony. To reach the door of the Mission Gallery, they had to walk around what had to be one of the largest and oldest cottonwoods in Taos.

As a trim, vigorous mature woman approached Iggy said, "The is the grande dame of art in Taos, Rena Rosequist. As she greeted them warmly, Mac admired the variety of paintings— abstract, representational, expressionist—that melded to created a calm, refined mood as individual lights poured down on them from the high ceiling.

Rena immediately began to tell them a story about how the pair of women who had just left connected to the Taos Arts scene, then offered them a cup of tea.

Once they were settled in Rena's office, an open sort of room between the two main gallery areas, Mac tried his same approach.

"Oh, I love stories," Rena said. "But I don't know what might help you...Let's see." And proceeded to regale them with entertaining tidbits.

"And, another story. When we went in to find the cause of the wood rotting out back, we discovered a sixty-five foot well."

Rena smiled at them.

Mac smiled back. "And what about our mystery and Dr. Bottoms?" he asked.

Rena said, "The big secret about galleries is they never, never have enough storage space. You can see my lovely paintings propped on the floor and sitting on chairs. I just *hate* to say no to talent..."

Iggy broke in, "Our main reason to be involved is that my friend Cindy disappeared from El Museo."

Rena looked concerned. "I'm so sorry," she said. "Of course, you have every reason to be worried. Let's hope she's simply in hiding. Oh, and one thing I don't believe anyone is concentrating on. There seems to be a rash of theft of church art. Now that's something to think about. We have so many treasures... and very little protection."

Realizing she was reluctant to say more, Mac thanked Ms. Rosequist and directed Iggy out he door. Iggy then took charge and led the way to a little hole-in-the wall sort of gallery.

After waiting amidst Western art, they were eventually welcomed by a large man who made himself taller with high-heeled cowboy boots. "Help you?"

Mac introduced themselves, then said, "We're working on that theft and murder that took place on the Plaza. Wondered if you might know anything about it or Dr. Bottoms?"

Keeping in character with cowboy drawl, the proprietor said, "Have more than just art here. All sorts of fine Western memorabilia. And if you're looking for something special...?

Mac waited, not to be sidetracked. "About Dr. Bottoms?"

"Well, there, I don't know. A newcomer. *Says* he's bringing back ancient Taos Spanish work. I've heard the rumors. Did he rob himself?. And, of course, everyone's asking if someone in the know was so hard up...Well, now though, I'm not one to speculate."

"But if you were..." Mac prodded.

"I wouldn't be one ready to blame his employee—Cindy, isn't it? I don't much like that way of thinking."

Iggy turned red but managed not to speak. Mac helped him out. "Iggy here is good friends with Cindy. He's sure she's not involved, except perhaps a victim."

Leaving there, Iggy showed Mac the way around the corner to a hidden courtyard that was all angles of different adobe walls randomly intersecting, huge lilac bushes, and, up higher, views of the large north windows the original artists had installed in this compound that once contained their homes.

They made their way around and down Gallery Alley to Ed Sandoval's studio. There was little outside light, but the paintings supplied it, filling the area with light and color. A friend of Iggy's, Marianne, showed them around, including the tiny loft area with galley kitchen below that Ed used to call home.

Many of the paintings featured a dark, bowlegged, rumpled, twisted character with cane walking away from the viewer. "That's Amarante, of course," their hostess said, but both Mac and Iggy were too new to the area to remember the harsh old man who used to walk the streets of Taos after a career as a concert violinist.

Unable to pick up any gossip, the friends left, wandering back toward the street.

A young man popped out of the door of the first gallery in the courtyard. "Saw you fellows roaming around. Good place for a murder, eh?"

Mac looked around, nodded his head and said, "We're trying to find out if anyone saw anything, knows anything about the robbery the other day."

"Oh, you mean Bottoms' place." The man smoothed his long pony tail. "Inside job for sure. That cute little piece works there let in some cohorts and they made off with the goods."

Iggy moved toward the man, his bulk menacing.

Afraid his friend was losing control, Mac took Iggy's arm, saying, "C'mon, Ignacio. You wanted me to meet some other artist."

"That's enough, Mac. I know some people are bound to suspect Cindy and I can't help reacting but I'm not going to mess up any chance we have of finding her."

Iggy paused, then said, "I just pray to God Cindy is still alive."

CHAPTER XVIII

Having spent the previous afternoon with Iggy, Mac was once again sitting on the cracked brown leather sofa in the lawyer's office.

Iggy looked better today: curly hair combed, rat tail neatly braided, clean pink knit shirt and Dockers the size of a tent. He seemed less depressed.

"So, what's Christy up to today?" Iggy asked.

"Off to her dream class. It's a group that's been analyzing each others' dreams for years. Yesterday she had lunch with the Brit but didn't have much to say about it." Mac added too casually.

"Is that getting serious?"

"Lord, I hope not!" Mac felt a wrench in his gut. "I still want to check out the bastard's Santa Fe story and his bona fides. Christy's so impressed with his line about returning religious artifacts to the moradas, and building that museum for the people, I think the attraction has more to do with that than with the man. Well, *I'm* not charmed. I think he's pulling some sort of scam, but can't put my finger on what."

"Christy know how you feel?"

"No way! That's why I have to sneak around playing super sleuth with you. If I say anything about the character to Christy, she'll just put it down to jealousy on my part, and I'll be worse off than ever."

Despite Iggy's desperation over Cindy, he could sympathize with Mac, wished that pair would quit tip-toeing around their feelings and get together. "I hear you, man, but..."

"Right," Mac answered. "I realize I want to go after the good Dr. Bottoms for personal reasons."

"Pretty goddamned personal with me, too!"

Mac refused to let Iggy anger him, answering calmly, "Yeah, I know. If he'd just looked that night...Well, we'll check out Bottoms and Santa Fe, but right now I agree that Cindy's the priority. To help her, we need to keep on seeing what we can find out. And so far we have nothing on Dr. Bottoms to indicate murder and robbing himself, only that he might not be what he claims."

Mac pondered a moment, then suggested, "How about we try other angles. For one thing, since Nesbit wasn't around yesterday, I'd like to see if we can locate him today. Then there's the bankrupt pair we did corral...What did you think of them?"

"Spunk and Horse? Only alibi each other, but pretty smooth, weren't they? Maybe too smooth..." Iggy drifted off, pondering. "That gives me an idea. Since their big auction's tonight, they might lose their cool today, be hustling around getting ready. Maybe, in all that confusion, we could get a look at their store room. See if we see anything..." Iggy trailed off again, then added in disgust, "Oh, I don't know."

"Yeah," Mac agreed. "We sound like the Rover boys or something. Don't even know what we're looking for."

"Cindy, for one thing!" Iggy snapped. "Sorry, Mac. I know what you mean. But, think. Not a word from the police. Don't know if they're doing a damn thing. And La Doña's got a theory. She says, 'Rattle enough cages and you're bound to stir up the tiger.'"

"Surely Garcia and his boys have been checking alibis for the robbery?"

"Whose alibis? The Chief can't very well canvass the whole Arts Community. That's just our pet idea anyway."

"See your point. And I like your idea about going back to Spunk and Horse, but what's our excuse?"

"Why, to see what we want to bid on, of course." Iggy actually grinned.

"Good!" Mac grinned back. Then, as he stood up, asked, "What about seeing some more galleries? The ones we didn't hit yesterday?"

Iggy came around from behind the desk and gave Mac a punch on the arm. "Don't want to miss a single gallery? You're becoming a real art lover, eh, Dr. McCloud?"

"Oh, that I am. That I am, Counselor Baca!"

Since it was on the way, Mac and Iggy first stopped by La Bonita, Ted Nesbit's gallery. Still closed.

Mac commented, "Nesbit doesn't seem able to afford any help when he's not there. You don't have to violate any confidences for me to know he's not rolling in money."

"Doesn't look like it," Iggy answered noncommittally.

With Iggy driving and listening to opera, Mac was able to enjoy looking out the window at the high country summer day. He appreciated colors: orange poppies, pink peonies, tall cosmos in shades of red, purple, lavender, even candy-striped. And the light and shadow! He still marveled at the contrasts created by the sun and Taos' clear air. Contrasts, Mac mused. Just as here the light was brighter and the shadows darker, maybe the good was more pronounced and the evil more violent.

As they had found yesterday, the Horse-Spunk gallery was off the beaten paths of the Kit Carson road and Plaza shops in a former home on Placitas. Beginning to look a lot like Santa Fe, Mac reflected. First a small area of galleries and shops, then spilling out farther and farther.

As they entered, Mac saw that Iggy had made a good guess as to the confusion, but even so, the commotion and busyness were more than he had expected.

Men and women, dressed for work in jeans and shirts, were helping set up chairs at one end of the large room. (Must have knocked together at least a living and dining room, Mac thought.) Some were re-hanging paintings so as to squeeze more on the walls. Other workers were covering what must be borrowed tables with the smaller items for the auction.

A number of them waved and smiled at Iggy. "Nice bunch," he said. "These volunteers are other artists and a few gallery owners. Good people, coming over to help out."

"Mmmm."

"Well, they are, Mac," Iggy answered. "Not many snots and very few bad apples."

Someone yelled, "How you want us to number these?"

Tad Spunk, still flexing muscle, called back from the other side of the room, "Wait until we have everything on display. The numbers have to correspond with the catalogue."

The shorter, slighter partner, Julian Horse, entered the room from the back. Catching sight of Mac and Iggy, he moved toward them.

Mac spoke quietly to Iggy. "You know too many people here, so you do the talking and I'll try to ease off, check out if that's a store room back there."

Iggy nodded as Horse reached them.

He looked up at Mac. "Dr. McCloud, isn't it? What brings you and Ignacio back again today?"

Mac tried to look like a prospective buyer. "Thought maybe you'd let me slip in for a quick glimpse before the auction. Don't know if I can get here in time for the preview at, uh, seven, isn't it?"

"Sure. Fine," Julian Horse answered quickly. "We're in a shambles right now, but try to overlook it."

"Will do," Mac answered and casually strolled away toward the display tables.

Evidently, the Horse-Spunk gallery also showed local jewelers. Mac picked up a beautiful necklace. With heavy silver and some finely cut pink stone, it was splendid. Maybe he could bid on it for Christy tonight. Or was that going too far at this stage of their relationship?

Still in ear-shot, Mac heard Iggy ask Horse, "But weren't most of these paintings on consignment?"

The gallery co-owner answered, "Of course, but we offered the artists a better split than usual if they left them here for the auction. Most of them went for the new fifty-fifty and..."

Horse's voice faded as Mac wandered to the far wall where he put on a good show of gazing, seemingly enraptured, at some works which appealed to him. Others he didn't care for, but they seemed professionally executed. Still more appeared embarrassingly amateurish. There were pretty Taos hollyhocks against adobe walls. Taos-blue doors and windows. Mac could see a painter unable to resist such a scene of loveliness and tranquility. There were also luminous paintings, ones of tension, inward-looking. As Mac looked, he kept moving toward the door that he was guessing led to the storeroom.

Finally, thinking that he would seem more guilty if he acted furtive, Mac walked quickly into the storeroom.

This had obviously been the kitchen. It still had a sink and a counter holding coffee supplies, but the rest of the room had been gutted to make space for built-in storage cupboards with fronts of heavy mesh. Mac tried to peer into one and found he could see deep shelves, far enough apart to house canvases. It was locked.

Mac checked another. Locked.

He noticed an old white kitchen-type door. Taos homes seldom had basements, but maybe?

Approaching closer, Mac saw the door was padlocked.

"Looking for something?"

Startled, Mac couldn't keep his body from the jerk of reaction. He did manage to turn slowly, in an attempt to appear casual. He was facing Horse's partner, Tad Spunk. Obviously angry, the fellow seemed bigger than before. "Hello there, Mister Spunk. Julian said it was all right for me to see what you had for the auction tonight."

"Not in here, buddy. Not in here."

Mac smiled pleasantly. "Sorry. I was looking at the paintings out there and...Well, I'll just wander on out..."

Mac made for the door, very aware of eyes boring into his back.

Chapter XIX

Christy used her foot to pull the ottoman to a good position in front of the big Taos-style chair in her room. She'd had a wonderful session with her friends at dream class, they and their leader were always so supportive and accepting of each other. Then the grocery shopping and home. No one here but Desire when she returned. Ellie had finished cleaning and left. Mac was off somewhere. She called Barnabe. Nothing much there.

"Following leads on the murder-robbery, the *first* murder," he said bitterly. "Working on the second. Checking out associates of our drug-dealing dead man, Castle, but no way to go after alibis when there's no time of death established yet."

Next Christy tried La Doña but her secretary reported Miss Jordan in court. She was happy to hear that. These days her old mentor grew bored with her mostly probate, non-trial practice, one reason for involving her in this investigation.

No luck at Iggy's either. Maybe this meant she should take time to do some writing, but it was difficult to be creative when so much was menacing but undecided.

She called and got the latest from Mama. Patricio and his family would arrive from California tomorrow. Strange to think her brother had not seen Grandmama's hacienda since Christy had turned it into Casa Vieja Bed and Breakfast. In fact, they hadn't been together since Patricio had come for her husband's funeral.

How she had mourned Jean Paul all these years. Now here she was with Mac as a friend, maybe more...And this attraction to Evelyn that she didn't want. Time to do some thinking, use this space of solitude, a luxury to have no guests.

Evelyn seemed to be pursuing her. He was attentive, complimentary, and certainly had magnetism, but…Use your head, Christy, you don't feel that wonderful, warm, comfortable, solidness that Mac offers. Evelyn is purely sexual, heat and electricity. It's just…Christy heard the soft clang of the cow bell that hung on the courtyard gate. She got up to go look out the window by the outside stairs. Mac was crossing the courtyard toward his little guest house. Christy stepped out onto the landing, called down.

Mac looked up and grinned. "Hey there, Juliet!"

"Wherefore art thou, Romeo?"

"I art just mooching around town," Mac called back. "Stopped by to see what Spunk and Horse would be peddling at the auction tonight. And almost got in a peck of trouble. What time are we going?"

Christy came down the outside adobe stairs. "Didn't want to yell this," she said. "Let's plan to arrive as soon as they open. Probably everyone we've talked about will be there, so let's have as much time as possible to talk around, see what we can find out."

Mac smiled. "How about an early dinner out, then Horse-Spunk by seven?"

"Thank you, Mac. That would be fine."

Jeans could be worn anywhere in Taos. Christy had debated with herself over her usual, or something with a skirt instead. Was she dressing for dinner with Mac or because Evelyn would surely be at the auction?

Now Christy sat with Mac over an after-dinner coffee-with-Baileys, once again at the popular and inclusive Trading Post, dressed in a becoming cotton top of pastel sunset stripes and a very full heavy cotton skirt that picked up a deep lavender in the blouse.

Mac had been admiring. Now it was time to take on the reception and auction.

Being very much the Southern gentleman, Mac held her chair, offered her her cashmere stole. "You know how chilly it gets at night, m'dear." She smiled up at him, took the stole and they left, passing very modern art on the wall and on pedestals, waving goodbye at their hostess, Kimberly

Once in the pickup and on their way, Mac said, "Well, we put off murder and mayhem for our dinner, but now do you want to talk about anything special we should do tonight?"

"There should be a big crowd, everyone there, so just mingle, I guess. See if either of us can pick up anything."

Mac had been feeling guilty all through dinner for not telling Christy of his morning escapade. Yesterday hardly counted. But better come clean, he thought, or you'll never digest that elegant Italian meal. "Somehow I'd like to get another look at their store room."

"What store room?"

"Well, I kinda wandered into the back when I was at Horse-Spunk today and—"

"You what!"

"Yeah, well...aah...Tad Spunk kinda found me there," Mac continued as Christy sputtered. "No, wait. There were lots of locked cupboards with that heavy security mesh and, get this, a big padlock on what looks like a basement door!"

"Mac!"

"I know, but interesting, hunh?" There was a heavy pause. "Will you look at that sunset!"

Although it was barely time for the preview reception to start, the bargain hunters were out in force. A considerable number of vehicles were in the parking lot that had been the side lawn of the converted home. Not, Christy thought, the usual Taos mix of pickups and basic transportation. Nor, she would bet, many Spanish despite their renowned artists such Veloy Vigil, Miguel Martinez, Amada Peña, Ed Sandoval and the sons and relatives of a number of these as well as others. Must be the new monied people along with tourists, maybe out-of-town art dealers driving S.U.V.s and Beamers, the former in the ascendancy though Christy bet they didn't do much four-wheeling.

Iggy's venerable Chrysler Imperial pulled up beside them just as Mac was getting out.

"Told her," he muttered to Iggy as he came around to open Christy's door.

Christy had already jumped out on her own and ran to Iggy. "Como 'sta, my friend?" she asked with concern.

"Not too bad, Christy. Cindy stays on my mind, but you know as much as I cared for her, our relationship still wasn't aaa…" He tugged on his rat tail.

"I understand," Christy answered softly, giving Iggy's arm a hug. And she *did* understand how difficult it was for some men to say the word love.

"So," Iggy said, giving his considerable bulk a shake, "Let's get in there and do some detecting."

"Just don't do anything stupid."

"Stupid?" Mac had come up on Christy's other side. "I resent that, madam!"

Christy grinned and the trio made an entrance.

Both Tad Spunk and Julian Horse were at the door, greeting their guests. Spunk's welcoming smile slipped a little at the sight of Mac and Iggy, but he quickly turned genial. He must have told his partner about Mac's foray into the former kitchen because Julian's automatic, "Hello there. Glad you could come" was also a little frosty.

"The gallery's looking absolutely gorgeous!" Christy said to both men. "And this many people already! I'm sure your evening will be a big success."

"We hope so, too," Julian answered her ruefully. "Too bad it's our last."

"Um, well…" Christy was at a loss for words. "We'll just wander."

They moved off a little way and studied the crowd. Worn jeans contrasted to a woman who appeared to be draped in black veils. Men with straight haircuts, pony tails, tams or berets, women with short, sleek hair or pulled straight back and caught up with ornate, Indian-style barrettes. The majority of the latter seemed to be wearing a uniform of Martha-of-Taos velvet broomstick skirts and wedding-boot-variety moccasins.

Many seemed posed, so enraptured was their attention to Art. Not old Taos types at all. They lacked the patina.

Chief Garcia and Doris Jordan joined the trio.

"Hello, my dears," La Doña boomed, resplendent in her good black silk suit, a diamond pin on her shoulder, black walking shoes on her feet.

"Your *prima* looks lovely, doesn't she, Barnabe?" La Doña asked the Chief.

"That you do," he said, hugging Christy.

"No slouch yourself, *Primo*," Christy hugged back. "All spiffed up for the big event?"

"On duty," Chief Garcia muttered to her as they moved away from the door.

"Collecting alibis?"

"Not exactly. But I would like to find out what I can in a casual sort of way. Listen to what certain people are saying. Something new has turned up."

The group had openly eavesdropped on the Chief's quiet words to Christy. Iggy opened his mouth.

"No, Mr. Baca, nothing about Cindy." Chief Garcia went on, looking about to be sure he wasn't overheard. "I was faxed a list of stolen items this afternoon. No one had put it together before now, but seems the Sheriffs' Departments finally realized that a lot of art has been missing from the churches up here in the North. Only got on it when Chama police reported the loss of a huge and very ancient gold crucifix. I understand it's set with jewels."

La Doña said, "My client up there had already told me about *La Conquistadora.*"

Christy exclaimed, "The Saint Francis santo! And today Mama told me about the Amado Peña painting that's missing!"

Mac took a gamble and said, "You might want to check the former kitchen here, Chief. Lot of locked doors back there."

Chief Garcia grimaced in disapproval. "How do you know, doctor? You doing more detecting?"

With a too-innocent expression, Mac answered, "No, siree. Just happened back there earlier."

The Chief seemed uninterested in Mac's locked door, but turned to Iggy, "I understand you represented Clive Castle, Mr. Baca. What can you tell me about him?"

"What is this, Chief Garcia?"

"Might be part of a gang," the policeman rumbled, his expression heavy. "No one seems to know the man, but I guess you knew him pretty well. His lawyer, eh? Happen to see him Friday?"

"Of course not. You know I was trying to find Cindy on Friday! And speaking of that—"

Christy intervened. "Is there something new on Clive Castle?"

"Nope. Just following up on a few things. Excuse me." He walked off.

Iggy was staring after him when La Doña said, "Come, Ignacio. Show me to the refreshments. They will be the usual cheap wine and dried up cheese, no doubt, but we can scope out the crowd, hmmm?"

Christy and Mac were left alone in the midst of what was becoming a real press of people. They tried to talk but Christy had to speak to many of the artists and other friends. "Hi, Linda, Susan. Hello, Faustine. Margaret! Good to see you! Nan, do you have your great jewelry here?"

Mac noticed the people familiar to Christy were mostly casually dressed. Here and there a Taos-type skirt was the extent of dressing up. Lots of bolos on the men. It was easy to pick out the tourists and newcomers: more labels, more jewelry, more styled hair. Speaking of which, here came Evelyn Bottoms all turned out in a well-cut banker's gray suit. He had that fellow Nesbit in tow.

Evelyn clasped both of Christy's hands, "We are the bearers of bad news, I'm afraid."

"What?"

"Mister Nesbit has just been telling me," Dr. Bottoms spoke for the artist. "His friend from the Archdiocese, the archivist, Virginia Warren, was in a dreadful accident Sunday."

Naturally, the news brought strangers crowding around with little cries and questions. "Where?" "How?" "What happened?" "How bad is she hurt?"

"Poor Ted here will have to answer you," Evelyn said. "I only now heard."

Nesbit stood a trifle taller, important, but with a break in his voice. "The hospital called me. Virginia had a little note from me in her purse or we never would have known. Chimayo doesn't make the news, you know."

"But what happened?" "How is she?"

"That's the awful part. She was killed. A fall in the Santuario."

The people grew silent at this.

Ted Nesbit took a sad breath. "But as best the police can tell, she was trying to balance on a window ledge—"

There were some embarrassed coughs, hiding guilty laughs, at this grotesque picture.

"Probably trying to date some artifact. I went down as soon as I heard on Monday, just got back."

"Where?" Someone in the crowd asked.

"State Police office. They called me because of the note. Wanted to know about next of kin. Her van was stolen, too. Some opportunist, they think. Someone hanging around when the priest discovered the body. A lot of crime in Chimayo now, you know."

The crowd was murmuring in mixed commiseration and excitement. They were all offering sympathy to Ted Nesbit.

Christy was saddened by this as for any needless death, having only met Virginia Warren once.

Mac put an arm around her and said, "But Chief Garcia didn't..."

"There was no reason for him to be notified of an accident in Chimayo. No connection for the State Police."

A gavel banged. The auctioneer spoke into a microphone on the improvised stage. "Ten minutes, people. Just ten minutes for your viewing and to make silent bids as explained in your catalogues. Bidding will start in ten minutes."

Most of the crowd lost interest in the death of someone they didn't know and drifted toward the tables of items and lined up in front of the paintings on the walls. Evelyn Bottoms and Ted Nesbit disappeared among the crowd.

Her mind making links, Christy asked Mac, "Do you think it connects?"

"We'll talk when we get out of here. Let me show you a necklace—" An ear-piercing shriek froze the room. Turning quickly, Christy and Mac saw a group in the center of the room, heard a woman still screaming. Chief Garcia pushed his way roughly through the crowd. "Dr. McCloud," he bellowed. "Get the hell over here, doctor!"

Mac moved toward the bunched people as rapidly as he could get through the crush. Christy followed.

Julian Horse lay on the floor. The slight man was vomiting and gasping for breath.

As Mac knelt beside him, Julian's body arched in a violent convulsion, then lay still.

"Call an ambulance!" Mac shouted as he felt for a pulse. There was none. He began C.P.R., breathing into Julian's mouth as he rhythmically pressed his chest.

"Let me! Let me!" Tad Spunk screamed, pushing Mac away.

Seeing that Spunk knew what he was doing, Mac stood up, and found Chief Garcia at his shoulder. "The ambulance is on its way. What do you think?"

"M.I., probably. Sorry. That's myocardial infarction. Often preceded by nausea and vomiting, respiratory distress."

"Will he make it?"

"I don't think so," Mac answered quietly for the Chief's ears alone. "I'm afraid he's already gone."

Just then, Tad Spunk fell away from his partner's body, grabbing at his mouth and doubling over where he sat on the floor. "Oh, God!" he groaned. Then he, too, commenced vomiting.

The same woman began screaming.

"Shut up!" Chief Garcia shouted. "Everyone quiet! I will have no hysterics in here! Understand?"

More quietly, but loud enough for all to hear, Chief Garcia added, "I want everyone to stay put. Something's going on— and it's no damned double heart attack!"

As Mac went to the aid of Spunk, the ambulance wailed outside.

CHAPTER XX

"Get this one to the hospital stat!" Mac ordered the ambulance emergency medical techs. "Oxygen now! Respiratory distress. Convulsions. Can Holy Cross handle a poisoning? Lavage? Charcoal?"

"Yes, sir," the technician answered.

Moving quickly and efficiently, the E.M.T.s loaded Spunk onto the stretcher, strapped him down, and started the oxygen.

"An E.R. would normally look for other causes," Mac went on, "but tell the doc on duty we've had one death presenting the same and I think it's most likely a poisoning. I'll be right behind you as soon as I can get samples of the vomit and anything he might have ingested so we can determine the antidote."

Mac looked around to find Christy and ask for her help, but saw that she, La Doña and Iggy had already anticipated his request an were putting bits of everything on the refreshment table in paper cups. Mac picked up a cup and scooped up some vomit. Then turned quickly to recheck Julian Horse for vital signs.

"What about this one?" asked the fourth technician, gesturing toward that body.

At the same time, Chief Garcia questioned, "Can you pronounce him dead, Doctor?"

"He's dead," Mac answered, "I've double-checked. No vital signs, but take him along to the hospital."

The ambulance driver said, "It's my call, whether the M.E, Martinez, comes here or I get him to the hospital if there's the slightest chance."

"Then get a second ambulance over here," the Chief ordered, "and have Mr. Martinez meet you at the hospital. I can get photos of the body and outline the position while we're waiting on it."

Mac looked around for Christy and found her beside him. "Christy?"

Voice a little quavery, but strong, Christy said, "Go ahead, Mac. I'm sure I'll have to stay here a bit. I'll get a ride later."

At the other side of the room, the now-silent crowd parted for the ambulance crew as they wheeled out Tad Spunk, closely followed by Mac. Then the noise rose again.

Evelyn had appeared in the group near the body. "I'll take you home," he offered in a concerned tone.

Shaken by death and the violent illness of the other victim, Christy needed the comfort of the familiar. "No thank you, Evelyn. I'll go with Iggy."

Knowing that now he couldn't be heard over the excited hubbub of the crowd, Chief Garcia strode quickly to the auctioneer's podium and appropriated the microphone. He banged the gavel for attention, then announced, "Listen here everyone. Listen to me. We have two apparent poisonings. I—" At this announcement, the noise of the crowd rose to a pitch that drowned out the Chief. He banged the gavel again and seemed to swell in size. "Control yourselves! Listen here!" The crowd quieted.

"All right. We must assume there's been one homicide. That makes this the scene of the crime. I've called for back-up. We'll take statements and get you people out of here as soon as possible."

The buzz rose again, but now more like angry bees. The Chief banged the gavel again. "That's right. No one is leaving until dismissed by me or one of my officers. In the meantime," Chief Garcia spoke the words slowly and clearly for emphasis. "Do not touch anything. Not anything!" He paused to make sure he had their attention. "And I would assume no one would even *think* of eating or drinking, considering the circumstances!"

Sirens keened to a stop. The few police had arrived who were on night duty in Taos.

Chief Garcia strode back across the room to give orders.

"Officer Trujillo, get started taking pictures of the body, then outline it and get it out of here. Call in Mary and Jaime from off-duty and tell Mary to accompany the body to the hospital, take charge of all clothing, etcetera. Next, I'll want photographs of the entire room.

"Officer Arnold," the Chief addressed his lanky sometime stenographer, "make the crime-scene sketch right now. You know the drill. Outline the room, all doors and windows, position of the body, refreshment table, cash bar, auction area. Then you can start taking notes while I interview certain people.

"Sergeant Vasquez, get some help setting up a couple of those display tables with chairs for interviewing *after* Trujillo and Arnold have them in their photos and sketch. So they can leave, start with any tourists, out-of-towners, anyone who doesn't have any connection with Taos. But hold anyone for me who might have seen anything at all. Your first question is 'Did you see Spunk or Horse eat or drink anything?'"

As they started to move to their assignments, Chief Garcia raised his voice to his men, "Remember. Nobody touch anything! We're going to have to clear out some of these people before we can start bagging evidence and that will be anything, anything at all that might bear on this mess."

Around the room, people clumped together like filings on a magnet, most seeking those they knew, a few wanting to be near the center of action.

Iggy and La Doña headed toward Christy, as had some of her other friends. Evelyn hovered nearby. But Christy felt encased in a glass bell. Voices came at her from a distance, and though she had turned away from Julian Horse's corpse, that seemed to be all she could see: the face contorted in pain, the body twisted in its final convulsion. Christy tried to make herself concentrate on the concerned faces around her, but only succeeded in replacing Horse's face with that of Tad Spunk in agony and trying to breathe.

Meanwhile the police sketched and photographed. More officers had arrived, as had another ambulance crew. Accompanied by Officer Mary Quintana, they took away the body of Julian Horse.

Christy's primo Jaime organized the crowd in two lines: one line trailing away from the table where Sergeant Vasquez was taking statements; the other from primo Barnabe.

Jaime came over to the group around Christy, gave his cousin a brief smile, then addressed La Doña Doris, saying, "Chief Garcia would like to speak to you now. Then the rest of you."

Together they moved toward the side of the room where the Chief's table had been placed near the wall out of the way. He sat behind it with Officer Arnold near by.

Christy gazed up at the painting over the Chief's head. An empty expanse of canvas focused the eye on two nipples apparently tearing through. The title was "Goddess Emerging". Christy looked back at her cousin whose glare seemed to challenge her to make a comment. She didn't. Nor did Chief Garcia address Christy, but said, "If you'd just sit down, La Doña? And the rest of you, back off some. I want to speak to each of you privately."

The Chief began his questions to La Doña. "First, let me ask, did you see either Spunk or Horse eat or drink anything?"

La Doña shook her head. "I did not. Ignacio and I were near the refreshment table until the incident took place, but I did not see either man in the vicinity."

"Okay, fine. Now, La Doña, I'm told you represent the two victims?"

"True, Barnabe," La Doña answered, then clamped her lips as if that was all she intended to say.

"What can you tell me about them?"

"I assume you will respect the attorney-client privilege?"

"Of course," Chief Garcia replied blandly. "But *I* assume you will want to do what you can to assist the investigation. After all, one of your clients is dead and the other is probably dying."

La Doña sat more erect if possible. "Ask your questions, Barnabe, and we will see."

"All right. Let's start with money. Who profits? Always the first inquiry. But before we get to that, where did their money come from? I understand Spunk and Horse arrived here from California flashing around a considerable amount of cash."

"I did not quiz them on prior assets," la Doña answered firmly. "I am attorney of record for the bankruptcy proceedings only."

The Chief pressed, "But before that? Before the bankruptcy? Cash to buy this place, set all this up?" he waved his hand indicating the large, expensively renovated room. "Drugs? Money laundering?"

"I do not have a criminal clientele, Chief Garcia," La Doña said coldly. "Nor does one hear of mobsters going bankrupt."

"Then you did satisfy yourself as to where all that cash came from?"

The old warrior seemed to falter briefly, then lifted her chin. "I did not."

"Oh-ho!"

"Don't oh-ho me, Barnabe Garcia! I had no reason to suppose my clients did other than sell a successful gallery in California."

The Chief shifted uncomfortably in the too-small folding chair. "We'll leave that for now. We may find that Tad Spunk did not mean to become so ill, that his poisoning, if that's what it is, was a smoke screen. So what about insurance? For instance, there's that partnership deal where one insures the other?"

La Doña remained mute.

A flush started at the Chief's neck, moved up his face. "That was a question Miz Jordan. Did Spunk and Horse have partner insurance?"

"Privilege."

The flush deepened. He leaned forward. "This is a police matter, Miz Jordan! Can I assume that *if* they had insurance on each other, the bankruptcy wiped it out?"

"No, you cannot. If there was insurance, the bankruptcy proceedings have just begun. I would argue to a putative insurer that the partnership is still in existence and thus the insurance coverage remains if the premiums were paid."

"Thank you, La Doña."

She nodded regally.

"Now, what about relatives? A will?"

"I know of none."

The Chief had paused to consider additional questions when Officer Trujillo moved in quickly. "There's a padlocked door, looks like to a basement, Chief. Want us to open it up?"

"Open it."

"Yes, sir!"

La Doña stood glaring.

"You're excused," the Chief said calmly. "Get Mr. Baca over here."

Iggy breathed steadily, determined not to lose his cool. He sat down.

"All right, Mr. Baca, tell me if you saw either Tad Spunk or Julian Horse during the evening."

"Of course I saw them both when we came in. That was with Christy and Mac. But not after La Doña and I moved over to the refreshment table."

"Did you leave the table?"

"Wandered around some. Checked out the paintings, looked at some of the small sculptures and stuff on the tables."

"And where were Spunk and Horse then?"

Iggy shrugged. "Beats me."

"What about the cash bar set up later? Did you get a drink there?"

"No."

"Did you speak to your client?"

"Which one?" Iggy's expression was that of a wide-eyed cherub.

Barnabe, too, resolved to keep his temper, but the effort showed as he said, "Your client Ted Nesbit."

"No."

"No? I understand he had quite a group around him when he was talking about the death of Ms. Warren."

Now Iggy was curious. "Death?" he asked in a startled voice.

Chief Garcia waved aside the question. "You can discuss that with Mr. Nesbit later. I don't have the details. I also heard about a fight between your client and Spunk and Horse, what about that?"

Iggy shook his head, now genuinely bewildered. "Fight? I didn't see any fight."

"You're defending Nesbit on embezzlement charges among other things, Mr. Baca. Was he into something with this pair?"

"Now, you're fishing, and far out, Chief," Iggy answered coolly. "Ted Nesbit has only been *charged* with failing to pay certain artists for paintings sold. That's hardly a crime ring. And hasn't a damn thing to do with Spunk and Horse!"

"Then why were they arguing earlier?"

Iggy's voice rose as he leaned across the table toward the Chief. "How the hell should I know? Maybe Nesbit didn't like their choice in art! Or the food! Hell—"

"Lower your voice, Counselor," Chief Garcia said firmly, "Or I'll think you have something to hide."

"What do you mean by—"

The Chief continued unperturbed, sounding self-satisfied as he ticked off, "You represented Clive Castle. He's dead. Murdered. Your girl friend worked in a gallery that was robbed. She's missing, maybe hiding out. Bobby Mascarenas dead. Murdered. Your client Nesbit here at an art auction where one man's dead, another probably dying. And why is he here? He's highly unlikely to buy any paintings seeing as how he's desperate for cash himself. And not exactly popular with the artists here. Nesbit fights with the two others also known to be strapped for money. They become victims."

The Chief paused. Iggy sat staring at him.

"And you let slip about a crime ring. Maybe you're the mastermind who—" Iggy was too shocked to be angry, but did start to sputter, "Crime ring! Me? I was being facetious. I—"

The Chief interrupted firmly. "Thank you, Mr. Baca. I'll ask you to leave now. I don't want you comparing stories with, uh, anyone until I'm finished here."

"I'm taking Christy and La Doña home. I—"

"Wait outside for them. I'll send Christina out when I've spoken with her."

Curls plastered to his head with sweat, wet under the arms of his shirt, Iggy marched unseeing across the room to the door.

Chief Garcia turned to the silent Officer Arnold who had been conscientiously writing it all down. "See that Mr. Baca goes directly outside. Don't let him talk to anyone. Wait! Get Miz Grant over here first."

"Yes, sir."

Seeing how upset he appeared, Christy had started after Iggy but was turned back by Officer Arnold. Now she quickly sat down in the metal folding chair across from her cousin. "What's going on, Barnabe? And what did you say to upset Iggy?"

The Chief grinned. "I'm sure he'll tell you at length, prima. I just offered him a theory...Now, what can you tell me?"

"Oh, I saw it, Barnabe!" Christy was near tears.

"Saw what?" He jumped on her words.

The question surprised Christy. "Saw him die! A woman screamed. Mac ran to help. I followed him and saw Julian Horse on the floor. He was—"

"Hush, now," Chief Garcia said sympathetically. "Don't think about that part. Tell me anything you can remember before that happened. Start with where everyone was when you heard the scream."

"I don't know. Mac and I had been with Evelyn—Evelyn Bottoms—and Ted Nesbit. He was talking about the terrible accident that woman, the archivist, uh, Virginia Warren, the accident she was in. Then Mac and I went over to the tables. He wanted to show me something. Then the scream and—"

"Where was Mr. Baca all this time?"

"I don't know. He and La Doña had moved away early. La Doña made a crack about cheap wine and stale cheese."

"Did you see who either Spunk or Horse spoke to, what they were doing?"

"No. After we came in, that was the last—"

"What about Nesbit? See him? Hear the fight he had with them?"

"Fight? No. Nothing. Just what I told you about him and Evelyn."

"I saw you and your friends gathering samples for Dr. McCloud. Was anyone hanging around the table then? Notice anything unusual?"

"No. Everyone was moving toward where...toward poor Julian and Tad."

Suddenly Officer Trujillo and Jaime appeared, moving behind the table to whisper to the Chief. He rose so abruptly, he almost turned over the table. "Well, I'll be damned! Show me!"

Chief Garcia turned back to Christy, "You can go home now, prima. Mr. Baca's waiting outside to take you."

Christy stood up. "Wait just a minute, Barnabe. What have they found? What's going on?"

The Chief looked at his determined cousin, realized that there'd be no keeping this a secret with so many people around.

"Looks like a garden in the basement, prima. Gro-lights and all. A marijuana garden!"

CHAPTER XXI

Once Iggy had La Doña seated regally in the center of the back seat of his ancient Imperial and Christy beside him in front, he started the car and asked, "The hacienda?"

"Of course, Ignacio. We need to confer," La Doña replied.

After that, there was little conversation on the drive, each too upset in their own way to talk. That would have been difficult anyway as loudly as Iggy played Wagner at top volume. Apparently he needed the release of great Teutonic *sturm und drang*.

Arriving at Casa Vieja, Christy wearily led the way inside. There were no lights on in the hacienda or Mac's guest house. He must still be at the hospital with Tad Spunk. She prayed for his recovery.

Christy turned on the kitchen light, then lit the kerosene lamps and the chandelier candles in the dining room. It was chilly enough for a fire and they all needed warming up after the night's horrible events. "Hot tea? Brandy?" she offered her guests.

"Brandy," La Doña ordered. "For the shock, of course."

Iggy nodded.

Christy brought the snifters, checking the clock. "It's not too late to phone Mama with the news, and I'll be in real trouble if I don't let her know." Christy took her brandy with her to the desk in the middle room. She needed to compose herself before the call.

Mamacita was apparently still up because her deep voice answered on the third ring. "¿*Que pasa?* What's the matter, m'hija?"

"I'm fine, Mama, but something terrible has happened." She added quickly, "Not to anyone you know."

"¿*Quien?* ¿*Que?*"

"At the auction tonight. One of the gallery owners, Julian Horse collapsed and died."

"¡*Que lastima!* What a shame. How? What happened?"

"At first Mac thought it was a heart attack."

"¿Si? Pero you are saying the doctor was mistaken?

"Yes, because then Horse's partner, Tad Spunk collapsed also, so Mac suspected poison. He's at the hospital with him now."

"Poison! But this man Spunk lives? What kind of poison? ¿*Quien?* Who? So many questions!"

"I know, Mama. We just don't know very much But last we heard Mr. Spunk was till alive."

"He lives. ¡*Gracias a Dios!* Poison. How can this be? What is happening to Taos? *La vida es un puño de tierra.* Life is a handful of dirt. And you, m'hija! You must not be associating with ones who would do this wicked thing. *El que se acquesta con perros, con garrapatas se levanta!* He who lies with dogs wakes up with fleas—or worse, Christina! Someone may hurt you. Are you alone now? Should I come to be with you?"

"No, Mamacita. Don't worry. La Doña and Iggy are here now and Mac will be home soon."

"¡*Ai! Pobrecita!* So much evil you have seen tonight. Stay away from those persons, Christina. I will pray for you."

"Thank you, Mama. Bueno bye."

"You pray also, m'hija. *!Cuando pegan los truenos, se acuerdan de Santa Barbara!*"

"It's late, Mamacita. What does Santa Barbara have to do with it?"

"When you hear the thunder, turn to Santa Barbara, *pero mejor*, a better way to say it is, 'When you are in trouble, look to the Lord.'"

"Yes, Mama. I will pray."

"Bueno bye."

Christy returned to the dining room just in time to hear Iggy's "I asked Nesbit if he wanted me to stay for his interview. With his usual charm he said he thought he'd do better without me."

Sitting across the table from him, La Doña commented, "Since you have neglected to explain to us why Mr. Nesbit is in need of any attorney, we can scarcely decide if your services might have been required."

Christy sat down at the head of the table between the two as Iggy answered La Doña, "The Chief has cooked up some crazy theory that I'm the brains of some ring responsible for robbing Bottoms' place, and that the deaths are somehow the result of thieves falling out!"

"Rubbish!" La Doña snorted. Then, "What does that have to do with your client, Ted Nesbit?"

Iggy had been holding his head in his hands, now he lifted it, saying, "His being charged with embezzlement isn't too far a step from robbery in the Chief's mind. I disagree. One is done secretly, the other involves possible violence. But the Chief heard that Nesbit had a fight with Spunk and Horse tonight."

"Interesting," La Doña mused. "However, if Barnabe Garcia considers you a suspect, I doubt you would have had much beneficial effect when he questioned Mr. Nesbit, though I dislike agreeing with the man."

"I would have seen that he didn't incriminate himself. I should have insisted more."

Christy intervened. "Stop berating yourself, Iggy. Nesbit wouldn't need you just for tonight's questioning. Not unless Barnabe has already settled on him as a suspect. We're not thinking, just reacting. Let's try to put what's happened in order."

"Precisely, my dear," La Doña said with approval.

Christy felt some of the shock and fatigue drain away as her mind went into gear. "Okay. I'll start and then, Iggy, you fill in with exactly what Barnabe's ideas are."

Iggy nodded.

"First, someone, probably at least two persons, break into Evelyn's gallery. At some point, Bobby Mascarenas apparently tries to stop the robbery and is killed in the struggle. Or maybe he pulled off someone's mask and had to be silenced. Cindy disappears. Perhaps gets away because she had hidden, been somewhere out of sight."

"More likely kidnapped," Iggy added somberly.

"We have been unable to establish either proposition," La Doña put in. "Our efforts to find a witness to Cindy's departure were to no avail."

"Leave that for now," Christy continued. "We do know that somehow, the pair, we'll call them that for now, did get away without being seen and with something they took from the broken empty crate."

"Which implies knowledge," La Doña contributed.

"That's what the Chief wants to blame on Cindy," Iggy said. Then with sudden realization, added, "And me! He's tying me to it through Cindy and Nesbit!"

"Not yet, Ignacio. Keep to the point." La Doña ordered.

Christy went on, "Okay. Good, La Doña. The pair knew something in Evelyn's gallery was worth taking a big chance on, this being what was most likely a daytime break-in. Not only that, but when employees would be on the premises."

La Doña shook her head. "Not necessarily daring. Could have been the only way they knew to circumvent the burglar alarm."

"Right on," Iggy acknowledged. "Now me again. My client, Clive Castle, is found murdered in the river. Shit! Am I supposed to be the one who beat him and wrapped a wire around his neck?"

La Doña fixed him with a stern gaze. "That is not worthy of comment, Ignacio."

Iggy looked abashed, "Well, maybe I'm over-dramatizing, but if not me, who?"

"Now that's a proper question, Ignacio. We are in need of a large, violent suspect."

Christy was ignoring this by-play. "You don't believe that Castle, for all his drug dealing, was a violent man, Iggy. But, knowing him, do you think the Chief could be right in figuring that Castle could have been one of the ones in the robbery?"

Iggy tugged on his rat tail, taken out of himself by the puzzle. "I suppose so, if Mac's wrong about time in the water, but it doesn't feel right. Clive got along okay as a small-time dealer and mountain-man type. I wouldn't expect him to do something so, hell, I don't know...Outrageous? Gutsy? Whatever it took to pull off that robbery.

"And don't forget what Christy mentioned. It took someone strong to garrote Castle."

La Doña held out her brandy snifter and lifted her eyebrows. Christy poured them all more brandy.

"But might Mr. Castle be one of the robbers If the spoils were great enough?" La Doña asked, then added, "And what's this about Dr. McCloud?"

Iggy shrugged. "I guess we didn't mention it to you, but, at the river scene, Mac's opinion was that the body had been in the water too long for Clive to have been alive at the time of the robbery."

Christy said, "So the big questions are when did Clive Castle die, what was in that crate, and who knew about it?"

"We haven't a clue," La Doña announced.

"Yes!" Christy was excited. "There *is* a clue, La Doña. Primo Barnabe told Mac they had found a coarse black hair in the crate."

La Doña snorted with disgust. "Charming! People are dying like flies and it all hangs on a hair! That's on a par with Holmes' dog that didn't bark."

Iggy slid a glance at Christy, then looked at his brandy. "No accusation, I just want to mention that Bottoms could have told all kinds of people about some of those treasures."

"Moving right along, children," La Doña said. "With these questions in mind, we reach tonight's affair and *my* clients. Chief Garcia seemed rather enamored of the idea that Mr. Spunk murdered Mr. Horse for the insurance, and, taking poison to avert suspicion, inadvertently gave himself too much."

"I like that better than me as prime suspect." Iggy actually grinned. "Spunk is a big guy, could have killed Castle. And tough! Just ask Mac."

"Just ask Mac what?" Mac questioned as he came in through the kitchen.

Christy jumped up to hug him. "Oh, Mac, you're home! What happened? Is Tad Spunk going to live? You want something to drink?"

"That brandy looks fine. And I don't know if he's going to make it. We tried to stabilize him. I say 'we' but, in fact, I don't have hospital privileges. I am allowed as a licensed physician working under the supervision of a doc with privileges, but I left them to it." He sat.

"Anyway, I was sure by then that we weren't dealing with a cardiac problem, especially considering Horse. Did an EKG anyway. Got the lab to run through what poisons they were capable of testing for, while we tried lavage—that's stomach pump—and then liquid charcoal. Tried to relieve the respiratory distress at the same time."

Mac took a couple of sips of brandy. "Well, the upshot is, no luck. We don't know what the poor bastard's got in him and Holy Cross called in the Life Guard helicopter to fly him down to Albuquerque to the University Hospital. They'll save him if anyone can. Have the latest toxicology equipment, but I don't know. We hadn't stabilized him when I left."

La Doña asked, "But you're sure it was poison, Dr. McCloud?"

Mac looked exhausted. "No, I'm not *sure,* La Doña. Y'all have that hantavirus that acts damn quick and on the respiratory system, but I don't know much about it. Otherwise, I'm not aware of any disease that would present like those two did, or kill Horse that soon with those symptoms. Except for cardiac and as the Chief said, 'We ain't got no double heart attack!'"

"But if it is poison, are you able to make a guess as to what?"

"Nope. We've ruled out anything common. So...I'm tired of hearing the sound of my own voice. What were y'all saying when I came in?"

Mac pulled around a second chair to stretch his legs out on, as Iggy grinned at him. "I was just ratting on you, telling these two you knew how tough Spunk could be."

Mac, too weary to rise to the bait, only managed an "Un-hunh."

"Spunk chased our doctor here out of the storeroom."

"Lord! I forgot," Christy exclaimed. "You don't know! There at the end, talking to Barnabe, my primo—"

"Primos and primas without end!" Iggy had regained his good spirits.

"Don't, Iggy. This is important. They found marijuana in the basement!"

That got everybody's attention. Even Mac woke up. Amid the exclamations, La Doña said, "This could throw a new light on the whole sorry affair. Total outsiders might be involved. And it creates a possible connection between Clive Castle and the partners."

"I wonder if Nesbit knew about the pot?" Iggy pondered. "And if that had anything to do with the alleged fight between him and the partners?"

La Doña said, "Since privilege would prevent you providing us with any insights on your client, Ignacio, I will offer observations made from years of contact with Ted Nesbit at openings and such.

"First, however, I will say that the artists he represented appear to have been seriously defrauded. It's so difficult for those starting out to obtain gallery representation, they were slow to bring charges.

"Secondly, although he doesn't appear violent, the man does have a supreme ego and those who take the life of another must be totally egocentric." La Doña nodded firmly, satisfied with her summing up.

Christy, however, was still engrossed in the marijuana angle. "But why would the pot or anything else be a motive for killing Horse and Spunk?" she asked. "Who is better off with them dead?"

CHAPTER XXII

"Cindy is dead."

Dead...dead...dead...dead...echoed through Iggy's mind.

Chief Garcia had said a bunch of crap first. Something about maybe being too hard on him...something about Search and Rescue...something about coming down to identify the body..."

The strong, low voice continued to make noises through the telephone receiver."Mr. Baca? Are you still there, Mr. Baca?"

You knew it, Iggy berated himself, knew it and pushed it down into your subconscious. Even started kidding around last night with the Crew. Get a grip, man. Time to show some maturity...Oh, God! I don't want her to be dead! It's not right. Cindy was so bright, in love with the world, interested in the least little thing. Loved working in that goddamned gallery, the beautiful stuff. Damn it, God! Why?

"I'm sorry, Counselor...Uh, Ignacio. Are you all right?"

No, no, not all right. "Yes, Chief. Tell me what I can do to help."

Barnabe Garcia sighed. "There's no easy way to break this kind of news. I wanted you to hear it from me, but again, I am sorry...Did you take in what I was saying?"

"No, I'm afraid not, Chief. Run it by me again." Iggy heard the break in his own voice. Didn't matter. That old bear understood. Had to take a new grasp on the telephone, hand slippery with sweat. Missed the first words, "...in the Rio Grande, down river from the gorge bridge."

"Did she drown?"

"No, son." Chief Garcia didn't elaborate further.

"C'mon, Chief. Nothing can be worse than knowing Cindy's dead."

"Okay. She was still partially in a black plastic bag. Search and Rescue are just now bringing the body up to the top. It was hung up on rocks in the water. But...ah...it appears she died from a gun wound."

Control yourself, Ignacio. Breathe. "I knew it! I knew the bastards killed her!"

The Chief sighed again. "I'm sorry to say you've been right all along. Lord knows it would be a whole lot better if she *had* skipped out. We'll know more when the M.E. can take a look, but I'm guessing the young lady was killed in the robbery. Of course, it might have been later."

"Are you sure it's Cindy they found?" Stupid false hope. Who else could it be?

"I'm afraid so, Ignacio. One or two of the men on the team knew her slightly...I didn't want the news getting out before you were informed, but if you could prepare yourself, then come on over to Holy Cross Hospital. Say about an hour? Don't know that I can reach Dr. Bottoms."

Iggy glanced at the clock. Eleven. Eleven on a Wednesday morning in July.

"I'll be there. And...ah...thanks, Chief, for letting me know at once."

"I'm sorry, son."

Iggy hung up and sat, unthinkingly rubbing his sweaty hands on his legs. He considered calling Christy or Mac. No, he didn't want anyone around. Right now sympathy would hurt too much.

Iggy stared numbly into space.

Then he prayed.

Christy hadn't heard the bad news and even Mama's sources had failed her. Unknowing, they waited impatiently for the arrival of Christy's brother Patricio and his wife Nicole.

The hacienda was shining. Always clean for guests and lookers, Christy and her great housekeeper, Ellie, had outdone themselves: even the vigas had been washed and oiled.

Of course, Desire had dressed for the occasion. Today, she was angelic in a froth of white ruffles threaded through with thin blue ribbons. "It's the innocent look, you know, Miz Grant? Your brother not having met me before?"

Desire sat at the desk in the Middle Room to take reservations while Christy and Mama sipped coffee in the dining room.

Mama fretted. "I hope Patricio didn't get lost, Christina. He should be here now, driving from Albuquerque this morning. He may go to my house. I should have stayed home to be there for him,"

"Now, Mamacita," Christy reassured her yet again. "Patricio and Nicole said they would come straight here. And you know he didn't get lost. He visited our grandparents here all the time when we were growing up."

"Perhaps he thought to go home first."

"No, Mama. He—"

A car honking, honking! Christy dashed to look out the high dining room windows while Mama darted through the kitchen and out that door. Patricio was here!

Christy ran out the back and across the courtyard. Across the way, Patricio was already hugging Mamacita. Nicole looked on, smiling. Then they were all hugging and laughing.

"I'm so glad to be here!" Patricio said. "I had to honk to let you know!"

"All the way from San Mateo, California," Mama said in awe. She turned to Nicole, "And you, m'hija, finally to be a grandmother! And me, a great-grandmother again, gracias a Dios!" She paused meaningfully. "Too bad you and Patricio had only the one daughter. How is Annette with her baby coming?"

Nicole ignored the customary dig and answered, "Fine, fine, Mama Garcia. The baby's due any time, so I didn't want to leave her. But Pat said that if we stayed home the baby wouldn't come til after Fiestas anyway."

Patricio held Mama off at arms' length. "You look great, Mamacita! Not a minute older." And she did indeed look pretty, pink and bright-eyed with love and excitement.

"Now your turn." Patricio eyed Christy. "Not bad, sister, not bad at all." He grinned, "And that little gray in your hair is quite distinguished."

Christy grinned back at her slightly taller older brother. "I guess your beginning of a little paunch is distinguished, too, grandpa-to-be."

"*Su hermano* is *muy* handsome," Mama scolded Christy, then belatedly added, "and Nicole muy bonita." And they were a good-looking couple, Patricio dark-haired with deep brown eyes; and Nicole, California-tall, slim, blonde and tanned.

Patricio patted his belly and answered Christy, "Too much slaving over hot computers and not enough exercise."

"Pero your job is very important, no?" Mama asked anxiously.

"Oh, Mama!" Patricio said embarrassed.

"His job is important, si!" Christy teased. "The head honcho of Silicon Valley."

"What is this 'Silicon'?" Mama asked in bewilderment.

Patricio hugged her again. "Never mind, Mamacita. It's the same old Christy, I see."

"Do you want to get your bags now or see the new-old Casa Vieja first?" Christy asked.

"Might as well take them in…" Patricio popped the trunk lid and started lifting out bags as Mac strode through the gate. Patricio lifted that family eyebrow at Christy. Slightly flustered she said, "It's a long explanation, but this is my friend, Dr. Mac McCloud. He lives in what was the old cow shed."

"Glad to meet you." They shook hands.

Then from Patricio, "Cow shed? You live—?"

"I said it was a long story, Patricio. Guest house now."

In the midst of the bantering, Christy thought Mac seemed awkward, not his usual easy-going self. All long legs, shifting from foot to foot, he said, "I was staying out of the way of the family reunion, but now something's…er…ah…come up."

Mac shook Patricio's hand again, avoided Christy's questioning eyes, and said, "Sorry, gotta run." He quickly fled to his pickup.

"Mac?" Christy called.

Pretending not to hear, he waved and backed out of the parking lot onto the road.

"Kind of abrupt fellow, isn't he?" Patricio commented.

"Not usually," Christy answered. Puzzled and more than a little concerned, she was once again gripped by foreboding. Then, giving herself a mental shake, Christy turned back to the joy of having her big brother back. "I'm really proud of what I've done with the hacienda," she bragged. "Come look!"

Meet part of the family and really make an ass of myself, Mac thought as he drove as quickly as possible down the curving dirt road. But that sort of thing is too trivial to bother with right now.

He'd been lying low in the guest house not wanting to intrude on the arrival and, face it, a mite self-conscious about meeting Christy's older brother, when the noon Hometown News came on the radio. Search and Rescue had brought up an unidentified woman's body from the Rio Grande.

Mac was jolted to his feet. Cindy! Oh, Lord! The poor kid. And Iggy. What would the news do to Iggy? He must go to him right now, but should he tell Christy? He didn't want to upset her with the news, not now with her so happy. Nothing for it but to light out of there and find Iggy…

Now Mac was driving on the Talpa highway. From there he looked off to the South, across the valley to the mountains beyond. It was such a splendid July day, the sky infinite and baby blue, the air clear. But towering white thunder heads were looming on the southern and western horizons.

CHAPTER XXIII

"You want to talk about it?" Mac had taken the chance that Iggy would have retreated from people, clients especially, and had tried the apartment first.

Iggy sat in the gloom, drapes still closed, operatic music bouncing off the white walls.

"Not much to say, Mac. The Chief called me, really decent about it...Well, then I went to the hospital. He wanted me and Evelyn Bottoms to identify Cindy for sure. Didn't look like..."

"Yes, I know. Several days in the water. Don't think—"

"Dead, she looked so little."

They sat in silence, Mac believing that just being there for the grieving was better than words. They always seemed to be nothing but platitudes.

"I've told you Cindy and I weren't serious. But we might...And she was a great person, Mac."

"I know."

More silence.

Finally, Mac pulled back the drapes and let in the July day. "Mind if I turn the music down a little?"

Iggy wakened from his daze, "Uh, no. Sure."

Another long period of quiet, then Iggy said abruptly, "Enough of this. I'm not going to sit around feeling sorry for myself. I want to find out who did this godawful thing!"

Relieved at the change, Mac asked, "The Chief have any ideas?"

Iggy answered, "Not really. The man's in a quandary. He thinks it's most likely that Cindy was shot during the robbery. But, of course, Bobby was stabbed, so different m.o. Trouble with her being shot then…" He cleared his throat. "God, this is hard! …is the same thing our crew was wrestling with. How the fuck did the bastards get her out of there?"

"When it's determined how long Cindy was in the water, that will help answer when she was shot." Mac said as gently as possible, then went on with a question,"You said Bottoms was at the hospital, too. He come up with any ideas?"

"Stroked that damned little moustache of his and said that surely 'the poor child had left the gallery with her accomplices who'—get this—'inexplicably it appears had a subsequent falling out'. Shit!"

"What do you think of Bottoms. Really?" Mac asked, hoping to keep his friend diverted.

"Really, Mac? Aside from hating his guts?"

"Yep, that's the trouble isn't it? The way you and I feel, it's hard to get a fix on the man."

"And Christy."

"What about Christy?" Mac asked sharply and, in turn, received a penetrating look from Iggy.

"Oh, nothing. she's just defensive. That's all."

"Hell, she can't see straight where that bastard's concerned," Mac grumbled. "One thing we can do, we don't have to take him on faith like Christy does."

Iggy was interested. "Whadda you mean?"

"Well, con men, promoters, have always been thick on the ground back in Florida where I come from. I'm used to hearing their schemes, taking them with a very large grain of salt."

Now energized, Iggy stood to pace around. "You're saying you think all this museum deal's a bunch of bull?"

"Evelyn Bottoms came in here acting like every con man I've ever met," Mac answered. "Talking big. Flying here and there in his own Lear. Galleries in Santa Fe and Taos. The big lie—and never tell a little one—of a huge museum to house all the Indian and Spanish artifacts he's reclaimed from all over the world. Ph.D. And what do we really know about him? Squat, that's what!"

Iggy's eyes were no longer dull with grief. "Yes!" he said with a punching gesture. "Who knows if he's even a Ph.D.? Who knows if he's spent a goddammed cent? Hell, we don't even know if he has a gallery in Santa Fe!"

Then his expression sobered. "But he does have the gallery here. So, if it's some scam, what's the point?"

Mac rose. "I don't know, ole buddy, but we sure as hell can try to find out!"

When Mac returned to the hacienda, he figured he could no longer put off telling Christy the bad news. He found her and the family gathered on the courtyard in the shade of the portal. This, despite the fact that Mama thought that the best way to enjoy a nice day was from inside.

The summer flowers made bright patches of color, while the summer air warmed the scent of roses.

The group had been laughing, but stopped to look as Mac came through the gate.

"Hi, Mac," Christy called out. "Come and join us. Have a glass of iced sun tea."

He wondered what to do. He didn't want to tell Christy now when she was so happy, but then she might hear it at any time.

Mac walked over, smiled and greeted Mama, Patricio and Nicole. "Excuse me folks," he said to the uplifted faces, "but I need to take Christy away from y'all for a minute...Christy? Can I talk to you alone?"

"Sure, Mac", she answered, her expression puzzled. "Come in the kitchen and I'll get more ice for the tea."

Within its thick adobe walls, the kitchen was much cooler than outside. Christy turned to Mac. "What is it? It's something bad isn't it?"

Mac put a hand on each of her shoulders, "Yes it is. They've found Cindy. She's dead."

Tears slid down Christy's face. "Oh, Mac, I'm so sorry. I didn't know her well, but to be cut off so young...What happened?"

"Shot," Mac answered reluctantly. "The M.E. had established that by the time Iggy got to the hospital to identify her."

"So that's what you went rushing away for?"

"Afraid so. I didn't want to tell you then, your brother arriving and all." Mac paused, then added, "Just like before, it was rafters who found the body. They saw a black bag and enough of the corpse...Well, no need to go into that. But Cindy had been shot and dumped into the Rio Grande."

"When?" Christy's one-word question was forlorn.

"That will be difficult to determine exactly because of the body's time in the water. Still, the O.M.I. in Albuquerque will have a pretty good notion if she'd been there since last Friday or several days less."

"Just like Clive Castle."

"Putting a body into the river, yes," Mac replied slowly. "But shooting compared to beating and strangling, no. To me, shooting can be a lot more—what's the word?—well, antiseptic, distant. Clive Castle's murder was more up close and personal."

A shout came from the courtyard. "Hey, little sister? Where are you?"

"I have to get back," Christy said and went to the sink to throw cold water on her face.

She turned back to Mac. "I'll have to tell them something. Mama will want to know, but I hate...Oh, Mac! How long is this going to keep up? Cindy. Clive Castle. Bobby Mascarenas. Julian Horse...I forgot. Is there any word on Tad Spunk?"

"I called and asked the Chief today. Not much. Still alive. The University's ruled out everything except poisoning, but still haven't found what poison. There's some screening device unavailable in any major hospital in New Mexico, so they're sending samples out of state." Pause. "You want me to tell your mama?"

"No, I'll do it."

"Then back outside with you." Mac tried to sound upbeat. "I want to shower and all...Can I take you folks out to dinner?"

"No, thanks, Mac. Patricio says he has a serious deficiency in real Northern New Mexican food, including Hatch green chile. Mama's going home in a little while to fix him traditional Spanish. I'd like you to join us."

"Thanks, but let's make it tomorrow," Mac answered, postponing the inevitable. "That's when you'll have everyone here, isn't it?"

"Yes, they all arrive tomorrow to be ready for Las Fiestas Friday."

Mac hugged Christy. "Hang in there. See you soon."

Christy got out the ice and filled a new pitcher of tea, composed herself, and started back out to the courtyard.

Mac went to his little house, took his shower, turned on his contraband television (Christy wouldn't have one in the house), and flipped to the Channel 7 news He stretched out on the bed in his underwear to watch Howard Morgan giving the usual forecast from Albuquerque for July in Northern New Mexico: moisture sweeping in from Old Mexico to provide the monsoons, so a fair day tomorrow until the heat triggered afternoon rain, then clearing in the evening.

Mac was dozing off when he heard the newscaster, Dick Knifing, come back with an item: The Archdiocese had no comment on the source of very old religious articles found in the van of Archivist Virginia Warren, which had been found abandoned.

The newscaster went on to say that Ms. Warren had died in an accidental fall at the Santuario at Chimayo on Sunday. The State Police had not been able to recover the stolen van until today.

The artifacts were alleged to be of an undetermined value, probably priceless, and Police speculated that the van thief had not understood the value of the items.

Lordy! Lordy!

Mac looked out to see if Christy and her family had left yet. Nope. They still sat around the table outside. He grabbed clean jeans and a short-sleeved shirt, dressed, and started out. Mac caught himself: Back to comb his hair still wet from the shower, shove bare feet into sneakers.

Christy must have told them about Cindy. The group was subdued, but smiled when he approached. Mamacita said, "Dr. McCloud! Have you changed your mind? Will you have dinner at *mi casa?*"

"No, I don't know. Sorry, but I'm not thinking straight." He turned to Christy, "We have to talk."

"Again?" Patricio asked suspiciously, protective of his little sister and this strange man.

"No, that's all right," Mac answered, "but it won't make much sense to y'all."

Mac then told them all what he had just heard on the news.

"*Castigo de Dios!*" Mama exclaimed when Mac finished the story. "This woman had stolen from the churches. That is why the accident. She is being punished by God!"

Christy said, "Oh, Mama. Maybe the poor woman was just taking the things to be repaired or restored, whatever, being the archivist…" Her voice trailed off as she thought, then added, "No, you're right, Mamacita. With our Saint Francis santo and the painting stolen, and La Doña telling us about things missing from the Church at Chama. Somehow this ties in with all the rest."

Patricio shook his head. "It's sure gotten violent in Taos since I lived here, complicated, too. Next thing you know, the CIA will be involved. You'll be discovering some sort of spy ring!"

Mac stared at Patricio blankly. Patricio fidgeted, becoming irritated with the stare.

Christy tried to lighten the situation, "Earth to Mac. Earth to Mac. Come in, Dr. McCloud."

Mac said, "Uh, sorry, Mr. Garcia."

"Pat," Christy's brother corrected automatically.

"Yeah, sorry, Pat, I was lost. You just made me remember…" Mac's usual drawl picked up speed with excitement. "That's it! That's gotta be it!"

Now Christy was exasperated. "Stop being so mysterious, Mac! What are you talking about?"

Mac beamed at Christy, then at Patricio. "What you said about spies. Remember in New York several years ago? During the Cold War? I forget who all was involved but a man collapsed and died on the street. They thought it was a heart attack, but then it turned out to be a James Bond sort of deal. The assassin had used an umbrella or cane to poison him! A tiny hollow ball inserted with poison in the tip."

Christy caught on immediately. "Spunk and Horse! You said they had symptoms of a heart attack!"

Mac stood up quickly. "And get this! The poison, ricin, was a substance taken from castor beans and well nigh untraceable!

"I remember, too," Patricio said. "It was so weird! And didn't they say the stuff is so lethal, just what you could put on the head of a pin could kill a man?"

Christy said, "Castor beans? Isn't that the plant with the big leaves?"

Nicole spoke up. "Castor bushes are used in ornamental plantings. I'll bet they grow all over New Mexico."

"I've seen them around here," Christy said slowly. "Anyone could get hold of castor beans. Anyone."

"I have to call the Chief," Mac announced. "Tell him to inform the treating doctor at the hospital. Maybe this will help Spunk!"

"*Castigo de Dios*," Mama muttered.

After Mac left, a heavy silence descended. Finally, Patricio broke it. "You say 'Punishment of God', Mama, and that makes me think about what Grandfather said about Talpa, the reason Talpa had so many witches."

"Aii!" Mama answered. "*Su abuelo* and his *brujerias*—your grandfather and his witch stories." She smiled lovingly. "Such stories he could tell."

"Remember how in the fall, we would see blue lights over here at night?" Patricio continued eagerly. "Balls of fire?"

Eager to be distracted, Christy jumped in. "The blue fire balls were the witches! By day the brujos changed themselves to tumbleweeds to travel. At night, they were burning blue lights."

"Well," Patricio's voice changed to that of a *cantadoro*. "You don't know, but one night Grandfather called me to the window. He said, 'Look, *m'hijo*. See all the blue balls of fire there across the road?' There were a bunch of them bouncing up and down. 'See how many blue lights are dancing in the night?' mi abuelo asked. I was frightened of the witches. 'Si, Grandpapa,' I answered all big eyes, looking at those fire balls.

"Grandpapa nudged me. 'Dancing like that, the brujos must be having a party, eh, m'hijo?'"

Christy smiled with the others, but felt a chill.

Chapter XXIV

Mac and Iggy were on their way to Santa Fe, Iggy driving, to see what they could find out about Evelyn Bottoms.

It had taken Iggy quite a while to wake up. Conversation had been sparse.

Now, Iggy said, "So how's Christy this morning?"

"Suspicious. I got quite a look when you called and asked for me instead of talking to her. Ducked out with the excuse that you had an errand in Santa Fe, and I was going along to get out of the way of family."

Iggy listened to a particularly brilliant passage of *The Magic Flute*, then answered. "Well, we hadn't worked out who was going to drive today and I wanted to pick you up in Diva here, so we'd have opera on my superior stereo."

"Naturally. And, back to your question, Christy's mostly fine. Having the rest of her family come in today helps. It takes her mind off of all this mess. But the big question is, how are *you*?"

After a long music-filled pause, Iggy got around to saying, "Not happy, but now I can mourn Cindy. Earlier, it was the question...and the godawful pressure to find her before...Well, you know."

"I understand."

There was silence between them and the music seemed empty to Mac. Finally he tried to help by making new conversation. "Well, Odelia and Gabe from Espanola will be here with their kids. You probably know them. And then the other brother, Juan, comes from Colorado with his family. Patricio and Nicole have already arrived from California, said it was such a long drive they wanted to stay a few days."

His emotions mercurial, Iggy seemed to perk up, but at Mac's expense. "So, Dr. McCloud, you going to take on the whole bunch tonight?"

"Yep. Big dinner for all."

"Going to ask the elder brother for Christy's hand?" Iggy glinted.

That wasn't funny, a veritable sore spot, in fact. "Don't be ridiculous! I'll ask Christy herself, if, and when, we ever get to that point. Anyway, those gallant days in the South are gone."

Mac found an outlet for his irritation in the Mozart. "Can't you turn that noise down some?"

Now it was Iggy who thought he'd better change the subject. "So let me tell you what I did yesterday."

"Mmmm," Mac was noncommittal.

"Your enthusiasm astounds me. I'll tell you anyway. After you left and I…er…got myself together, I went out to the Millicent Rogers Museum. I'm always surprised what a great place it is, usually only go with visiting tourists. Anyhow, I talked to the curator about Bottoms. She's very strong on Hispanic art, Native American, too, of course. The curator's highly educated, well-connected. And just like Jason Kelly at the other museum, she didn't know anything about our Evelyn other than the stories he's put out himself."

"So he's not known in the very circles he claims." Mac crowed.

Iggy paused to listen to a graceful moment in an aria as they went through the horseshoe curve. "That's right. She'd naturally be in touch with other curators, especially in her areas of expertise which, supposedly, are Bottoms', too. But nada. Same thing with conferences and all. Nothing."

"Hot dawg! We're going to nail the bastard!"

"Yeah." Iggy grew somber again. "But it won't mean anything other than a con of some kind." He angrily spat out the words one by one, "I hate the bastard, but I have to know who killed Cindy!"

"Well, maybe if we can dig up something about Bottoms, we'll find a motive that ties in Castle, Spunk and Horse as well as Cindy."

Falling silent again, they passed the hostel at Pilar, heading down to the point where Clive's body had been found. The same river, Iggy thought, that had held Cindy. Cindy in these cold, dark waters. Cindy bundled up in a black, plastic bag and tossed away like a piece of garbage. Cindy frightened...No, I mustn't think about that. Think instead that maybe she was shot quickly, so unexpectedly that she didn't know it was coming. Iggy turned up *The Magic Flute*. Loud.

Mac didn't comment.

They were quiet until past Dixon, before Velarde, when a pickup heading south came whipping past them on one of the many blind curves. "Goddamn! Will you look at that bastard!" Iggy braked to avoid what looked like disaster: a car was coming north. For a few seconds it seemed certain that the pickup was going to hit it head on. The north-bound car had nowhere to go but the narrow shoulder next to the rock cliff with the pickup in its lane, yet somehow the two vehicles managed to squeeze past each other.

An adrenaline surge had hit both Iggy and Mac, lifting the depression that had filled the car. "God!" Iggy said. "The damned fools do it all the time! I hardly ever make the Santa Fe trip without some hot-dogger passing where there's no way to know if he's going to meet someone coming the other way."

"Save a few seconds and take a chance on wiping out someone else." Mac commented. "I guess that explains some of the little crosses along here."

"'*Descansos*', they're called" Iggy explained. "The word means 'a stopping or resting place'. Someone died at that spot marked by the descanso."

Mac's heart beat was about back to normal as he said, "Well, before that excitement I was going to tell you...We were all talking yesterday and something Christy's brother said jogged a memory about a weird New York story. It was about that guy who was killed with an umbrella used to stick him with poison. The poison was ricin from castor beans. Looked it up last night."

"Yeah?" Iggy looked at Mac quizzically.

"They first thought the man died from a heart attack."

"Yes!" Iggy finally got the point and hit the steering wheel. "Sure. I remember now. But why didn't the hospital find out immediately if that was it?"

"Because this ricin can't be spotted with the usual toxicologic tests. I asked the Chief to pass it on to Spunk's treating physicians. Same symptoms—vomiting, diarrhea, convulsions, respiratory distress."

"Castor beans," Iggy mused. "I think they've got some growing around my apartment. Big leaves?"

"That's it. Grows most everywhere in New Mexico. Like oleander shrubs, you just don't usually think how toxic they are."

"How much would a person need?" Iggy asked.

"An amount no bigger than the head of a pin." Mac replied. "That's the straight stuff, the ricin taken from the bean."

"Wow! So you could poison anyone however you wanted? Food, drink, or zapping as in the spy case?"

"Yes," Mac answered, "but we still don't know how the ricin was administered, if it *was* the poison. My guess would be that Spunk and Horse were each pricked with it. Easier in that crowd. I figure Spunk's still alive because he's much bigger, taller and heavier, than Horse. Had to have gotten less into his system, too. He could have taken it intentionally but overdid it. Toxicology never entered my practice after med school, but I know that to have survived, Spunk would have to have had a much smaller amount as lethal as ricin is. One of the most deadly poisons."

After passing Velarde, the landscape opened up, the mountains drew back into the distance, dotted with juniper and twisted pinon, and the Rio Grande became broader and flatter. Low cacti, flowering in vivid shades of magenta and yellow, were interspersed with the balls of sage and straight sprays of golden chamisa. As they swept along the now four-lane road into Espanola, Iggy asked, "Want to stop for a cup of coffee?"

"Sure," Mac agreed. He bet himself Iggy would have more than coffee.

And yes, as Mac came out of the restroom at Burger King, he saw Iggy was already demolishing a breakfast burrito.

"We can have lunch in Santa Fe," Iggy offered, planning ahead.

Back on the road out of Espanola, Mac said, "I looked up the Museum of New Mexico. They have an office and the Foundation at the same address on Lincoln."

"We have time to try there before lunch."

Mac grinned. "I hear you, man, I hear you. You're not going to starve between that burrito and the next food. But we have to stop at both El Rey Motel and the airport to check Bottoms' alibis. Yeah, and his gallery—that was where the good man supposedly spent Friday. Anywhere else you can think of that we can do quickly? I can't be late for the big dinner tonight."

Iggy refrained from any more cracks about the family dinner. He just said, "That should cover it, but let's play it by ear. See if we get a lead on anything else."

Approaching Santa Fe, the mountains were close again and the hills spotted with deep green pinon growing from the thin, fragile covering of earth. They passed the flea market, called Der Fliedermarket since it was next door to the Santa Fe opera. Iggy glanced over wistfully. "I haven't been able to get to a performance since opening night."

Mac grinned at him. "Hey, I haven't met anyone yet who went to those famous tail-gate parties."

"Kind of 'social' for me, but you should see it, Mac! Elegant, catered, sumptuous food laid out on damask with silver, fine wines, on tail gates of S.U.V.s, vans, trucks!" Then he added sternly, "People do forget the whole point is the opera!"

"Never!" Mac answered.

They passed the prestigious adobe-colored north side homes on the hills overlooking the city. Mac amused himself by translating the street names that sounded so fancy in Spanish but not in English, such as *Camino Tierra* meaning Dirt Road.

Iggy turned on the road to downtown Santa Fe and they were soon crawling through heavy traffic, approaching the Plaza and the intersection of Lincoln and Palace.

Mac said, "The Museum must be that Pueblo-style building up ahead. Why not drop me off and you check out El Rey Inn? You'll never find a parking space this near the Plaza in July, and that will save us time before you have to eat."

Iggy let Mac out and then slowly fought the tourist traffic through the Plaza area, aiming for Cerillos Road.

The old adobe El Rey looked pleasant enough from the street, but Iggy knew that the rooms were especially charming. Each was unique, many with fireplaces, and most had antique furnishings, unlike the usual motel.

An attractive young woman smiled at Iggy in a friendly way as he entered the small lobby. Her name plate said LISA LITTAU, MANAGER. "May I help you?" Lisa asked.

Iggy pulled on his rat tail and looked forlorn. "Well, I hope so."

Lisa waited, still smiling and attentive.

"I'm from out of town and trying to track down a friend of mine, a Dr. Evelyn Bottoms. I know he usually stays here and wondered if he's here now?"

The woman looked rueful. "Oh dear, what a shame. Yes, Dr. Bottoms was here, but something came up in Taos and he had to leave us unexpectedly."

Iggy appeared dejected. "Shoot! Did I just miss him?"

"No." She shook her head, then turned to the computer. "Let's see. I don't quite recall...Ah, here we are. Dr. Bottoms came in on Thursday, here Friday. Oh yes, I remember he was particularly pleased with the croissants at breakfast that day. He said that he'd overslept and had been afraid we'd be out of his favorites."

Iggy controlled his excitement, asking casually, "That would be Friday morning? The twenty-eighth?"

Lisa still looked at him curiously. "Why yes, that's what I was saying. He had breakfast with us Friday. Saturday, too, of course. It was Saturday afternoon when some emergency in Taos forced him to cancel." She suddenly seemed to be suspicious of his motives, "But if you're looking for Dr. Bottoms now...?"

"Um, right," Iggy tried to recover his credibility. "It's just that I've been traveling around the state, up in Taos last week, you know..."

Ms. Littau seemed relieved at his answer. After a quick goodbye, he was outta there. Damn! Looked like the bastard Bottoms had an alibi after all. Well, he'd make a quick check of that gallery Bottoms owned on San Francisco, then back up to Mac on the other side of the Plaza.

Sure enough, there was a gallery, El Museo Primo—nothing shy about our boy—and a young man who glided toward Iggy. He had no name plate and offered no name, simply, "If you have any questions, sir."

He seemed displeased with Iggy's girth, jeans, and jewel-tone deep purple silk shirt. This irritated Iggy who said, "I'm looking for a Dr. Bottoms, Evelyn Bottoms."

"I'm dreadfully sorry sir, but Dr. Bottoms is not here at present."

Iggy tried to restrain his impulse to mimic as he asked, "Dr. Bottoms does own this place?"

"Oh, yes."

"I need to talk to him personally. Is he here often?"

"Dr. Bottoms keeps in close touch always."

Iggy thought it was safe to go for the real question now. "I should have tried earlier...Would he have been here last Thursday or Friday?"

The young man seemed flustered. "I'm not sure I should be discussing Dr. Bottoms, sir."

Iggy put all the authority he could into his voice. "This is important."

"Oh, dear. Well, one can never be sure what days he'll be in. But, Dr. Bottoms was here the day after he arrived in Santa Fe. That would have been last Friday. All day."

Shit. Iggy thanked him and left.

Mac was waiting on the corner when Iggy finally made it back through traffic. "Sorry you had to wait," he said as Mac climbed in.

"No problem. I was finished so fast in there, I checked to see if you'd arrived yet, then took the time to call the airport, saved us a trip. You don't have to file a flight plan to fly in here. Leaves Bottoms open."

"Nope." Iggy bit off the word.

"Why not?" Mac looked over as he fastened his seat belt. "El Rey provided an alibi?"

Iggy nodded. "They give him an alibi for Friday. The manager clearly remembers him having breakfast there. He had checked in Thursday. I tried Bottoms' gallery, too, and he really was working in Santa Fe like he said until La Fiestacita Friday evening. Came back for that damned appointment he claimed kept him from opening El Museo that night. That night, Mac! Motherfucker wouldn't..." Iggy choked with pain and anger, thinking of Bottoms and how he'd pleaded with the bastard to open the gallery that night. When he regained control, he added, "Bottoms didn't come back to Taos until I called him Saturday morning."

Mac gave his friend time, then said, "Well, cheer up. He's still mighty fishy. I looked at directories of museum curators and directors for several years. No Evelyn Bottoms. And no Evelyn Bottoms that any of the Museum people had ever heard of. Thought they would have, just from his buying up heavy-duty stuff."

"Oh, hell. Who knows?" Iggy despaired. "Let's eat."

Iggy chose the Zia Diner for lunch and found a parking spot in back of the restaurant. The Zia was packed, but since lunch was also being served outside, the two men didn't have to wait long for a table. The menu was solid, ranging from meat loaf or liver and onions to an Italian-type quiche.

As they waited for their food, Iggy said, "I keep getting depressed, Mac, but I'm not giving up on that sumbitch. Can you check out the Ph.D.?"

"I just believe I can," Mac drawled. "I remember he said his degree was from Harvard. I have one or two buddies who went the doctoral Ph.D. route. They might have ways to find out if he was there."

Iggy brightened. "Good deal. And I haven't been thinking straight. Well, you know...Anyhow, I completely forgot that Cindy had me cash a check for her once. I know where he banks!"

"You think you can get a look at his bank account?" Mac asked in disbelief.

"We need to know if he's got the kind of money he claims, don't we?"

"We surely do," Mac answered, getting more Southern by the minute.

"Well, I just happen to know that bank has files on the net worth of everyone in town, not just their depositors. And a few favors are owed me."

"And you...?"

Iggy grinned and tugged on that rat tail. "Don't ask. Then ye shall receive."

CHAPTER XXV

Thinking he'd rather take a lickin' than walk into a houseful of family, Mac ran the gauntlet just before dinner.

First he got the eye from assorted children who were setting up trays and arranging chairs on the courtyard. Then Mac entered through the kitchen and immediately felt overwhelmed.

Mamacita and her sister Porfy were scooting about. Both were so tiny that Mac was afraid he would step on one of them. He had already met the older sister, Odelia, from Espanola, and Nicole, the blonde Californian. Now Christy, looking downright beautiful in deep turquoise with a full skirt, introduced him to Dolores, whose happy little round face belied her name. She was married to Juan, the younger brother, from Colorado.

Feeling as tall and gawky as an adolescent, Mac was rescued by Patricio, who braved the dining room and kitchen busyness to get more beer from the refrigerator. "Here," Pat said, handing Mac three cold cans, "take these and I'll carry the rest. The men are in La Sala."

Mac gratefully followed, and was introduced to Juan from the San Luis Valley. Then, good ole Gabe broke the ice by saying, "This is Christy's friend who lives in the sheep shed."

Tall, solemn and wordless, Tia Porfy's elderly husband Eli came from his solitary stance by the window to silently shake Mac's hand, and get another beer from Pat. Tio Eli was dressed in new jeans and a blue dress shirt, its collar closed by a big silver bolo inset with large chunks of turquoise. Mac noticed that Juan had on jeans and sports shirts (as he had finally decided to wear), Patricio in white Dockers, green Izod knit shirt, and sneakers.

As the men all stood around, reminiscing over past Fiestas, Pat, the California high-tech sophisticate, decided to return to his big-brother routine. "So, doctor," he said. "Christy tells me you're a widower from Florida?"

"Um, yes, I am." Real swift, McCloud, Mac thought.

"Have you moved here permanently?" Pat's dark eyes looked up at Mac sternly.

"Well, yes, I believe so." Mac answered but continued his internal dialogue, The brothers are going to think you're not quite bright. Remember you were a highly esteemed Fort Lauderdale surgeon. Yeah, but this is Taos.

"Are you going to practice medicine here?"

"I'm looking into it." Now, don't twitch nervously.

"How long do you plan to stay in the guest house?"

Juan, a little taller and stockier than Patricio took pity, "Hey, bro," he said to Patricio, slapping him on the shoulder. "You're treating Dr. McCloud like one of your computer chips. Chill out!"

The slang from Juan was so unexpected that they all laughed. Mac joined in and tried for a light note by saying, "And I assure you my intentions are honorable!"

Pat didn't seem to think that was very funny, but luckily Christy entered just then, saying, "Dinner's ready. Come on in. The kids have already taken their plates outside. We're too many for the dining room table."

Still wordless, Tio Eli thrust out a bony elbow for Christy to take his arm and, beer in the other hand, formally escorted her into the dining room. Once there, he pulled out a chair at the side for Christy, then installed himself at the head. Wondering what third degree the brothers had given Mac, grinning at his subdued state, Christy took pity and motioned Mac to sit next to her.

Hmm, she thought, didn't need to feel sorry for Mac: the beautiful Nicole was seating herself next to him. Patricio was on the other side of Nicole, and then Dolores. Mamacita had, of course, appropriated the other end of the table, Dolores on one side and Mama's beloved baby son, Juan, on the other.

As a college girl, Little Odie was much too old for the outside children's party, so she sat next to her Uncle Juan. Then Odelia and Gabe. Finally, all the way back around, Tia Porfy sat across from Christy, ready to supervise Tio Eli. He looked over the table and rose. The others followed suit as Tio Eli prayed in Spanish, "In the name of the Father, the Son, and the Holy Spirit. For these Thy gifts which we are about to receive from Thy bounty—and for family—we give Thee thanks. Amen." They crossed themselves.

Trust Tio Eli to be brief, Christy thought, but that was downright sentimental for him to add in family. And she was certainly feeling sentimental herself, looking at the beloved smiling faces, seeing them all here. And Mac! She gave his hand an unexpected squeeze under the table. It was good to have his warm presence beside her at this family dinner.

Christy had brought in red roses and pink and lavender sweet peas from the garden. They had looked beautiful when the table had first been laid, contrasting with its shining dark oak. But now, the flowers were lost amid the many silver bowls and platters of food.

Mamacita had insisted on a traditional meal for the boys so long away from home: *posole* with tender pieces of pork in the broth, red chile for the mashed potatoes and roast beef, green chile stew, tamales, beans, green salad, and last a platter heaped with the *sopaipillas*, as light as only Mama could make them.

Dishes were passed and there were exclamations and happy chatter all around the table, except for Tio Eli who remained silent.

As everyone began to eat, Christy, and especially Mamacita, were lavishly praised. Carefully, sparingly picking at his food and looking down at his plate, Tio Eli muttered something. No one would have noticed but Tia Porfy exclaimed, "Eli!" and slapped his hand.

Mac who had taken an immediate liking to the gruff old man with the beer, asked, "What did he say?"

Tio Eli glared at Mac and answered, "I say, '*Cuando hay hambre no hay mal pan*'."

Juan and Gabe laughed, Juan translating, "When you're hungry, there's no such thing as bad bread, well, food."

Mama was incensed, rattling off a return fire of Spanish.

Gabe said, "Oh-oh, when someone asks, 'Just what did you mean by that?' at a family gathering, there's trouble!"

Tio Eli ignored them all, sipping on his beer.

"Gabe!" Odelia said to *her* husband.

Now they are going to fight, too, Christy thought. She tried to figure how to make peace, but little conversations started up all around the table as the others rushed in before her, and little Angela, Juan's three-year-old, drifted in from outside to lean against her grandmother for some loving.

Soon the rest of the children were inside, too, propping themselves against walls, sitting on the dining room bancos, afraid of being left out of happenings at the grown-up party.

At their end of the table, Christy heard Tia Porfy again scolding Tio Eli, telling him that wasn't even the proper use of that *dicho*, that saying. Little Odie was flirting demurely with Mac, asking him if he'd been rafting yet.

Christy grinned at her friend, knowing how adverse he was to what he called "that damned-fool sport".

"No," Mac answered little Odie, not looking at Christy, "Afraid I missed the good Spring white water."

Christy couldn't stop the giggle as she said, "But Mac, my friend Mary says this year's run-off is still great. You could go rafting today."

Then at the other end she heard Mamacita who seemed to be explaining the Church theft to Juan. "...pero our padre, Father Joe, says that nuestro santo San Francisco was not in the car of that woman."

From his place on the banco, eleven-year-old Gabe Junior chimed in bravely, "In Espanola we have a priest who won't stay buried!"

That stopped all conversation.

"No, hijo," big Gabe corrected. "That's at the mission at Isleta Pueblo. In Espanola, well, Santa Cruz really, we have the ghosts of Fray Francisco and Fray Juan who come back to shoot pool!"

Laughter and the children shouting, "Tell us! Tell us!" while Mamacita sat back in satisfaction and sighed, "Ah, *los cuentos*, the stories."

The other adults stopped eating and waited. Gabe smiled and took a drink of iced tea to prolong the suspense in true storyteller fashion.

"You can find out on your own why the sound, cues hitting balls, clicks through the rectory," he said sternly.

Groans.

"But," another sip of tea, "I will tell you about the padre you spoke of at Isleta who lived and died many, many years ago...

"You must go back to the year of 1776 because in that year, who can tell? Some say that this padre, Fray Padilla his name was, was killed by Indians. Others..." Gabe widened his eyes and looked around the table, "That a jealous husband stabbed him!"

"Ai, no!" Mama and Tia Porfy both exclaimed, shocked.

Gabe nodded slowly. "In mistake, of course!"

"Ahhh!" Relief.

"You know what happens when one dies violently?" Gabe turned to look over his shoulder at the children. "He will not rest!" he said so loudly that they jumped.

"Si, Fray Padilla had been wrapped in a shroud and placed under the altar. There he stayed for twenty years or more. But..."

More sips of tea.

"Then he rose up thorough the hard-packed earth!"

"Ai-ee!"

Now, Gabe's voice soothed, "Not to fear. It is said that even the children"—another look over his shoulder—"were not afraid of this still-soft body of the priest.

"The people of the parish thought perhaps Fray Padilla did not like sleeping in the cold ground.

"They took a big log from *los alamos*, the cottonwood trees that grew about the Mission, hollowed it out, and placed the padre in this coffin. Perhaps now he would be happy in the ground?"

"C'mon, Dad. What happened?" from Mary the high-school daughter.

Gabe smiled at her. "More years pass. It is now toward the middle of the eighteen hundreds..."

"Again!" someone groaned.

Gabe nodded. "Again. And again the people prayed over the body and again placed it in the earth.

"Now we come to Christmas Eve, eighteen ninety-five, and the Indians are dancing before the midnight mass. Ai, you should see them dance, their feet pounding the floor." Gabe's voice grew very quiet and the room was silent.

Now loudly, "A knocking! No one pays attention. They dance. A more noisy knocking! The drums beat. Now the altar itself begins to shake!"

"Ai-ee!" from Mamacita as she crosses herself.

"Yes, *Comadre*. When they pry up the floorboards, for now the Mission has put wooden floors over the earth, Fray Padilla in his coffin, has risen once more!" Gabe sat back, his story over.

"But what happened?" several voices asked.

"Oh," Gabe says casually, "the Bishop of Santa Fe was called. He came and looked. They again buried Fray Padilla."

Gabe smiles and shrugs, "*Quien sabe?* Who knows? Shall we go see?"

"Nooo!" chorus the children, and everyone claps.

Mamacita was happy. "Ah, *los cuentos,* as in the old days. Can you put *las adivinanzas*, the riddles, also, Gabriel?"

"No, I'm afraid not, Comadre," Gabe was answering when there was a sound from Tio Eli. The rumble grew louder. Everyone looked to his end of the table in surprise.

"*Era una bruja*. That is how one is supposed to begin a story. 'There was a bruja,' a witch."

Christy was delighted. "Tell us, Tio Eli. Tell us the bruja story."

Uncle Eli nodded at her and handed her his empty beer can.

"I'll get it, Tia," little Odie said, jumping up quickly.

Tio Eli waited until the new beer was in hand. "*Ahora, era una bruja* and this story is about my uncle-by-marriage who has the name of Miguel. He had been married to a good woman, my tia, but she died."

"Oh," sadly from the group.

"Soon a strange woman comes around la casa of my uncle-by-marriage. 'She must be a bruja,' say the neighbors, so enchanted was Miguel. And indeed he takes her as his wife!"

"No!"

"Ah, si. He marries her." A drink of beer. "Was she a good wife to him?"

"No," they answer.

"No and no again!" Tio Eli confirms sadly. "This woman who shall be without a name, soon showed her wicked ways to my uncle-by-marriage and to all the neighbors.

"Pero what could Miguel do? Nada."

"Nada." The word echoes around the table and from the children who have crowded up close to their parents.

"Nada," Tio Eli repeats. "Ahora, you know that a bruja can take many forms...a tumbleweed, a ball of fire, an owl, perhaps?"

Nods.

A sip of beer. "It is so. And so it is one night, just before dawn, when the neighbors see an owl flying over la casa of my uncle-by-marriage." Uncle Eli's voice rumbles louder. "They shoot it down!

"My uncle-by-marriage had been sleeping alone in his bed."

Wise looks and nods from Mama and Tia Porfy.

"He runs to the front door to see what is the shooting. Nada. Miguel can see nothing outside. Ah, that is *outside*. But *inside* he then turns to the fireplace..." He pauses for suspense. "Si. This woman, his wife, lies bleeding on the floor, wounded in the shoulder. She is covered with *las cenizas*, the ashes that come from a fireplace." Tio Eli again stopped dramatically, drank his beer, then added, "And from the chimney of the fireplace comes falling down slowly, the feather of an owl!"

Applause.

Tio Eli stood up slowly but with determination. "Time to go," he announced.

Mama was nodding. "You are a true cantadoro, Hermano Eli."

Tio Eli nodded an acknowledgment and then bowed slightly saying, "*Las penas con pan son buenos.*"

Accepting this as an apology for his earlier comment, Mama proudly addressed the group, "He says, 'If you eat a good meal, things look better!'"

Tio Eli was already heading for the door regardless of whether or not Tia Porfy was coming along behind him. Mamacita called to his back, "Remember, Fiesta Mass tomorrow night!"

Without turning, still moving, Tio Eli waved a gnarled hand back over his shoulder.

CHAPTER XXVI

The bread and homemade cinnamon rolls were in the oven and Christy sat alone at the big oak table, drinking a cup of coffee.

Juan's and Dolores' kids should enjoy the rolls, she thought. Surprising that such young children should be sleeping late, the two youngest, Matthew and Angela on sleeping bags, while John Junior and Joe had the single bancos there in the Curandera's Room, and their parents had the big bed. Christy wondered if Juan remembered that was the area where the Healer laid out the dead.

Odie and Gabe were getting a sort of honeymoon in the Don's Room alone, Mamacita having taken little Odie, Mary and Gabe Junior home with her. Too bad their oldest sons, Tito and Alex, could not get home from the Navy.

Patricio and Nicole had been happy to tuck themselves into La Escondida, Patricio saying that when he was a child visiting Grandmama here, it had always been his favorite room, so little and secret.

There was no need to worry about dinner tonight, what with no food an hour before Mass, and everyone sure to buy hamburgers and stuff from the Plaza booths later. Actually, this bunch better be getting up soon, she was supposed to help set up the St. Francis booth this morning. Then there was that lunch date with Evelyn. Should she go ahead and ignore that hint of danger? Should she be sensible, listen to her feelings and break it?

Christy had left the kitchen door open to enjoy the early morning air. Now, she was pleased to see Mac come in, ducking under the low lintel. He then bent again under the viga above the dining room step-up. They smiled happily at one another.

"Hey, this is some surprise," Mac said as he poured himself a cup of coffee and joined Christy at the table. I never expected to catch you by yourself. Where's everyone?"

"Sleeping, and I'm enjoying the solitude, but I'm glad you're up. It seems like we haven't had a chance to really talk for days."

Mac nodded. "I agree. I like your family a lot, but feel like I haven't seen you since all the hellacious stuff started last Saturday...Why are you smiling?"

"Oh," Christy said, "not because of those terrible things. Just that's such a funny Southern word. But, yes, we had fun at La Fiestacita..." Charlie's words trailed off as she felt the touch of evil, and added, "Only it started for poor Cindy on that Friday, didn't it? We just didn't know."

The mood grew heavy, but then Christy caught the aroma of baking bread. "Ooops! I forgot the bread!" She brought her feet down off the other chair where she'd propped them and ran into the kitchen.

"How is it?" Mac called after her.

"Perfect. I got here just in time. You can have toast or a hot cinnamon roll as soon as they rest on the rack a little."

"I'd like an unrested one straight out of the oven. They smell so good!"

Asbestos fingers, Christy thought as she gingerly picked a roll out of the pan and quickly dropped it on a plate for Mac.

"Thank you, ma'am," he said, and poured them both more coffee.

"Now, where were we?" Christy asked, settling down and pulling the chair back around for her feet.

"Talking about this week. No time together."

"Right. But it's not just my family coming in and getting ready for them. You've been disappearing on mysterious errands for days."

Mac busied himself eating. "Sure is a good roll!"

"Mac." Christy demanded.

"Well, yeah. I've been kinda involved with Iggy."

"Doing what?"

"Now, don't start sounding like a lawyer."

"I get so sick of that comment," Christy snapped. "If I ever start asking intelligent questions or thinking logically, somebody's sure to say I sound like a lawyer!" She fumed, thinking Mac sure punched a button on that one.

"Sorry, m'dear. I agree it wasn't fair. I felt defensive because Iggy and I have been doing a little detecting."

"May I ask what?"

Mac squirmed a little. It did sound pretty silly: a currently retired physician chasing around after clues with a young lawyer. But better come clean. This relationship with Christy had to be based on honesty. Well, maybe not all the way. There was *his* feeling about Evelyn Bottoms, after all.

Christy waited.

"Well, you know how Iggy felt about the Chief trying to nail Cindy as part of that robbery...Say, have you talked with your primo? Found out about how Spunk's doing? Or news about any lab reports?"

Christy decided to let go of her irritation. "No, I'm afraid not. I kept meaning to call Barnabe, but there was all this..." She waved in the direction of her sleeping family. "So what have you found out?"

"Nothing much. I relayed the information about the possible poison to the Chief. Haven't heard any more about what was in Virginia Warren's van."

"Mamacita found out that one of the holy objects recovered was *La Conquistadora*, like the one stolen from the Cathedral in Santa Fe and—"

"Sorry, m'dear, but I don't know about her."

"Oh, she's the representation of the Blessed Virgin who saved Santa Fe during the Indian revolt. I think she's been renamed—many of us are uncomfortable with that conquering aspect. I guess La Conquistadora was stolen because she was dressed with real jewels in her crown. Maybe not. Maybe worth something to some sick collector who'd buy stolen religious art. Anyway that's what two other pieces appear to have been taken for—each by early famous artists, the Quill Pen painter and Pedro Fresquez."

"What were those?"

"*Retablos,* religious paintings on wood or tin. Mama thought one was from the Santuario at Chimayo. The artist Pedro Fresquez died over a hundred years ago, but the Santuario was already a holy place then. He petitioned to be buried there. I'll ask Evelyn more about it at lunch." Casual.

"You're going to lunch with that—" Mac caught himself.

Christy felt herself growing stubborn even though a little while ago she'd been thinking of canceling. Evelyn had been his most charming, even a little wistful, when he called to ask her. Wanted to get better acquainted, all alone in her delightful town. But she wasn't sure about what lay under the charm. She had a feeling...Yet, knowing she was being perverse, Christy said, "Just because you don't like him, Mac, there's no need—"

"It's not just that. The guy's a phony."

"You don't know that."

"I do. I—" Mac broke off, thinking he'd better shut up.

"What? What do you know?"

Mac was saved from answering as Juan's four came racing out of the Curandera's Room and wrapped themselves around Christy. "We're up, Tia! We're up!"

Christy laughed, hugged back, and stood up. "So I see. And good morning to you, too. How about a cinnamon roll for breakfast?"

Mac also rose. "I'll leave you to deal with the little ones and run on downtown for a while."

Realizing she was more miffed with herself than with Mac, Christy said, "Are you going to the Fiesta Mass with us tonight?"

Mac hesitated, thinking of Patricio's quizzing, but making up with Christy was more important than that. "Sure thing. Wouldn't miss it."

Damn! Christy thought, as Mac sauntered out. I act noble and he doesn't volunteer to tell me what he's up to!

Chapter XXVII

As Mac carried out his private mission by walking into the Police Station, he saw Louisa at the counter. Once again, she glanced behind him as if looking for Christy. "No, ma'am," he grinned at her. "I'm still all alone. Is it possible for me to see Chief Garcia?"

"Just a minute, Dr. McCloud, I'll check and see."

Louisa moved over to her intercom, and in less than that minute was saying, "You can go right on back, doctor."

In an office bright with morning, the Chief stood to shake Mac's hand and they exchanged pleasantries.

"So, Dr. McCloud," Chief Garcia said, gesturing to a chair and sitting down himself. "You come without my prima again today. How can I help you? I don't have much time with Las Fiestas getting under way."

"Oh, right," Mac said. "I hadn't thought about that, but I guess you do have a lot to do, what with crowd control and all."

The Chief started to grin. "You remind me of what they were doing for crowd control when I started here. I had worked my way up pretty high with the Sate Police when I was asked to take on this job as Chief." His grin widened. "I had only been here about a week before we had a meeting—me, one of my staff, a few key Fiesta people to discuss security arrangements, traffic, the parade, and so on.

"In all innocence, I started out with the Plaza problem and the need for more police to patrol, keeping the peace. You know there's always the danger of trouble, drinking, fighting. Now, remember, we run a pretty tight ship down there at State, go by the book, so imagine me when my own officer speaks up and says, 'No problem, Chief. We don't have to pay any overtime for our men, we use volunteers.'

"Volunteers? I ask.

"'Sure', he says, 'Same ones come in every year, off the street. They're happy to work for a meal and a beer.'

"I'm speechless.

"'We give 'em a nightstick, shirt with a police patch on it, wear their own pants,' this character tells me proudly.

"I feel all the blood leaving my face, see visions of some yahoo beating hell out of a tourist with his police-issue nightstick, wearing his TOWN OF TAOS POLICE patch.

"He's still talking, 'See, the thing is, Chief,' he says, 'Department don't have to pay, Fiesta Council don't have to pay, volunteers able to eat good, sit up on Oglevie's deck so they can watch the crowds while they eat. Each one gets a whistle, too!'

"Finally, I'm able to speak and I ask, Are they insured?

"Who?

"These volunteers of yours. Insured? Trained?

"No.

"I'm having more visions of lawsuits, start trying to educate the man. What if one of them hurts a civilian? Hurts himself? I ask."

Now the Chief was laughing out loud. "The guy misses the whole point and tells me, 'We haven't given them guns before, but I guess we should for certain locations!'"

Mac had been chuckling all through the story, imagining the spit-and-polish State Captain hearing about Taos' crowd control for the first time.

Now Chief Garcia sobered. "You can bet your ass, excuse me, doctor, well, you can bet my people got educated real fast, and trained, and no guns. And there damned well weren't any volunteers around on my beat!"

They grinned at one another, then the Chief said, "Sorry, I took up too much time storytelling. Back to what I can do for you."

"I thought we might talk a little but first both Christy and I wondered how Spunk was doing."

The big man grimaced at the idea of a little talk, but he answered, "Well, Spunk's still out of it, but thanks to your brainstorm the hospital thinks it's on the right track treating him. Mighty sick man."

"Right," Mac agreed. Then, hoping he wasn't pressing his luck, asked, "What about Warren, the archivist who was killed. Anything found in her van...?"

"Ah, my tia, the madre of Christy, always knows, and spreads the word. Then finally the State Police fill me in. Yes, her van was found and it seems the archivist had private plans. She was doing more than working for the Archdiocese!"

"What's the explanation from the Archdiocese?"

"'No comment', they say. But *I* say, we seem to be getting somewhere, doctor!" The Chief ticked off points on his big, blunt fingers: "We have Miz Warren dead by apparent accident, but her vehicle found with La Conquistadora and priceless retablos stolen from two Churches. Under guise of her job to inventory for the Archdiocese, she visits all the Churches up here and can decide what's worth stealing. We are just now putting together how much is missing."

Chief Garcia paused and looked at Mac sternly, as if expecting argument. "And I myself saw how close she was with Mr. Ted Nesbit at La Fiestacita." Now the Chief snapped one index finger against the other. "Nesbit has already been indicted for fraud and embezzlement. And, don't forget, this person was heard quarreling with two men who were later poisoned. It makes one wonder, does it not?"

"You're tying it all together?" Mac asked. "The Church thefts and the murders? Nesbit and Warren? And what about her death?"

The Chief seemed to withdraw some as he answered, "You ask a lot, doctor. I don't know about tying it all together, though, as to Warren, she does seem to have truly fallen. She was probably reaching when she should not have."

Although the Chief seemed done with providing information, Mac tried another tack. "Back to my area of expertise..." Christy's cousin lifted that family eyebrow. "Or lack of expertise. Has the pathologist determined times of death for Cindy or Castle?"

The Chief's broad forehead furrowed. Interested in the puzzle, he answered, "Preliminary only. So far, he insists, as you did, that Castle's body had been in the Rio Grande longer than we thought, considerably prior to the robbery. I don't know what to think about that.

"And Cindy? More difficult for the M.E., but he believes a week. Also, and this I would not say to Mr. Baca, so many bones of her body were so badly broken, he thinks she must have been thrown from the Gorge Bridge."

"The bridge?" Mac questioned. "But there are tourists stopping there all the time. When could someone throw a body off the bridge?"

"Exactly, Dr. McCloud. That is why I think our Mr. Baca may have been at least partially correct as to Cindy's innocence. Given the time in the water and the injuries, it may be that she was somehow abducted, shot, and thrown off the bridge the night of the murder-robbery. It would have to have been very late to avoid the *turistas*."

Mac had an objection. "I understand, but somehow I can't see Nesbit involved in so much violence. Poison, yes, but this other, I don't know."

Chief Garcia rocked back in his chair, "Yes, yes, I see your point. But how about this? If the M.E. is wrong in Castle's time of death, then Nesbit could have managed the affair with Castle doing the dirty work—killing Bobby Mascarenas and Cindy—then getting himself killed by his cohort."

Mac sighed. "It's too much for me! And how does Bottoms come into it?"

The Chief thumped his chair forward. "Come into it, doctor? His gallery was robbed. That started the whole chain of events!"

Mac was too caught up in the discussion to be careful. "Yes, but we've found out he's probably pulling a total con on this town and Christy, and I wouldn't be surprised if—"

"We, sir? Who is we and what have you been doing? Running your own investigation?" The Chief was a bear now, and not of the teddy variety!

Mac answered uncomfortably, "Well, Iggy, Mr. Baca, and—"

"I'm well aware who Iggy is. And you mentioned my prima along with Dr. Bottoms. Your personal affairs wouldn't be influencing you, would they?"

Mac was defensive."I can't say anything to your cousin for fear she'd jump to the same conclusion you did. But Iggy and I have been checking, yes. And not a single person in the business ever heard of this Bottoms character!"

Mac paused for breath but plowed right ahead regardless of consequences. "On top of that, sir, I talked to Iggy right before I came here. His bank contact can't get a lead on any other assets than what Bottoms is making through his gallery."

"Your *investigation* leaves a few questions unanswered," Chief Garcia said sarcastically. "Our banks aren't exactly world centers of finance. Dr. Bottoms undoubtedly only uses the local bank for his gallery here. And what about the robbery-murder? Are you saying he robbed himself?"

"Well, no, but—"

"And his alibi? What did your investigation reveal?"

"Well, that seemed to hold up, but—"

The Chief grinned that ferocious grin again. "It did, did it? And Spunk and Horse? What if Spunk poisoned Horse for the partnership insurance. He's in a bad way financially. Then overdid it on himself, got more than he bargained for in his attempted cover-up?"

Mac was feeling very uncomfortable. "Yes, Chief, I see there are some questions—"

Some questions?!" Chief Garcia exploded. "Pot growing in basements! Dead people all over my town! Taos does not have knifings and shootings and poisonings and bodies jumping out of the Rio Grande!" he roared. "*Madre de Dios*! Taos does not have this sort of thing. *I* will not have this sort of thing!"

"Yes, Chief. I, uh, see your point." Mac answered weakly, feeling personally responsible for the corpses.

The Chief took a deep breath and his face returned from dark red to its normal warm olive-tan.

"Thank you for your input, Dr. McCloud," Chief Garcia said coolly, picking up some papers. Mac was dismissed.

Chapter XXVIII

The crowning of the Queen and all her Princesses took place at the Mass for Las Fiestas de Santiago y Santa Ana at Our Lady of Guadalupe Church. Burned and rebuilt in the sixties, the Church did not carry the prayers of the centuries, but the ceremony crowning *La Reina* did. The old ways came alive as the young Spanish Queen knelt before the priest, her sweet face upturned and serious. The priest solemnly placed the crown on her head and the past Queen draped the royal robe over her, while dark-haired princesses knelt by her side. The priest laid his hands on her shoulders and the candlelight from the two altar candles reflected in the tears shining in her eyes. The Spanish guitars sang out with joy.

Now, marching the short distance to the Plaza, were La Reina and her Court, pretty teens in crowns and robes, escorted by their young men in fancy white shirts, red cummerbunds, and black pants. They were traditionally protected by the Conquistadors (from the Kiwanis Club) wearing cardboard and tin silver helmets and breastplates, red cloaks swirling.

This colorful, formal part of the procession to the Plaza also included the Queens and Courts with their escorts and Conquistadors from neighboring communities—Espanola, Questa, Penasco and Santa Fe.

The Garcia family was farther back among la gente and created a crowd by themselves with Christy and Mac, Mamacita, all the brothers and sisters and in-laws and children. Tia Porfy and Tio Eli weren't here. Tia Porfy had explained that Tio Eli didn't like to go out at night, but Christy wasn't sure whose rule that was.

Nor was it quite night yet, the summer day holding on to the last bit of light in a sky of Prussian blue, green tinged, darkly subtle. They walked between old adobe walls, Christy knowing it was that time of dusk when the veil lifted between worlds.

Moving in procession, though speaking softly, Mac broke the mood as he addressed Christy. "We haven't had a chance to talk...Uh, how was your lunch with Dr. Bottoms?"

"I didn't go."

"Oh."

"How was your mysterious errand?"

"I saw your primo, the Chief."

"Oh."

"And not so mysterious," Mac explained to break the impasse. "I just wanted to go over a few things with him. Instead, did I ever get reamed out! He seems to think it's my fault that people are dying in his town. Probably includes even natural deaths.

Christy chuckled. "So I heard."

"You knew all along!"

Feeling just a little self-satisfied, Christy smiled up at him and said, "Primo Barnabe and I had a little visit when I helped set up the Saint Francis hamburger booth. He was checking out Plaza arrangements. And you weren't really reamed out. Barnabe just likes to puff and blow sometimes."

Mac thought how appealing Christy looked with her face up-turned to him, eyes twinkling, dark hair shining in the streetlights. Her shoulders were bare above her ruffled white blouse, her Fiesta skirt swaying. But he wasn't going to let her get away with stopping there. "And?"

"And, my primo said that he did get a bit irritated with you and Iggy and your investigations."

"A bit irritated," Mac complained. "Then I'd hate to see the man when he's really angry!"

"I already explained that. Wasn't anything."

Mamacita had been walking ahead of them, her tiny self holding the arms of both her boys, Juan and Patricio. Now she

wheeled around, twirling her classic old Fiesta skirt. "*¿Que pasa?*
Who is angry with the doctor?"

Christy laughed. "Oh, Mac got in a little difficulty with
your nephew Barnabe, Mama. No big deal."

"What is this big deal? Is there more trouble?"

"No, Mamacita. Calm down."

"Calm down, you say. Who is it that cooked and sold to
make the money so that you could be La Reina all those many
years ago? ¡Si! Tu madre! And for your sister Odelia, *tambien*, eh?"

"Oh, Mamacita," Christy said gently, thinking what was
really behind Mama's fussing was her sadness that those two
young girls had grown up, moved away, and suffered losses.

Mac improved the situation by teasing, "What did you do,
Señora, buy the votes?"

"Si," Mama said proudly, "I buy the votes—and much
money went to the Church!—so *mis muchachas* could each be
La Reina in their time. Muy bonita, they were so pretty, too."

"Just like their mama," Mac answered and Christy was
pleased to see Mama sparkle up at him from her five foot
nothing, before turning back to her boys.

By the time their part of the procession had reached the
Plaza, the Taos Queen and her Princesses had already ascended
the steps to the bandstand and the speeches had commenced.

People crowded around and the mariachis played periodi-
cally. As the Mayor spoke, Christy's mind wandered. There
was something tickling her mind, some connection she should
be making. It had to do with the procession, but what?

"Viva! Viva!" interrupted Christy's thoughts.

Now, as Fiesta Council President, La Doña Doris Jordan
was making her speech and once again leading the people in
cheers of "Viva La Reina!" "Viva!" "Vivan Las Fiestas!" "Vivan!"

La Doña remained up on the bandstand with the other
important people, so there was no chance to speak to her.
Instead, more speeches and applause, applause and speeches.
Christy could feel Mac growing restive beside her.

"Shall we roam around a little? Get a hamburger or burrito?"
she asked.

"Good deal!" Mac answered enthusiastically. "When do you
go on duty?"

"Not tonight. I work the Saint Francis booth on the morning shift tomorrow through the parade, and then Sunday afternoon. Just a volunteer this year. The Mayordomos are the ones who have to take turns covering every shift."

Although there was still a crowd around the bandstand, many others were strolling the outside perimeter of the Plaza along with Christy and Mac. Booths encircled the square, most selling food and soft drinks. Some, however, offered tourist-type things such as tee-shirts, caps, fancy-handled knives, and inexpensive jewelry—lots of beaded earrings.

Christy wondered why the darkness seemed to make even the most tawdry booths appear romantic, festive. Then Mac asked, "Why are so many booths closed?"

"Most of the tourists come tomorrow. Then you'll see everything under the sun for sale. And a really fine crafts show over in Kit Carson Park with beautiful handwoven ponchos and serapes, for instance, and pottery, wood carving, on and on. Tonight it's mainly food for us locals."

"What would you like to eat? I see hamburgers and tacos and corn dogs and corn on the cob and—"

Christy laughed. "The only choice you get to make is what kind of hamburger! We have to give our business to the Saint Francis booth."

Christy and Mac added a little more purpose to their steps as they headed for the booth on the north side of the Plaza. Reaching it, Mac saw a menu nailed up on the outside. He ordered two deluxe green chile burgers while Christy exchanged all the ritual greetings with the parish workers inside.

Once they had their hamburgers and Pepsis, Christy and Mac continued their stroll as they ate. "Judging by that crowd around your booth," Mac commented, "Saint Francis must make a pretty penny over the three days!"

"After expenses," Christy answered. "And you'd be amazed how high they are! We have to pay for booth space to the Fiesta Council and the booth itself has to be built to spec. We build it ourselves, of course, but there's the lumber and all. Then the cost of hamburger, buns, condiments…"

"I hear you!" Mac replied with a chuckle. "A lot of work, too, hunh?"

"Last year, I helped cook on the grill. When I got home I could run a fingernail down my arm and scrape off the grease. But fun! You get to see all the people you haven't seen for ages."

Christy and Mac continued their peregrination toward the east side of the Plaza. As they turned the corner, Christy naturally glanced toward Oglevie's and the shops underneath. Suddenly that niggling thought fell into place. "That's it! That has to be it!" she exclaimed.

Mac was startled. "What? What's it?"

Christy was excited and her thoughts tumbled over each other, so that she didn't know where to begin. "The hair," she said.

"Hair?"

"In the crate. Barnabe said they found a long black hair in the crate. A coarse black hair!"

"Christy," Mac complained, "tell me what has you in a snit."

"I've had something in the back of my mind all evening and couldn't think what it was. Then seeing Oglevie's, I naturally remembered Bobby's murder down there and...Anyway, it was the procession."

"Christy!"

"Yes, I know I'm not making sense. It was the procession from Our Lady of Guadalupe. That made me think of other processions, the Good Friday walk and the Hermanos carrying the Cristos."

Heavy sigh.

"Okay, okay. I'm getting there. The old, old Cristos were made with human hair, black hair!"

"Got it," Mac declared.

"That crate would have been the right size for some of the Cristos I've seen. Gosh, Mac. The first ones had the hair, even real teeth! Los Hermanos could move the arms. I remember hearing they were able to reach through from a hole in the back of the Cristo and palpitate a heart!"

"They must have been something! Would the new ones have human hair?" Mac asked with growing excitement.

"Golly, I don't know. Maybe. Or maybe horse hair?"

"But if it was the Christ figure in the crate and if it was one of those old ones, that would be priceless!"

Christy didn't answer because she was thinking and she didn't like where her thoughts were leading.

"Christy?"

"Oh, Mac. I don't understand. That kind of Cristo comes from the moradas. You've been here long enough to know those are the holy places where La Hermandad pray. The very things that Evelyn is bringing *back* to restore to the moradas."She paused for several beats. "Why in the world would one be in a crate that Bobby and Cindy were apparently shipping *out?*"

Mac's mind was racing: knock wood, say a prayer, something. This could be it! But let Christy reach it on her own, try to at least *sound* fair. "I don't know, m'dear. Maybe Evelyn forgot that he had one arriving. Maybe it was being shipped in."

"Yes, maybe," Christy answered slowly. Then her logical mind returned to the look of the crate and the comments made about it. "No. Don't you remember, Mac? No shipping labels. And Evelyn said that Bobby and Cindy must have been preparing a purchase to *send* to a customer?"

As they walked and talked, Christy and Mac continued around the south side of the Plaza. They were almost back to the bandstand, when they saw Mama, Patricio, and Nicole approaching through the Plaza itself.

"We need to see if Mamacita's had something to eat," Christy said absently, then returned to her thoughts. "Maybe a local *santero* is making them. Carving new Cristos, I mean. I'll ask Evelyn tomorrow."

Warning bells rang for Mac. "I wouldn't do that, Christy," Mac said and immediately regretted it, knowing her stubborn streak.

"Why not?"

"Well..." he answered slowly. "Well, let's just ask your *primo* if he has a lab report. That would tell us more, whether the hair was human or horse hair, the age of it and all."

Christy didn't answer, thinking it would be more direct to simply ask Evelyn if he'd had new Cristos in stock to sell.

While Christy and Mac were silent with their own thoughts, Mama reached them. She was complaining about all the changes she had seen in this night before Las Fiestas. The old ways were all dying out. Nothing was at all like the old days. Nothing at all.

Chapter XXIX

Christy woke to the softest of breezes stroking her cheek, but panicked when she opened her eyes and saw the bright blue summer sky. Late!

Sitting up quickly, she remembered Las Fiestas. No guests, well, no paying guests to worry about. Still, better get on with it: feed the family, gather up the cleaning supplies for the St. Francis booth and be ready to get to the Plaza by noon.

As Christy went through her morning routine in the bathroom, she remembered her weird dream of the night before: beautiful music that became a cacophony each time evil prepared to chase her down, while a black hair grew strong and twisted about her throat. Some of it was pretty obvious but she wished she was meeting with her dream discussion group to ask about it now. She *did* feel surrounded by evil.

The crate in Evelyn's El Museo...A coffin? Had it held the life-size body of the Cristo? And what should she do about Evelyn? Too bad she canceled lunch with him yesterday. Then she could have simply asked him about the hair and if he were shipping out a Cristo. She had pleaded family and lack of time, but was she afraid of questioning Evelyn?

You know, Christy acknowledged to herself, that your excuses aren't the real reason you broke the lunch date. There's a dark side, something hidden...Like in choosing a jury, a potential juror could be giving all the right answers, but she would pick up on animosity, anger, lying...Evelyn. He did have an attraction. Face it. A sexual pull. Made her feel lovely and feminine and not just because of his compliments, but in the way he looked at her. Maybe she and Mac had become too comfortable together. Maybe their relationship wasn't going anywhere.

Then Christy smiled, thinking of Mac waggling those black eyebrows, their shared humor, his strength, how much he meant to her. And what was Mama's line? "A good rooster can crow in any hen house?" Better not take Mac for granted.

Stop mooning around like a teen, Christy, old girl. Get yourself downstairs and get this day going!

Although the customary bed and breakfast demands made Christy feel late, it was only seven-thirty as she stepped quietly down the wrought-iron steps.

No need for quiet after all. She heard the noise of Juan's four children fighting and giggling. The excitement of going to Las Fiestas must have them out of bed just as she used to wake early, ready to take her twenty-five cents and go to Fiestas. That quarter would last the whole day. Rides and food and all.

The noise was coming from the dining room where John Junior and Joe were rolling on the floor, banging into chair legs in some kind of scuffle. Matthew yelled and little Angie giggled piercingly.

Angela was the first to catch sight of Christy and came running to wrap her arms around Christy's legs, "They're fighting, Tia! They're fighting!"

John Junior and Joe jumped up off the floor to loudly proclaim, "We are not!"

"Are too," Matthew reported.

"It doesn't matter," Christy said. "Why don't you guys help me set the table and get breakfast ready?"

They liked that and soon the two oldest boys solemnly and carefully lifted plates down from the trastero and laid out the place mats. Matthew and Angela noisily dragged chairs across the old brick floors so they could climb up on a level to help Christy at the kitchen counter.

It took longer than usual, but Christy soon had both blueberry and bran muffins mixed and ready. She let little Angie place the paper muffin cups in the tins and then gave older Matthew the honor of helping fill them, he having a bit more dexterity. John Junior and Joe wanted to help in the kitchen, too, so they got to slide two fat loaves of bread into the oven, one cinnamon, one sesame.

Pandemonium again when the adults straggled in and the children tried to out-shout one another, telling what they had done to help Tia. Hugs and good mornings were exchanged, chairs were moved back to the dining room, and coffee was poured.

Mac arrived, grinned at Christy and asked, "How're you doing, Tia mia?"

She smiled back. "I think I'll survive, but just barely, doctor."

"Can I help?"

"You sure can, since I've lost my little helpers. How about slicing the melons for me and finding out who wants cereal?"

"You got it."

But then, the family left the dining room for the kitchen. "Buenos dias, little sister. Where's my hug?" from Patricio and then a big squeeze from Juan, too.

Like most men—thank God for Mac!—Patricio and Juan offered a perfunctory, "Can I help?" and before Christy could answer, had disappeared back to the dining room. After more greetings, Odelia, Nicole and Dolores stayed. Nicole asked, "What can I do?" Dolores and Odie went to work without asking.

Finally, they settled back at the table, absorbed in drinking juice and eating their melons and cereal, as Christy brought the fragrant loaves and muffins from the oven.

"We're here!" Gabe Junior and little Odie yelled from the Middle Room, high-schooler Mary being too cool to shout like that.

Mamacita had been behind Gabe's and Odie's three, but, as usual, somehow zipped through everyone and was first into the kitchen.

Christy bent to hug her little mama who then pushed her back to arms' length, looked her over, and said, "Not dressed yet, Christina? I hope you do not wear this robe when you have strangers in the house!"

"I am completely covered, Mama. A long robe. It zips up the front."

"It is not proper."

Mac had retreated from all the bustle to lounge against the back door frame and sip his coffee, but now, from hard lessons learned in his prior marriage, he stopped an imminent quarrel by straightening up and coming over to Mama. He took her arm, led her to her place at the head of the table, and said, "Tell me about Las Fiestas, Señora."

Relieved Christy followed along.

"Ai!" Mama answered, her eyes shining. "In the old days we all dressed up in our best jewelry and fiesta dresses." She paused to survey her daughters and daughters-in-law. Odelia and Dolores received a nod of approval for their white ruffled blouses and broomstick skirts, but not Nicole in her elegant fawn pants and cream blouse, nor Christy in her inappropriate robe.

Then, happy once more in her memories, Mamacita continued, "La gente would come from many miles in their wagons and the bachelors on fine horses. We would see all the amigos and *vecinos* and primos and primas and tios and tias we had not seen all year. The little ones would eat ice cream and ride Tio Vivo, the merry-go-round. And we would dance! Ah, *los bailes!*"

Mama's little face suddenly saddened. "*Mi esposo*, my husband Edmundo would look so handsome…" Silence fell as the grown children remembered their father. Their children, even the littlest Angela, caught the mood.

"You had many happy years, Mamacita," Christy said gently, wishing she were near enough to embrace her mama.

Showing her new maturity, little Odie tactfully said, "We still dance to the same music, Grandma."

Perking up, Mama answered, "It does not sound the same as when the old *musicos* would fiddle." Then her eyes sparkled again, "Ah, how your *abuelo*, my Edmundo, would whirl me in the valses. *Valses, cuadrillas,* and *varsovianas.*"

"I can do that!" Gabe Junior offered, and sang out, "Put your little foot, put your little foot, put your little foot right there!"

Little Odie wasn't to be left out. "They say," she addressed Mac sagely, "that Taos didn't have electricity until the fifties."

"Eighteen?" Mac played along.

"*Nineteen*-fifty! Of course that was simply ages ago!"

"Of course."

"We'll have fun, Mama," Patricio said. "We, your sons, will dance with you."

"No," she answered sadly. "No more. We danced in La Plaza, but now, filled with things to sell *las turistas*. No more dancing."

Christy said, "The merchants are closing their shops this year, Mamacita. That will be like the old days when everyone celebrated Las Fiestas."

"And, mi comadre," big Gabe came in, "there'll be music and dancers on the bandstand. We'll find us a corner and all dance with you!"

Her happy little round face smiling, Dolores added, "Just look at all these men! They'll take turns making your beautiful skirt twirl!"

As Mama looked down with satisfaction at her faded blue broomstick skirt, Desire startled them all, appearing at the Middle Room doorway. Standing dramatically where the sun lit her golden hair, Desire announced, "Me, too, you know? I'll be varsoviana-ing with the rest of you at the big dance tonight! Hi, Miz Grant, Dr. McCloud, Missus Garcia, ma'am. And all you folks. I'm Desire!"

The family who had not met Desire were stunned and the ones who had were still impressed as Desire pirouetted to show off her white wedding boots with silver concha snaps, her red fiesta skirt edged with silver rick-rack, her ruffled white blouse pulled low off her shoulders to show happy rounds of breasts, and her long blonde hair loose in a wild tousle. Mac grinned widely as Gabe, Patricio, and Juan were quick to jump up and ask Desire to join the group.

"No, I can't," she answered. "I am giving up most all of today's Fiesta and the parade to help Miz Grant, you know?"

Desire made a slow exit, then glancing back, blue eyes serious over one bare shoulder, "I have work to do! *Adios, amigos!*"

Desire had effectively broken up the breakfast gathering. Chairs were being pushed back, the children clamoring, "When can we go?" "Can we go to the Fiestas now?"

Enjoying her role, Mamacita said firmly, "There are dishes to do first" and the family began clearing the table, while Mama moved gracefully out of the way. Christy and Mac were left behind in their corner by the high windows.

"When do we go?" Mac asked Christy

"Pretty soon," she answered. "I need to dress, of course, but want to get the cleaning things to the booth before my shift starts. I'd like it if you could take me in your pick-up. We can put the broom, mop, and bucket in back."

"My pleasure, ma'am. I'll be ready when you are."

Patricio came back from the kitchen, ready to organize. "Are we all going together?" he asked.

"No," Christy answered. "You all go on so you don't have to be tied down to my schedule. I'll need to come back and check on things as soon as I'm finished at the booth."

"I'll ride with you," Mama announced to Patricio, taking his arm, and everyone scattered: Christy upstairs to dress and Mac out to his little house to make a phone call.

Mac quickly crossed the courtyard thinking that he wished he didn't have to worry about anything but enjoying himself at the Fiestas.

The bright flowers, flamed by the morning sun, seemed an intrusion on his glum thoughts. And although the sun was striking part of the courtyard, the front of his tiny bed-sit was shaded, the inside shadowy. Probably unconsciously made it cave-like, Mac thought, for this old bear to hide in and grieve. But the good times in between were getting longer and longer. It was Christy.

Mac dialed Iggy's home number, knowing his proclivity for sleeping late and that he probably wouldn't be going to the office on a Saturday. Mac took the mumble at the other end of the line to be a hello from Iggy. "This is Mac, Ignacio. How soon can you meet me on the Plaza?"

This apparently woke Iggy because he replied sharply, "Why? What's up?"

"After the procession last night, Christy realized that the black hair the police found in the crate—you know, in Bottoms' place?—well, that it might have come from one of the Cristos—"

"What Cristos?" Iggy interrupted.

Mac had scarcely ended the explanation when Iggy's quick mind leapt through the connections: ancient, rare, priceless, should be being retained for proposed museum or returned to the morada, not shipped *out* for sale. "Shit, Mac! the bastard's selling contraband, maybe the stolen stuff from the Churches!"

"Exactly."

"But what've you got in mind on the Plaza?"

"Christy just happened to mention that all the shops will be closed today, I guess for the parade and all, and I thought—"

"Gotcha," Iggy broke in again. "A shop that's closed—"

"Dammit, Ignacio! Surely that character's left some kind of—"

"Evidence lying around. And, Mac? I just happened to have defended a guy with a set of tools. Never came back to pick 'em up after the trial."

"Yes!" Mac said. "So how soon can you meet me? I'm driving Christy and she needs to be at the Saint Francis booth before noon."

Iggy was still thinking, "Look, Mac. No rush. The best time to use those tools would be during the parade. It circles the Plaza and everyone will be watching it. Why don't I meet you at the Saint Francis booth shortly before, like around one-thirty or so?"

"Good."

"Wait, Mac. What about a burglar alarm? The value of what's in there. Our figuring that's why the daylight robbery?"

"Damnation! I'm not using the brains God gave me. Let me...Well, hell. I'll get in and we'll just see what happens!"

"I don't...Well, see you at one-thirty, Mac."

"See you then."

They hung up. Then Mac slammed his fist against the table. "Yes, sir! We're going to nail you, Evelyn Bottoms, old man!"

CHAPTER XXX

The rest of the family had already left by the time Christy dressed and Mac loaded the cleaning paraphernalia into his Chevy.

Anxious anticipation pumped so much adrenaline through his veins that Mac could scarcely contain himself. Driving down the road with his dear friend he couldn't speak, knowing he was likely to blurt it all out. Christy was increasingly the person he wanted to share everything with. Now, here was this law-abiding, eminent surgeon about to do something damned stupid and risky with a certain up-and-coming attorney as accomplice, and he couldn't say a word to Christy!

Christy felt the excitement emanating from Mac but was immersed in her own thoughts. When she cancelled their lunch date, Evelyn had said that he would probably drop by the booth today. She would ask him then if a precious Cristo could have been in the crate and, if so, why. She knew the probable conclusion to draw, but then logic failed: if Evelyn were shipping out what he shouldn't, why draw attention by staging a robbery on himself? It didn't make sense and it sure raised that old reasonable doubt as to Evelyn's guilt. No, she wouldn't prematurely condemn the man, not with his splendid plans for returning what had been lost to the people and to Taos!

Heavy traffic came into Taos from the South for Las Fiestas. Tourists, friends, family, former Taoseños as in the old days, but now truck, S.U.V.s, and car replaced horses and wagons.

Christy admired the low riders, vehicles that had been lovingly and expensively customized with tiny tires to bring them close to the ground; hydraulics to raise and lower the body, and even to tip the vehicle side to side; and usually some fifteen coats of paint or lacquer, sanded and buffed each time, now shining in the sun. The windows were usually tinted black; the steering wheels little rounds of rigid chain-link; the dash and seats upholstered in plush and velvet and zebra stripes. The seats were also lowered so that just enough of the driver's head was above the bottom of the window frame to coolly nod "Hey, bro," while his boombox reverberated like thunder, vibrating through the soles of your feet.

Today these low riders would be part of the parade and also compete in a variety of categories, slowly passing the judges' stand with trunk lids open to show fancy rugs, tapestries, and paintings, such as ones of Our Lady of Guadalupe.

Mac and Christy had plenty of time to observe the low riders as they crawled along in bumper-to-bumper traffic toward the Plaza. To Mac, they were moving all too quickly. To Christy, though, it was a snail's pace because she just wanted to get there, speak to Evelyn, and have it over with.

Finally, Christy broke the long silence by saying, "Turn left up here and take the back way to the Plaza. I have passes for parking at Our Lady of Guadalupe, the Church parking lot."

"Good deal," Mac answered, sounding phony to himself. "I didn't think to ask where we'd park."

"They tell us every year to guard these Saint Francis passes with our lives. People are parking in every possible, and impossible, place for miles around."

"Mmm," was Mac's only comment as he found it difficult to breathe properly this near their destination. Just stage fright, McCloud, he counseled himself. Get a hold, man, or you'll blow the big one.

There was no let-up in the traffic as he turned left, then around the curve into the three-way stop, past the bank, new shops on the backs of old ones to his right, and again on his left. Our Lady of Guadalupe Church was coming up.

Several parishioners, doing duty as lot attendants, sat on over-turned crates in the shade of a big cottonwood tree. They waved at Christy and motioned Mac to a space. Mac spotted Bottoms' elegant Infiniti parked on the other side, and hoped Christy didn't notice. Once out, Mac loaded himself down with mop, broom and a bucket full of rags and supplies as Christy led the way over to the parishioners.

Louis, Alex, Tony—the volunteer attendants—were a blur to Mac as Christy first hugged, then went through the set steps of the greeting dance:

"¿Como 'sta?"

"Muy bien, gracias. ¿Y usted?"

"Bien, gracias. ¿Y su familia?"

"Bien, bien."

That done, Christy was instructed on how many hamburgers she was to bring back to the men at noon.

"That's the big Father Joe ones with green chili and the works."

"I know."

"Don't forget us!"

"I won't. We'll see you."

"See you."

Christy and Mac walked up to the corner and crossed the street, up the short block past the Variant Gallery to the Plaza.

What a sight! What a contrast to last night's Mass and then the rather quiet crowd in the dark. Today just the tops of the booths were visible above the noisy mob. Mac tried not to bop or jab too many people as he struggled to get through their number with his mop and broom poking every which way, attempting to hold them up out of the way, but hampered by the bucket in one hand. Christy made an effort to run interference through the pushing, jostling throng.

They finally reached the Saint Francis booth midway along the square, across from the fine shops on the North side of the Plaza. Inside was orderly bustle: cooking, serving, taking orders and making change. The shift was just changing and Mac was introduced to the Vigil and Martinez couples as he gratefully dropped his load in a corner.

Christy put on an apron and someone handed her a cap with a picture of the Church and the words SAN FRANCISCO DE ASIS on the front.

"We're selling the caps, too," an attractive young woman explained to Mac, seeing him watching Christy. Mentally, Mac corrected that it wasn't the cap, but how Christy looked in it. She was so appealing with the white cap tipped back on her dark hair. And, Mac added to himself, I hope I see her smiling at me again soon! "Need me for anything else?"

"Nope. Go enjoy the Fiestas while I flip hamburgers."

Christy started to edge through the crowded booth to the grill, but Kathy said, "No, Christy. Over here. Right now, we need you to take the money and make change at the front."

From then on she was inundated with the noon-hour rush, seeing up close every variety of Fiesta-goer: bearded men with long hair and sandals; lots of obvious tourists, young and old, male and female, in shorts and tank tops or wild tee-shirts making every sort of statement or Western style in too-new, too-blue jeans and Stetson-type hats, some expensive, some straw; local older men and women, dressed for Fiestas, the women in broomstick skirts of every gay color, plain and printed, with wonderful old silver concha belts and turquoise and silver earrings, bracelets and necklaces; mountain men with leather, knives, soft shoulder pouches, berets or round hats and moccasins and strangely wan mountain women in long faded skirts; Taos hippie types still trailing pseudo ethnic skirts; and other Anglo Taoseños and Taoseñas distinguishable by—what had John Njieto said? "A look like that wonderful patina of old bronze"—wearing lived-in clothes, usually faded blues, maroons, purples, and greens over even more faded jeans, the women's faces most often innocent of make-up.

Christy took all this in as she smiled, spoke, accepted money, made change, passed orders to the crew and handed food out to the customers in a daze of non-stop activity. All this was done over the loud background noise of various groups playing their kind of music on the bandstand on the western end of the Plaza.

Mamacita and the rest of the family arrived in a bunch, turning in so many orders that Christy had a minute to visit. Peering up from her short height to Christy on the booth platform, Mamacita complained, "Too much food! In the old days *toda la gente* brought sandwiches for the picnic, *los hombres* with their beer. We had only the posole, maybe a burrito or tamale. Now look! In all these booths are hamburgers and corn on the cob and Indian tacos and hot dogs and—"

"But you're having fun, Mama. Admit it," Patricio urged.

"And we'll have that dance," Gabe offered. "Just listen to that flamenco music!"

Christy turned to look at the bandstand and saw a flamenco dancer gallantly doing her swirls and foot stamping to a mostly inattentive crowd. By then the food was ready and Christy started delivering their orders to her family.

"I'll find you somewhere to sit, Mama," Odelia said protectively.

"And then we'll buy you some long, beaded, dangling earrings," Patricio added, and the group moved away.

The main lunch rush had ended, though Christy had learned from earlier experiences that crowds ate all day, starting as soon as the booth opened mornings. The booth workers were beginning to look at their watches to see if the parade was about to start when Evelyn appeared. "You look quite charming in that cap," he said and Christy was suddenly conscious of her stained apron and perspiring face.

"And you don't look like a man who would eat a hamburger," Christy retorted. Nor did he: smooth cap of blonde hair shining in the sun, no jacket for once, but a pressed blue, obviously custom-made, Oxford-cloth shirt, regimental tie in dark blue and red, and beautifully tailored gray slacks.

"Are you workers allowed to take a break and stroll about la Plaza for a bit?"

David overheard him and said, "Sure, Christy. Take a breather before the parade. We've got it under control now."

Feeling nervous, Christy removed her apron and came out the side of the booth to join Evelyn. "There's everything here," she heard herself chattering. "See over there balloons, then hand-crafted jewelry, and next to this food stand, Taiwan tomahawks and fake Indian headdresses.

"A letter to the editor complained the Plaza was taken over by turistas and Taiwan tomahawks so Charley there ordered a dozen gross and plastered his window with signs advertising Taiwan tomahawks. Claimed he sold them all."

Evelyn looked and smiled and made small comments while Christy's stomach fluttered as she babbled and wondered how to casually bring up the question she wanted to ask.

Perhaps unconsciously, Christy had directed their steps to the right, away from Oglevie's and Evelyn's gallery underneath, toward the Northwest, taken up by that same Charley's Corner, Taos Mercantile, and other shops.

The police blocked the Plaza from auto traffic during Las Fiestas, so the streets were free to fill with people. Despite the variety she'd seen at the booth, it now seemed to Christy that all were young tourists in mostly grungy outfits—lots of legs and waving arms.

Christy paused to look at hand-thrown pottery, picking up a mug from a set of blue clay with earth tones. "This would fit in nicely with my Mexican plates," she said, admiring the mug.

"Here. Let me buy it for you," Evelyn offered reaching for his wallet.

Christy replaced the mug quickly. "Oh, no, please. Thank you, Evelyn, but I don't want you buying it for me."

"I insist," he smiled at her and gave the nod to the vendor.

Christy saw from the hand-lettered sign that the potter was Mary from the arts community in nearby Dixon. "The mugs are seven dollars apiece, discounted ten percent if you buy six or more," Mary told Evelyn in a gentle voice.

Christy was feeling unreasonably cornered, all out of proportion to what was happening. She didn't want to ruin a sale for a hard-working artist, but she did not want a gift from Evelyn!

Still struggling for the right statement, Christy saw Evelyn handing over a hundred dollar bill. "We'll have a dozen," he said smoothly. "Keep the change."

Seeing the delight on Mary's face, Christy knew she was stuck with the mugs.

"I'll carry those," Evelyn commanded as Mary from Dixon handed over the bulky brown package.

"Uh, thank you, Evelyn," Christy said tonelessly, more irritated with herself than him.

They returned to the crowd in the street and passed the corner shop where Claire Haye used to show her lovely little fey sculptures, now Wolf Creek Gallery. Such a bunch along here on either side of La Fonda: Rainy Mountain Trading Post, Stewart's Fine Arts, Western Heritage, Taos Candy Factory. The last had a cotton candy stand in front of it today and Evelyn asked, "Would you care to be absolutely ridiculous and attempt some spun pink sugar?"

"No, thank you." That was all Christy could bear. She had restrained herself, tried to keep in her training as an attorney, but now emotions took over. Christy blurted out, "Are you selling Cristos from the moradas?"

Evelyn looked taken aback, but that was natural considering her sudden pounce. Then he asked quizzically, "Whatever are you talking about, my dear?"

Elbowed one more time by somebody in the throng, Christy didn't answer but suggested, "Look, that bench over there is empty. Let's sit down and talk for a minute."

"Of course," Evelyn replied, his eyes round with confusion.

They managed to make their way between booths and people to the scrolled iron bench before it was taken. They sat down facing the back of the St. Francis and other booths, Oglevie's to their right.

Evelyn took both Christy's hands in his, and looked into her eyes. "Now, my dear, please explain what you are asking me."

The mood was broken by the bundle of mugs in their sack starting to slip off his lap. Evelyn grabbed at the package and Christy had her hands free again.

"The hair," she said. "You remember. Primo Barnabe told us that the police found a long black hair in the crate."

"Yes?"

Somehow by small look and gesture, Evelyn was making her feel ridiculous, but Christy plowed ahead. "After the procession last night, I realized that the hair could be from a Cristo, so—"

"Los Hermanos Penitentes utilized human hair in their creations of Cristo at one time, true," Evelyn said helpfully. "These Cristos were carried in procession, but resided at the moradas."

"Yes, Evelyn," Christy sighed, "I know. But I'm asking you if one of the old ones was in the crate to be shipped out?"

Puzzled, Evelyn shook his head. "I simply don't understand your urgency, Christina. Is this not totally repetitive? Material covered with Chief Garcia? We discussed the fact that I have absolutely no idea of what poor misguided Cynthia and Bobby had packaged for shipping. So I fail to see—"

Evelyn interrupted himself as he gazed across the Plaza to the corner across from Ogelvie's. "I say, isn't that your chum, Mr. Baca, simply standing over there in front of Magic Mountain Gallery? I've always thought it quite nice."

Christy followed his indication and did see Iggy there, looking around as if he were lost. "Yes, it is. What...?"

Evelyn abruptly stood. "I'm afraid I have kept you too long. Your fellow workers will think you're shirking your duties, my dear." He took Christy's elbow, escorting her through the mob in the center of the Plaza. Over the noise of people and music, he bent to put his lips close to her ear. "Is your Southern gentleman not in attendance today?"

"Mac?" Christy replied, uncomfortable with Evelyn's tone. "Oh, he's around somewhere. We came together. But, Evelyn, I wanted to ask you about human hair and horse hair..." Christy's words were drowned out by an ear-splitting shriek, moan, wail of sirens and a clanging of fire bells. The parade had begun!

Chapter XXXI

When Mac left Christy at the booth, he tried to act casual by strolling around the Plaza some. The appetites of Fiesta-goers must be voracious to support so many food booths. Well, here was a person who had no appetite, a physician with never a parking ticket now planning on breaking and entering! He was a damn fool. Iggy, too. But how else to get the goods on Bottoms? By all signs, the Chief was ready to arrest famous artist Nesbit, thereby allowing Bottoms to go scot free.

Mac had been doing his aimless wandering at the Western edge of the Plaza so as to stay away from the other end housing Bottoms' gallery. Superstition, he supposed, afraid someone would somehow intuit his guilty intent. He also just happened to keep Christy's booth in view, wanting to see if that bastard Bottoms came mooching around there. Damn, but he'd like to get on with it, hated waiting for Iggy.

Maybe he should case the joint as his soon-to-be buddies in prison would say. Wouldn't hurt to see if the shops were truly closed. Check whether there was a burglar alarm. But no, better wait until time to do the deed before…It was a good idea to make himself scarce anyway, be sure Christy didn't catch sight of him heading toward the gallery. Well, maybe just check the shops…

Now, Mac sauntered through the jostling crowds along the south side of the Plaza, passing La Fonda. He cut catty-corner to where new galleries had been built in a little cul-de-sac.

One of the first had been a retail shop for the Millicent Rogers Museum. Was that where Bottoms got the idea for his scam?

Elbowed and jostled by the crowds, Mac worked his way toward Oglevie's, finally reaching a tiny shop packed floor to ceiling with a fantastic array of Indian jewelry. Pretending to be studying the display through the window, Mac looked into the next windows. They were the ones by the lobby doors under Oglevie's. Good deal! It seemed to be dark inside, the shops closed. Surely, though, those outside doors were unlocked, so that people could go upstairs to Oglevie's. Didn't want to risk someone seeing him check. What he'd do was walk around the corner to the restaurant's main entrance on Santa Fe Road. That way, he could have an innocent cup of coffee at Oglevie's and then come down the inside stairs past Bottoms' place and out these doors. He would insure that the other shops were closed and that the outside doors were really open—for escape!

After all that checking, it still wasn't one-thirty, but in a fury of impatience, Mac made his way through the crowd to the Saint Francis booth where he and Iggy were to meet.

Usually tardy, Iggy must have been anxious, too, because he was already there. They exchanged a conspiratorial glance before Mac looked around for Christy.

"She's not here, Mac," Iggy said, interpreting the look. "They say she went off with a tall blonde man."

"Bottoms!"

"Bottoms. So what say we don't wait for the parade and do it right away? We know Bottoms is with Christy now, but we may not know where he is later on."

They had automatically moved away from the booth, finding a little pool of isolation near the Veterans' Tree.

"Did you bring the stuff?" Mac asked.

Iggy patted his jeans' pocket. "Right in here. A little bag of burglar's tools. Highly illegal just to possess them. Never thought the cops would give them back."

"Then let me have them and—"

"Whaddaya mean?" Iggy was incensed. "Let you have them? I'm the one going in!"

"Oh, no!" Mac answered. "You have to practice law in this town! What if you got caught?"

"I'm—"

"No, Ignacio. Listen here. To be right blunt, you're pretty heavy. What if you had to run? Besides, one of us has to be a look-out."

Grumbling, Iggy assented, and they decided that the corner in front of Magic Mountain Gallery was the least obvious place for him to stand. There, Iggy could keep an eye on the lower entrance to the shops and also the street leading to Santa Fe Road. "That way," Mac said, "you'll see if Bottoms leaves the Plaza and goes around through Oglevie's from the other side like I did...In fact, like I'm going to do again. I don't want *anyone* seeing me go in over here."

Iggy said, "You know you're crazy, doctor."

"I know, Counselor," Mac answered, and they solemnly shook hands.

Mac strode briskly up the street and, at the corner, crossed over to Oglevie's. He quickly walked through the place like a man with a purpose, then ran down the inside stairs.

It was eerily quiet down here. Since the shops were closed, no one was in this small lobby, and no one would be except for someone using the stairs to Oglevie's. The outside noise of the crowd was muffled and little sound drifted down from the bar and restaurant upstairs.

Was this how it was when the bastards broke in and murdered Bobby? Did they kill Cindy then, too?

Was Bottoms one of them? No break-in at all? But why, dammit! Why? He could make all the other pieces fit the puzzle, but not the robbery-murder.

While he thought, Mac took out the small bag of burglary tools. Iggy had had no more idea than he how to use them. Breathing deeply to quiet his nerves, Mac moved over to the door of El Museo. He saw no evidence of a burglar alarm on the outside of the door. He couldn't see inside. Hopefully the police would be prevented by Fiestas from any quick answer to an alarm if there was one. It was time to commit.

Mac examined the bunch of odd-looking metal shapes. Well, this pick ought to do it...Steady there. Remember you're a surgeon. Dexterous fingers...Just wiggle this little gizmo around in there. Pretend it's a probe. This is just a surgical procedure to find...

Sweat streamed down Mac's face. He used his arm to wipe it away so he could see. His hands were slippery wet. Feel...Feel and probe...There! By God! he had it!

Mac eased the door open. No audible alarms went off. Probably rang through at police headquarters. So, do it and get out! He took the final step in commitment. The final step, all right.

It was pretty dark in here. Not much light from outside through the frosted windows. God! McCloud. Some burglar. No flashlight. Keep cool. Breathe. You can see enough to get through this showroom. Now down this hall...Damn! it's dark. Easy. Easy. Remember when you picked up Iggy: the office was to the left.

He banged into the door frame. Must be the office here.

Time! Too much time. Were the cops answering the alarm right now?

Mac felt around for a light switch. This far back no one in the lobby was going to see a light. Found it! Neon flickered on. Pretty sparse office for our elegant Evie. More like the storeroom. He tried not to think of the body that had been on the floor in there. Utilitarian metal desk. Plain sort of wheeled typist chair behind it. Lamp.

Tensely aware of passing time, Mac quickly crossed to turn on the lamp and then back to turn off the overhead light...

Jerome Kelly! The museum director had apparently darted behind the door when he heard Mac approaching.

Kelly held a small plastic baggie in one hand; a gun, with a silencer, in the other.

"I'm going to kill you, you know," he said pleasantly in his trans-Atlantic English.

"I don't think so," Mac answered, trying to sound equally cool despite the spasm in his stomach. "Were you here to plant poison in Bottoms' desk? Is that what's in the baggie?"

"Yes, it is. I don't believe the police ever searched the office area. Now they will when they find your body in here, shot with the same gun as Cindy. I must. You would have seen me."

"Are you carrying the knife you used on Bobby?"

"I didn't kill Bobby!" Kelly replied indignantly. "That was Tad Spunk."

He leaned against the door jamb negligently. "You see I came up here very early in the morning to pack up the Cristo, priceless, you know, along with a most valuable Spanish monstrance of pure gold." He chuckled, "As required, I had completed that little chore before staff arrived, but then they came in early because of plans to leave for that damned party..."

Insane conversation. Mac wondered if he could he take Kelly one on one? His only option was to keep him talking. Time and the burglar alarm were on his side now. "So?"

"So,"Mr. Kelly mimicked him. "Oh, you surgeons. Always want to cut to the chase. No pun intended.

"As I said, poor little Cindy and Robert arrived, forcing me to lock myself in here and then my boys jumped the gun and came in to do a little burglary on their own."

"Your boys?" Mac tried to prolong the conversation. He was going to die unless he could think of something. "You were the one running a theft ring?"

"Bravo, doctor. Got it in one!

"I subsequently heard an inordinate amount of noise, opened the door a crack, and looked out." He paused dramatically. "What should meet my eyes but Cindy running this way for sanctuary. Unable to close the door without discovery, I darted over there to the screen by the desk. Cindy entered unaware of my presence. She watched the storeroom events from my prior position at the door crack."

"Then how do *you* know that Spunk killed Bobby?"

Jerome Kelly smiled indulgently, "Dear chap! Before I shot her, Cindy was quite cooperative. Reported that my sometime employees, Spunk and Horse, forced entry, pried open the crate, and then stopped poor Robert as he ripped off Spunk's ski mask, stopped his impetuous attempts with a sharp instrument to the throat." Mr. Kelley shook his head. "That's why I had to poison the two of them, you see. One can't have one's peccadilloes bruited about or risk blackmail or a plea bargain to save their worthless lives.

"Now I set up Evelyn Bottoms and I'm home free today with my priceless Cart of Death!"

The murderer looked at Mac, as if for understanding, then moved closer aiming the gun. One more question and then he had to do something to get the hell outta there. When—if!—the police arrived, they could deal with the madman!

"But why kill Cindy? Why not just go along with the robbery?"

Christy appeared behind Kelly in the doorway!

Mac tried to freeze his face.

Thank God! Kelly was unaware, answering in a tone of pity. "No, no," he said. "Cindy had seen me here where I had no business being. And my traitorous partners..."

Kelly's words washed over Mac. He focused on protecting Christy, getting them both out alive.

Kelly talked on. "Our conscientious Cindy had also seen the face of one of the men I knew I would have to kill. When Horse and Strunk had left, I shot her after a little conversation. Had to leave the body, I'm afraid, but I thought there was little risk of discovery if I locked up and left the closed sign up. Bottoms had plans to come up for the party, Cindy said, but no one else would check El Museo during the day on Friday. I returned that night after your Fiestacita, and quickly disposed of her. Just another merchant carrying out a load of trash in a bag."

Mac nearly lost control. Peripherally he saw Christy's body react.

What to do? Lead Kelly on? "And Virginia Warren?" Mac asked.

"She was my first assistant, relieving the churches of treasures they had no business possessing." Jerome Kelly shook his head sorrowfully, "Poor woman. Dead."

Mac rose slowly, never so much as glancing at Christy behind Kelly, thinking, easy McCloud, easy.

"Then Bottoms is innocent?"

Jerome Kelly laughed. "How do you think we were making the money we were? We stole from a thief. Bottoms was running a scam. Shipping out antiquities."

Mac moved to the side of the desk as he spoke. "Give it up, Kelly. Bottoms' burglar alarm has the police on the way, and too many are dead. You'll never be able to keep on killing until everyone is silenced. Spunk still alive, me. You're going to jail."

"You're going to hell!" the museum director lost it, raising the gun to shoot Mac.

Christy leaped at Kelly's back, striking the knife hand with a slab of wood from the broken crate.

Jerome Kelly shrieked, dropped the gun and bent to retrieve it.

Mac shoved the wheeled chair in front of him. It hit the museum director in his crouched position, making him stumble.

Together, Mac and Christy rushed for the door, then down the hall. Kelly was close behind.

A shot thundered. Missed.

The doctor's hands were slippery again on the outside door. C'mon!

Then they were out through the lobby. Out that door.

Mac yelled at Christy to get the police and turned away from her, praying Kelly would follow him. He was the one who had grabbed up the baggie of poison.

Mac turned left across the street toward La Fonda. Where was a cop? Supposed to be so damn many covering Las Fiestas.

Mac pushed, shoved, elbowed through the crowd filling the sidewalk, lined up to watch the parade still passing this side. He caught glimpses down the block: the last horseback Honor Guard for some Queen and court disappearing, bright crepe paper on floats on pickups, pretty women waving, and some brown-robed monks. There were outraged shouts and yells from those Mac left in his wake.

He took a look back to see how close Kelly was. Gone! My God! Had he gone after Christy? Was he escaping? Where the hell were the cops? Nothing but a street full of horses!

Where was Christy?

Here came Iggy! His belly was bouncing as he fancy-stepped through the prancing horses of the Sheriff's Posse. "God, man!" Mac yelled. "Where were you? It's not Bottoms! It's Kelly. Kelly like to killed us!"

"Us?!"

"Christy came in. There's no time—"

"He must have spotted me," Iggy answered "He went through the alley on the other side. I saw you running—"

"I'll bet he's heading for his car—and a plane in Santa Fe. The museum has one. He killed them all! Find Christy! Call 911, Iggy, and then come after me. We'll get the bastard!"

"What about Bottoms?"

"Screw Bottoms!"

Mac dashed into the middle of another contingent of horses and riders. Seeing this creature unexpectedly under its nose, a horse reared and neighed. Women screamed.

Chapter XXXII

Christy ran the opposite way from Mac, toward the phone across from the St. Francis booth. Was Jerome Kelly pursuing her? Mac? How stupid she'd been! Attracted to Evelyn, total phony...Well, at least not a killer! *Where* were the police? She had to get help for Mac. For all of them.

Christy was barely aware that the parade passed in front of their booth, then on up to Oglevie's corner where it turned right to circle the Plaza.

A horse neighed fearfully. A woman shrieked. Christy quickly turned to look behind her at the opposite side of the Plaza. A horse was rearing. There was Mac! He was running across the square toward Charley's Corner. Iggy was jouncing along toward her from the same direction. Iggy actually running!

There was no time to wait for Iggy. She had to help Mac. Find the police.

Iggy, seeing Christy dash from the booth toward Charley's Corner, turned to intercept her.

Mac tried to reach the Guadalupe parking lot before Kelly took off in his car.

A cop barred his way. "Sorry, sir. You can't go down there. The low riders are just coming up."

Probably some primo of Christy's. "Damn it! There's a killer loose!"

He received a look of disbelief. Feet planted apart, the officer kept one hand on his baton, the other on his gun butt. Mac tried another tack, "Look, I'm a doctor. I have identification—"

"No."

With both hands, Mac shoved the young cop in the chest. Hard. He landed on his backside. Now they could add assaulting an officer to Mac's other felony.

He took off down the side street, past the low riders coming up, barely aware of their yells "Hey, bro!" "Wayta go!"

Christy and Iggy came together at the fallen policeman.

Iggy grabbed Christy's arm as she ran by in pursuit of Mac. "Stop, Christy! Mac's after Kelly. Thinks he's taking off for Santa Fe."

Christy yanked away. "I'm going with Mac. You call 911."

The young cop got to his feet, ready to pursue that big guy who'd knocked him down. Iggy shoved the officer against the plate glass window. "Get the police!" Iggy yelled.

"I am the police!"

Torn between staying to assist and running after Mac, Christy quickly made the logical choice: find someone who could really help Mac against the danger of chasing Kelly.

"Jaime," she pleaded with her red-faced primo, the officer who was trying to free himself from Iggy. "Look at me. It's your prima, Christy.—Let go of him, Iggy.—This is an emergency! Jaime, call Barnabe, Chief Garcia, on your walkie-talkie. Tell him—"

"Tell him," Iggy interrupted, "It's crazy, but that Museum Director Kelly is the killer. Dr. McCloud has the proof. He's chasing Kelly. Try to stop Kelly before he gets out of town, or he'll head for Santa Fe. He's got a plane there."

Totally bewildered and still unbelieving, Officer Jaime Archuleta looked from one to the other.

"Do it, Jaime!" Christy urged. "First get someone to the parking lot. Our Lady of Guadalupe."

"C'mon!" Iggy shouted at her, pulling her the other direction.

"Where?"

"My car. It's down the alley across from the old Cantu building.

They ran back toward the St. Francis booth, heading east, Christy having to slow herself for Iggy. He panted, "I don't know if your cousin understood!"

"Neither do I. That was a lot to take in out of the blue."

Christy spotted Mama and the family. Juan was the cool one, Patricio more excitable. "Stop, Iggy. Wait a minute."

Mama started to speak, questioning, but Christy cut her off. "No time, Mama. Listen. And you, too, Juan, pay attention! Mac's chasing a killer. Find a cop, a phone. Make sure Primo Barnabe has an all-points out for a red sports coupe, BMW, I think. Mac's driving a tan Chevy pickup, Florida plates. Tell Barnabe to try to stop them in Taos, but if they get away, Jerome Kelly is heading for the museum plane in Santa Fe. Need Sheriff, State Police, everybody!"

Thank God for Juan! No questions. He was already off, dodging low riders, trying to cross to the shop side to a phone.

"Christina Garcia y Grant!" Mama sputtered. "You do not go, m'hija! Stay. Stay!"

"Sorry, Mama," Christy called back, running after Iggy who hadn't waited to chat.

Mac raced down the side street past the low riders coming up.

Long legs carried Mac to the corner opposite Our Lady of Guadalupe. Starting to run across the road, heedless of cars, Mac almost collided mid-street with a red sports coupe, its tires squealing. Mac caught sight of Kelly in the driver's seat. Alone thank God! Christy was safe!

Something in the back of the guy's car. Something...Lord, Lord. That's why he hasn't been chasing either of us, Mac thought. Kelly went back for the Carreta de Muerte, the priceless death cart.

Yikes!

Mac jumped out of the way as Kelly swerved. He was trying to hit him! Luckily, the car was already too far past. Mac started running again.

The attendants in the parking lot, Christy's friends whom Mac had met this morning, were all on their feet. They were staring aghast after the murderous BMW, now out of sight.

Then they turned puzzled stares on Mac as he raced toward them.

"That's the guy been killing everybody," Mac shouted, somewhat insensibly, pointing after the red car. "Help me get outta here. I'm going after him. And call the cops. Tell 'em head south."

The men, not young but spirited, exchanged looks, then remembered this wild man had been with Christy. They sprang into action—as much as aging muscle and bone would still allow a spring. Alex shooed aside pedestrians heading for their cars now that the parade was ending. Louis and Tony loped toward the main street, bravely standing like traffic cops, arms outstretched in front of on-coming traffic, stopping it.

Mac jumped in his pickup, gunned it, and headed out.

Thank God! The last of the low riders was into the Plaza side street. And will you lookee there! Christy's friends had cleared the street for him. Standing there in front of the cars, the two gentlemen calmly accepted the horns blaring at them.

With a wave at the gallant pair, Mac whipped the Chevy out onto Placitas, down to the corner. Would Kelly head straight out to Santa Fe Road or take Placitas and the new faster back way? He probably didn't know about the local short cut. Straight it is.

There were still more vehicles bumper to bumper coming into town, but the traffic wasn't so bad heading south. Mac strained to see if he could spot Jerome Kelly anywhere up ahead. No goddammit! The thing to do was get through town as fast as possible and catch the bastard on the highway.

Mac used all his driving skill to pass cars and pickups, illegally swerving in and out of traffic to get farther ahead. After a quick look, he ran a red light. No worry. The best thing that could happen right now was for him to get a cop on his tail.

Ha! Center turn strip coming up. He was able to speed down the middle turn lane. Ooops! Some s.o.b. thought he'd turn into Wal-Mart's from this lane! To avoid hitting him head-on, Mac was forced back into traffic. But now there was enough of a shoulder to use it as a race track.

Mac saw he was approaching the hill down to St. Francis Church. He could pass those characters ahead on the right.

Now, the blinking light at the Church coming up. Watch for congestion in front of post office.

Check for Kelly...Yes! There he went up ahead, just cresting the hill past Llano. Starting to move out fast to catch him, Mac had to slam on the brakes. Some jerk cutting across to west Llano Quemado.

Off again and highway from now on. But that bastard's got more power than I have. He's going to out-run me. Indian tipis at Taos Drum flashed by on the right, white against infinite blue sky.

There he was again! Pulling away on this long stretch, and, Mac realized, Kelly would be able to take the curves faster than he could. At least, there would be traffic leaving town to slow him down.

Mac glanced right. Gorge snaking along in the sun. Sagebrush gray-green, greener than usual from the monsoons. Yep. There were the thunderheads piling up, towering white mound upon mound. Would be raining soon...Here came the long sweep of the horseshoe. Take it careful. Search and Rescue have to haul too many bodies from the drop-off.

There! There was the sleek red coupe up ahead, ascending the far side of the horseshoe.

Mac caught up with the car in front of him. Colorado plates. Maybe Colorado would drive this faster than some tourists.

Up to where many stopped to look over Taos and the great sweep of valley to the mountains. Then down. There were a bunch of cars ahead and too many coming North to pass. Down, down toward Pilar. Didn't ask the bastard if he killed Castle, too. Like to see him smell that body after it had been in the water so long. Find out what killing does.

Should be able to see him. Did he cut off? Slow to look down the road into the community of Pilar. Nope. There! There was the top of a red coupe, must be Kelly's BMW, turning down to that same beach where they'd dragged out Castle's and Cindy's bodies.

Slam on brakes! A flagman! No no no no. The two cars ahead were stopped. A big caterpillar was pushing rocks off the road. Too many cars were approaching to run around these.

Now! Go dammit! Go!

The flagman stepped back as momentarily the cat was off the road. Just take your sweet time!

Now!

Mac turned right, down the dirt road to the beach. There was the BMW parked. Door open. Empty dammit! Empty! Where in hell...?

Mac jumped out of the pickup, looked around desperately, ran down to the water. Rafts pulled up. Red ones and gray. People behind him. Rafters ready to put in, he guessed.

No Kelly. What? Where? Mac looked downstream and saw a red raft just rounding a curve.

His mind fogged with the scarlet blood of pursuit, adrenaline coursing through his system, unthinking Mac shoved a little gray raft into the water and jumped in. He saw fat rubber sides, a middle seat in the metal frame of the twelve-footer. There were oars in oar locks like a row boat. Mac had been in a rowboat before, and thought this shouldn't be too hard. The river seemed to be flowing calmly, not too fast.

Mac heard shouts behind him. Someone must want their raft back. Mac began to row like crazy, determined to catch up with Kelly.

Then there was nothing but the sound of the river, loudly echoed back by the canyon. Mac had time to look around. Fat boulders climbed up the steeply-sloped cliff to his right. Smaller ones to his left led up to the highway. Small green-leaved trees clung to the thin soil. Short, bushy red willows lined the bank. Piñon and spruce hung on farther up.

Red raft ahead! Ohmigod! It was bobbing along, bouncing against the cliff. Empty!

Zingggg! Plop. Mac instinctively ducked.

Kelly! Kelly stood up there on top at the pull-off, rifle in hand! It had been a set-up. Kelly had pushed off a raft, then hidden. Maybe he had crouched on the other side of the car.

Mac tried to concentrate on the river hazards, but couldn't stop himself from taking quick glances up at Kelly. The killer was loading the rifle.

Paddle, man. Paddle like fury! And, ohmigod! Here's the white water! Rapids. Rocks. Noise. Water in his face. The raft jumping and bucking. Trying to find a rhythm for that, Mac

felt it scrape bottom. He used his oar to push off from the rock. There's another! Lordy, Lordy! He'd never make it through this. Yeah, old man, and how about a bullet in the back, too?
  Crack!
  Bullet must have hit a rock. Otherwise he'd never have heard it over the awesome river noise. Row. Push. Rocks. White water leaping steaming, spraying! Dropping! Holes. Down. Up. Down. Mac hated water. He had never learned to swim. Now, he would die by drowning or freezing to death—if he wasn't shot first. Where in the world were the other rafters, one of that friendly bunch to rescue him?
  A number of factors conspired to leave Mac alone on that particular stretch of river which, in high season, would be teeming with rafts and kayaks: season's end, the lateness of the hour, and, of course, Las Fiestas drawing the crowds.
  A puny little gray raft bobbing and leaping below the immensity of raw, naked rock walls, only now and then possessing a sparse skin of earth and vegetation. Even the Rio Grande and the road alongside it were small cuts in the great stone mountain.
  The raft stuck! Wedged in between two boulders. Was Kelly going to get him now? A sitting duck! Mac peered up toward where the road would be if he could see the damn thing. Nobody. Mac tried to figure...Kelly must have had the rifle and some shells in the trunk. Not many or he'd be shooting more. After missing those first potshots, Kelly disappeared. Where? Was he waiting somewhere ahead?
  Mac looked up the cliff. It wasn't sheer, but so near perpendicular that its rocks and boulders seemed to defy gravity. Wet tan rocks close at hand, then black volcanic stones farther down there, tossed by a random immense force. Thick red-limbed swamp willows rimming the banks. Gray-green Russian olives. Nowhere to climb out. And don't be a fool. If he came upon one of those little beaches, he wouldn't dare risk it, be a stationary target. Okay, McCloud, get yourself unstuck here and paddle like crazy!
  Shoving with the paddle, straining, Mac pushed against the rocks until he freed the raft. Back into the racing swirl. Rocks everywhere! Water. Falling, falling down the rapids. How far did the river drop from Taos to Espanola? Thousands of feet!

The Rio Grande, crushed between steep sides, rushed over its stone bottom and fallen rocks, sweeping past Mac. He was desperately trying to stay afloat and think: how many turn-offs? Where was the next one? Kelly waiting. Death waiting.

You've got to miss this next boulder. Paddle that way! Ooof! Hit the sombitch! Don't turn over. Please God, don't let it throw me in this churning hell!

Still obsessively looking to see if the road was visible, Mac saw a figure up above. Kelly again! But there weren't many turn-offs left. If he could live through Kelly shooting from this one, there were only two more to go. Well, as best he could remember there were only four pull-offs altogether before the river left the road. He hadn't planned on it being life and death to know!

A great boom rolled through the river canyon! What's he got? A goddamned cannon?...Mac felt more water on his back and shoulders. Hell. The boom was thunder.

He had to take a quick look up. Kelly was taking aim. He couldn't watch. He had to get through these sharp black boulders. Stay low. Present a smaller target. How the hell stay low and paddle, push, get around rocks?

Thank you, Jesus! Kelly must not be much of a shot. There was no sound of any bullets hitting. All this bouncing and bucking must make him hard to hit.

Splat! Hiss, hiss, hissing. Crappy shot, hunh? Sombitch just got the raft! Mac could hear the air rushing out. Oh Lord! He'd rather be shot than drown! Who said you get your druthers, McCloud?

Deflating! That front side was deflating! Stay cool. He could make it. Just keep paddling, bouncing off rocks. Maybe stay afloat...Ha! Look there! That end's down all right but the rest of all that gray rubber's still nice and fat. Must be separate cylinders or whatever. Mac could fly with three engines.

His momentary hope turned to despair as he remembered the pull-off. The bastard could stand right at the shore and fire off one deadly shot!

Spray and rain. Good rain. Thank you, Jesus! I mean it. That's a prayer, Lord. It's harder to take aim in the pouring rain. Gray, gray.

Gray rain falling past pearl-colored stone, splatting on gray raft on silvery-gray river. A monochrome, hiding the green of occasional mountain meadow, the red, ocher, and black of the striations, screes and boulders.

Hard to see through the water. No silhouette in the blinding rain. Okay. Push! Paddle slipping against the rock. Yike! Almost tipped over. Out again. Glen Woody bridge coming up. Would Kelly risk that narrow shaky contraption in a car? Would he run down to stand on that swinging bridge to get a real close shot? What did they call it? "De-cap bridge." When the water was high the river was so close to the bottom of the bridge a rafter's head was endangered. Now, he didn't even have to duck. What had Mary, expert rafter, said when Christy called to ask? "800 C.F.S. max this time of year." That's cubic feet per second. So how fast was he going?

Oh-oh. Big Rock coming up! A boulder fell in a few years ago, sheared off as it came down the cliff and this half landed in the river. Tons and tons of it! He must wind around Big Rock and those other huge boulders...A great place to shoot from the pull-off right here at Big Rock! Can't look, Mac thought. I can't see if Kelly is waiting for me again. Got to get through here. Lord Gawdamighty! Big Rock's the grand-daddy but these others are huge. Huge rocks!

Mac's world shrank to nothing but the feel of spray against his face, rain pelting on his back, beating wind. He saw nothing of the look of the canyon: the black boulders, the occasional juniper growing out of a tiny pocket of dirt. His ears did take in zingggg! Crack! but Mac couldn't absorb the meaning. His mind functioned only on finding a way through the impenetrable wall of boulders ahead.

Suddenly Mac was clear, swept through the slot by the rushing water, dropping! The raft bounced like mad, then hung up once more, and Mac was ready to give up. He was so tired. His arms ached. His back ached...But he was alive and there was just one more place where Kelly could shoot from. After that, the river moves away, then comes back at La Iguana, just before Embudo station.

Despairing, Mac argued with himself: I do not have the strength to push off again. Yes, you do. Think of Christy. You don't want Christy to see you dead. Christy who lost a husband. Christy, Christy, Christy.

Shoving, pushing, grunting, eyes blinded by spray and rain, Mac got the raft off the rocks, back into the main stream again. It bucked over rocks and rough water like a rodeo bronco. And Mac was exhausted, so terribly exhausted.

Chapter XXXIII

Running, Christy caught up with Iggy before he reached the corner where the road into the Plaza became Kit Carson Road across the street. She heard a stentorian bellow of "Christina! Christina!" and looked round to her right. La Doña moved briskly up the sidewalk from her post down the hill at the parade reviewing stand. The beautiful old velvet fiesta skirt swung above sensible black walking shoes.

Iggy groaned, "Oh, no! We've got to catch up with Mac."

"What are you two up to?" La Doña panted. She had hurried so much in the heat that some gray hair had dared loose itself from its severe bun in back. "Saw that godawful purple silk shirt of Ignacio's. Both of you racing—"

In such an emergency, Christy dared to interrupt. "Can't stop, La Doña. Mac has found proof that Kelly's the killer and gone after him. We—"

"Jerome Kelly? The museum director. Lord love a duck! What proof?"

"I don't know. Mac grabbed a baggie, the poison maybe. I'm not sure. But *I* heard Jerome Kelly confess."

"You! Then we've got corroboration!"

Iggy, visibly twitching in impatience, said, "Don't worry about it now. Have to run."

"Settle down, Ignacio," the lady lawyer commanded brusquely. "Have the police been informed?"

"Yes!" Iggy exclaimed as the light changed. "I'm going!"

La Doña grabbed Christy as she started after Iggy. "Where are you children off to?"

"Following Mac. He told Iggy that Kelly would be heading for Santa Fe and is after him." She pulled loose.

With a glint in those piercing, elderly eyes, La Doña said, "Absurd. But I wouldn't miss it for the world!" She grabbed Christy's arm again, this time to hustle her across the street.

Iggy cut through the parking lot, Christy and La Doña close behind.

Reaching Iggy's ancient Chrysler, where a buddy had allowed him to park illegally, La Doña quickly clambered in the back, Christy in front. They backed down the alleyway, Iggy leaning on the horn as they came back out on Pueblo Norte. Luckily the first car in the creeping line was from Taos, knew Iggy, and did the hometown routine of stopping to allow a friend in line.

Iggy pulled out, up to the corner, and whipped his great boat onto Kit Carson. Mercy of mercies, there was no traffic ahead. Everyone was headed toward the Plaza. "Faster this way," Iggy muttered. "We'll turn up ahead and head south til we have to get back onto South Santa Fe."

"Yes, Ignacio," came from the back seat. "I'm quite aware of that. I've lived here somewhat longer than you have been alive!"

"No scolding today, La Doña," Iggy shot back. "I'm flashing my trouble lights and leaning on the horn as soon as we hit traffic, so don't bug me."

The big car rocked around a corner, taking it nicely. "Well!" La Doña rumbled. "To paraphrase, 'Fasten your safety belts, children, there's a bumpy ride ahead!'"

Now no one spoke as lights flashing, horn blaring, Iggy weaved in and out of traffic heading south toward Santa Fe.

Sitting, Christy felt fear for Mac grow in her. A knot in her stomach spread tentacles of electric panic through her body.

Behind them and ahead of them, sirens were beginning to wail and moan all over Taos, Taos County, and Rio Arriba, the next county south of the county line and Big Rock.

Jerome Kelly drove back onto the road from the last pull-off. There had been too many cars in a non-stop stream to attempt even one shot at that jackass doctor. He couldn't let some rubbernecker see him shooting toward the river and call the police. And this damned rain! He'd like to see anyone, hit in the eyes by rain, who could shoot a target leaping about on the rapids!

As the windshield wipers kept up their irritating snick-snack, Kelly peered ahead to find another pull-off. No place no place no place! Nowhere to park the BMW sufficiently far from the road. Nothing but a damned narrow shoulder.

Consider it coolly, Kelly informed himself. He must now be a considerable distance ahead of McCloud. He could find the perfect spot to lie in wait, take his time, fire off a fatal shot.

This delay in doing away with the doctor was not his fault. Who would have thought that one would have to employ the rifle from the trunk? Had he known he would have had a box of shells rather than that handful. But he had rationed them. Discipline had brought him this far. Now, he needed that discipline to dispose of the good doctor. No more than two shots at each of those pull-offs on this bloody road. Of course, the first one would suffice. Careful marksmanship and a dead enemy.

Curve after curve on the rain-slick road, and never a place to stop.

Grimly, Jerome Kelly saw that now the Rio Grande took itself away. He was coming into Rinconada. The river was over there across the fields.

Jerome turned down a dirt lane. Blast! A fence. Should he risk becoming stuck by turning in the grass? He took a chance. The luxury coupe bumped over the long grass, hillocks and rocks. He managed a turn and drove back up onto the highway...A few hundred yards and there was another lane.

Kelly had barely started down it when a pack of dogs came racing toward the car, barking. That settled this one. No fool he, not about to exit the automobile and be attacked by those beasts. Anyway, he could see now that the lane led to a house.

He must make it to the airport and fly out before some kind of pursuit was organized.

Of course, McCloud might well be dead now. The fool obviously had no conception of how to maneuver a raft.

Drowned, hopefully. Or perhaps overturned and freezing to death in the icy water.

His was obviously the superior mind. How cunning to push that raft in the river, then crouch behind the BMW's back rear wheel side. Then, yes then! the inferior fool, hot with blood lust, took the bait while Jerome Kelly, stood, smiled, and removed the rifle from the trunk.

Earlier perhaps he should not have returned to El Museo for the Carreta de Muerte. One should not be too greedy. Oh, but it was such a lovely thing, so old, so precious. Death, La Doña Sebastiana, sitting with drawn bow.

Now Comadre Sebastiana, old friend, sat in his back seat. We'll see how you would like to meet her, my dear Dr. McCloud.

Mac had somehow survived the rapids. Were there more ahead? He didn't know.

Finally, daring a long look up toward the road, he saw that this lovely river had swung away from the highway. Thank you, God. No more shots for a while.

Don't stop your paddling. You can rest when you've made it out of here. Paddle. Paddle and think. Where does the Rio Grande come back in next to the road?

Mac could not think. He was too tired, just plain exhausted. No you're not, he argued with himself, trying to survive. Paddle like crazy and picture the drive to Santa Fe.

Eight hundred C.F.S. plus paddling. How fast did that get him down river? What? Seven or eight miles an hour? But with the help of God, maybe by some miracle he could reach Embudo Station, beach the raft there. Oh, splendid thought: to be out of the water! Out of the water and able to call the police there.

The police. Everywhere the police were pulling onto roads, sirens blaring, whooping. Sheriffs and their deputies. State Police. Taos Police. Espanola Police. Some were headed north, some south as the manhunt began. Some were racing to the Santa Fe airport, probably the only capitol city in the country where big jets couldn't land.

Coffees were left undrunk, donuts uneaten, as officers hot-footed it to their squad cars. Fiesta-goers were left on their own as the entire Taos Police force took off in their patrol cars. Cavalcades and convoys raced up and down the Santa Fe road.

The Pueblos of Tesuque, Nambe, and Pojaque, crossed by the highway, thought they might as well join in, so Native American cops hit the road, too.

Iggy, Christy and La Doña heard the sirens closing in behind them at the same time that Chief Barnabe Garcia shouted to his driver, "That's Attorney Baca up ahead! The maroon Chrysler! Pull him over!"

Iggy saw the flashing lights, but they'd been flashing all the time they were catching up with him, hadn't they?

La Dona's gruff voice came from the back seat. "He wants you to pull over, Ignacio. Don't do it. We'll miss all the fun!"

"Good for you, La Doña," Christy exclaimed, doubled over her stomach. "We have to find Mac, Iggy!"

"Think I don't know that?" he exclaimed. "And my Diva here can make it as fast as any squad car. They can damn well follow me!"

And with Chief Garcia raging, they did. Iggy's wide, heavy Chrysler Imperial, taking up more than one of the two lanes, led the long parade of flashing lights and brown, white, blue police cars out the straightaway, past the amazed looks of oncoming Fiesta traffic drivers, swooping around the horseshoe, down into Pilar and into the first canyon.

Brakes squealing, Iggy suddenly slammed to a stop. A chain reaction followed. Squad car after squad car was violently braked. The road ahead was blocked. Construction caterpillars moved ponderously back and forth in front of them.

Chief Garcia jumped out of the lead police car and came striding up. He stuck his head in the window and shouted, red-faced, "I'll get you, Baca! Now's not the time. But when this is over...!"

The trio watched as Barnabe waved his arms at the road crew, gesticulating.

Christy hopped out of the car to see what was happening. Chief Garcia was coming back. "Tell your idiot friend to pull over and let us by! There's been a landslide. It's almost cleared, but no way to get past til they've got the rocks off the road."

Christy got back in the car and relayed the message, all of them frantic to move on.

Iggy drummed on the steering wheel, Christy fidgeted. La Doña grumbled, "Just what one would expect. Spend a trifling million or so of the taxpayers' money against the taxpayers' express wishes to put up those damnfool fences and blankets of wire mesh—except of course in the gullies, where, my dears you can see the slide came down.

"Slides when the snow melts. Slides when the ground warms. And slides, now, of course, in the monsoons."

"Speaking of which..." Iggy said with a grimace, as rain began to beat on the roof.

Kelly gave up on getting to the river any farther along in Rinconada village. Dogs and people and dead ends and fences! He sped up a hill, down another, up again. Into the next canyon. Damn, damn, damn! How much time had he wasted? An hour! One frigging hour of frustration!

What was next? Embudo Station where he and Virginia once had a clandestine meeting and a drink. Virginia. Dead.

But Embudo...

He gave up on finding a good place to get to the river. He would merely stand on the Embudo bridge and wait for the good Dr. McCloud to come to him!

In a haze of exhaustion, the good doctor paddled on, rhythmically, dully. Mac had lost all track of time. He had no thoughts, didn't even worry about getting shot The rain had stopped, but Mac's eyes were still blurred. Ahead? What was...? It was the big new bridge at Embudo Station!

With blistered hands and aching arms, Mac directed the raft over to the beach below the white chairs and tables. He clambered out into the shallow water, stumbled and fell to his knees. He stood again and splashed to the shore. He fell and lay there.

"Shoot me here, Kelly, you bastard," Mac mumbled to himself. "I'm too tired to care."

As the canyon widened just before Embudo, Jerome Kelly's anxiety heightened to get there before his quarry. He pressed his foot harder and harder against the accelerator. There was La Iguana up ahead. Next would be Embudo Station.

He looked to his right to find whether he could see the raft coming downriver. Trees were flashing by too fast to see. Faster!

Past La Iguana, he looked back. He could have gotten to the river there.

Suddenly, he lost his concentration on the chase as he swerved to avoid going off the road. Kelly become aware of the sound of sirens, many, many sirens. He swore aloud, then saw the empty raft bobbing ahead.

"Well, well, McCloud. I didn't get you, but the river did."

Knowing capture was racing to catch up with him, Kelly hit the gas. He and his beloved Lady Death had to make Santa Fe and his plane!

CHAPTER XXXIV

Embudo Station smoked meats and shipped them out as well as running a restaurant and bar in season, so there had been a sizeable staff sheltering in the rain. One of them saw a man lying near the edge of the Rio Grande water. Not another drowning! They rushed out to look.

As this group was circling the body, Iggy's car came hurtling down the road.

"Stop, Iggy! Stop!" Christy yelled.

God almighty! Iggy saw the body on the ground, too. He braked and swerved into the turn-off as police horns blared and sirens cried. The convoy swept on by.

Out of the car and at a dead run, Christy beat them all to that familiar lanky shape. "Mac! Mac!"

Shaking his head, Mac sat up.

The staff moved back as Iggy, La Doña close behind, quickly joined Christy and Mac.

"Mac! Mac! Are you all right?"

Mac wrapped Christy in a bear hug as they knelt together.

"You're soaking wet! What happened? You were chasing Kelly to Santa Fe."

"Turned out to be a river chase. Rain storm. Falling down in your damned cold Rio Grande!"

"Chase!" Iggy came out of the shock of finding Mac. "If you're up to it, let's follow the troops to Santa Fe. See if the police catch Kelly."

"Do it!"

Making his exhausted body lope, Mac joined the others in running back to Iggy's car.

They were interrupted by a tiny figure hopping from a car stopped by Iggy's.

"I made Juan bring me," Mama announced as she reached them. "The others did not want to come!" she added in a tone of astonishment. "Tell me what happened to *malcriado. Muerto?*" she ended in a tone that was simply interested.

"No time now, Mama. Juan, follow us to the Santa Fe airport."

Planting herself to hear the story, Mamacita had to surrender for once as Christy and the others plunged into the Chrysler.

There were so many sirens wailing ahead, Christy and the crew could still hear them while they raced to follow.

As they sped toward Santa Fe, Iggy and La Doña demanded an explanation from Mac.

He took them through the suspicions of Dr. Bottoms and breaking into his shop, Jerome Kelly, and why the crew had found Mac collapsed on the ground in Embudo.

Caught up in the story, Christy added, "I saw Evelyn notice Iggy lurking. That clued me in. I figured what you were up to and went to the shop."

"Thank God you did!" Mac held her hand tightly. "So anyway. Kelly was in the office planting evidence. He pulled the gun that no doubt killed Cindy."

Mac heard a muffled sound from Iggy but continued, "It had a silencer on it and is either with Kelly or on the floor in Bottoms' office. Christy knocked it out of Kelly's hand and we ran."

"Good for you!" La Doña exclaimed.

Mac showed his prize. "I also found this!" He tried for the big gesture but the baggie and his pocket were wet. It took some doing to drag the thing out without tearing it. Finally, Mac produced the sodden baggie with a powder in it.

"What is it?" La Doña asked.

"That is probably the ricin that killed Horse and left Spunk near death. Kelly wanted to plant it in Bottoms' office.

"Lord love a duck!" La Doña exclaimed, as Mac was provided with satisfactory astonishment from the rest of his audience.

"Meanwhile, back at the gallery—" Mac explained the confession and that "Horse and Spunk were the robbers, Spunk knifing Bobby in the struggle."

"An artist's tool." Christy jumped ahead. "They were robbing Evelyn—"

"And," Mac concluded, "Kelly said that because they saw Bottoms was shipping *out* a precious old Cristo and a Spanish gold monstrance, they knew his scam. Bottoms had no part in the robberies and murders. He was simply defrauding, maybe stealing.

"Simply!" Christy said bitterly.

Mac thought it better not to comment on Dr. Bottoms so he returned to the museum director. "Kelly was vulnerable to Spunk and Horse, and subject to a death penalty. He had to poison them."

"But since Spunk killed Bobby, he'll be charged with murder if he recovers," Iggy finally spoke. "Hope to hell I don't get assigned *that case.*"

Christy remained silent, thinking of Bottoms and how close she had come in her attraction to a slick dishonest con man. All those wonderful words about returning artifacts—all false. The man had been nothing but a thief and phony. He was making a fortune from selling off what others donated for the cause.

Iggy wanted it all wrapped up. "Virginia Warren must have been part of it. The State's holding those stolen treasures they found in her van.

"Miz Warren was Jerome Kelly's *first* assistant, using her job to get into the churches and her expertise to know what to steal—"

The sound of sirens and ear-splitting emergency horns increased. They could see the end of the convoy made up of squad cars from the different Pueblos.

"But what about Nesbit? I thought Chief Garcia had him pegged for this."

"Nesbit's out of it," Mac answered.

"Except for the old charges of fraud and embezzlement," La Doña added dryly.

"And my poor former client, Clive Castle?" Iggy asked.

"I think the final pathology report will conclude he'd been in the water several weeks. Probably bumped off by an angry coke-head."

"What a sorry epitaph," La Doña commented.

They were all suddenly thrown to the side of the car as Iggy raced through the turn onto Airport Road in Santa Fe. Enthralled by Mac's story, the others had barely noticed that they had been breaking all speed limits and running all lights as part of the police convoy.

Through the gates and into the airport. Across the tarmac.

Police cars were slewing to stop every which way, lights still flashing in the dark afternoon.

Iggy stopped, too, and then they all saw that familiar little figure darting through the police who, guns drawn, aimed at a Lear Jet on the runway. Some were behind open squad-car doors, some hunkered down.

"Mama!" Christy cried. She ran after her, closely followed by the others.

Jerome Kelly was on the portable steps, fighting with the Cart of Death, trying to push it up and ahead of him into the door of the plane.

The weight was too much. Kelly slipped on the rain-slick stairs. He plummeted down the steps, the Cart falling with him. On him.

The arrow of La Doña Sebastiana pierced her abductor's neck.

Christy saw that her Mama did not turn away from the bizarre sight of Kelly face down, Lady Death atop him. Christy knew her Mama. And so it was that Christy murmured, "Punishment of God" at the same time that Mamacita nodded in satisfaction and pronounced, "Castigo de Dios."

GLOSSARY

This glossary should be read with the understanding that the spelling and usages may differ from modern Spanish in that this Spanish put down its roots in Northern New Mexico 11 generations ago and developed in isolation from the mainstream of Spanish.

abogada (f): lawyer
abuelo, abuela: grandfather, grandmother
acequia: irrigation ditch
adivinanzas: riddles
ahora: now
alabados: hymns, sacred songs of the penitentes
alamos: cottonwood trees; Los Alamos, name of town
aqui: here
bailes: dances
banco: bench (usually attached to wall) made from adobe
bien: good, well
bruja, brujo: witch (f. & m.)
brujerias: witch stories, witch lore
bueno: good
bulto: carved wooden statue of saint
cantadoro: storyteller
capilla: chapel
carreta: cart
casa: house, home; *Casa Vieja*, Old House
castigo: punishment
cenizas: ashes

chile: our spelling of chili and normally means the red sauce only, no meat or beans

chamisa: a desert plant

comadre: mother-in-law; in Taos, close woman friend

como: how

¿Como 'sta? : Idiomatic from, ¿Como esta usted? How are you?

concha: shell; a concha belt is the leather belt decorated with round pounded silver "shells" usually incised with decorations

cuadrillas: a kind of dance

cuentos: stories

curandera (f.): a healer with herbs and prayers, not to be confused with a witch (bruja)

descanso: lit. a stopping or resting place; taken to mean where someone died or a cemetary; from the days when the pall bearers, walking a long ways, marked the spot where they had to stop and put down the coffin

dias: days

dicho, dichos: a saying, folk wisdom

Dios: God

La Doña Sebastiana: folk, Lady Death

Don, Doña: higher social strata than Mr or Mrs; almost Lord, Lady; the one who owned the hacienda and lands

El Señor: God

escondida: hidden, secret

esposo: husband

familia: family

Fiestacita: little Fiesta

la gente: the people, taken to mean Spanish people

gusta: pleasure

Hermandad: Brotherhood

Hermano: Brother

hombre: man

lastima: shame, pity (Que lastima! – What a pity!)

latilla: a slim wooden pole used in fences and ceilings

malcriado: evil one

malo: evil

Mayordomo: a Catholic Church title and position (cf. Deacon), assisting at Mass, tending the physical plant, taking communion to shut-ins, giving Eucharist at Mass; also, a title given the ditch boss

morada: the prayer hall of the penitentes/hermanos, also their meeting place

mis: my (pl.)

m'jiha: contraction of my daughter (m'jiho: my son)

muchacha: girl

muerte: death

muerto: dead

nada: nothing

nicho: a curved open space in a wall in which to place a statue of a saint

nuetro,nuestra (m. & f.): our

penitente: a member of a lay society of St. Francis

pero: but

piñon: a variety of low growing, evergreen tree

porque: because

posole: a Spanish dish with hominy corn (Eng.) and pork bits in a broth

primo, prima (m&f): cousin

que: what

quien: who

reina: queen

reredo: the Church altar screen

retablo: painting of saint on wood or tin, sometimes incised

ristra: garland of red chile

sala: room, used here as living room

santero: one who carves saints

santo: carved statue of a saint, cf bulto

Santo Nino: lit. Blessed Baby, always used to mean Baby Jesus

sopaipilla: puffy, deep-fat fried little pillow pastry

tambien: also

Taoseño, Taoseña: one living in Taos (m. & f.)

tengo: I have

tiempo: time

tierra: earth, dirt

tio, tia: uncle, aunt

toda, todo: all (f. & m.)

trastero: a free-standing cupboard, cf. armoire

tu: you or your (familiar)

turista: tourist

usted(es): you
valse: waltze
varsoviana: a kind of dance
vecinos: neighbors
velorio: a wake in which mourners sit all night with the
  deceased
vida: life
viejo, vieja: old one (m.& f.)
viga: a round ceiling beam
viva, vivan: from verb vivir, sing. and pl. of idomatic "long
  live" or "hail!"
y: and